# The Lady in the Tower

Other books by Marie-Louise Jensen
*
*Between Two Seas*

# The Lady in the Tower

## MARIE-LOUISE JENSEN

OXFORD
UNIVERSITY PRESS

# OXFORD
UNIVERSITY PRESS

Great Clarendon Street, Oxford OX2 6DP

Oxford University Press is a department of the University of Oxford.
It furthers the University's objective of excellence in research, scholarship,
and education by publishing worldwide in

Oxford   New York

Auckland   Cape Town   Dar es Salaam   Hong Kong   Karachi
Kuala Lumpur   Madrid   Melbourne   Mexico City   Nairobi
New Delhi   Shanghai   Taipei   Toronto

With offices in

Argentina   Austria   Brazil   Chile   Czech Republic   France   Greece
Guatemala   Hungary   Italy   Japan   Poland   Portugal   Singapore
South Korea   Switzerland   Thailand   Turkey   Ukraine   Vietnam

Oxford is a registered trade mark of Oxford University Press
in the UK and in certain other countries

British Library Cataloguing in Publication Data

Data available

ISBN: 978-0-19-275531-5

1 3 5 7 9 10 8 6 4 2

Printed in Great Britain by CPI Cox & Wyman, Reading, Berkshire
Paper used in the production of this book is a natural,
recyclable product made from wood grown in sustainable forests.
The manufacturing process conforms to the environmental
regulations of the country of origin.

*For Paul*

Acknowledgements:
*Thank you to my wonderful writing group,*
*Karen Saunders, Kelley Townley, Karen Priest*
*and Julia Draper, who gave me invaluable support*
*in the writing of this story.*

# PROLOGUE

1540

I used to be happy here. In the days when happiness still dwelt within the castle walls. Mother's merry laugh could often be heard ringing out in the great hall and Father's voice echoed cheerfully as he shouted orders to servants and played games with us.

Four years ago, when I was just eleven years old, a day came that altered everything. A day that is burned into my memory like a brand that will never fade. It changed my life and it changed me.

These days I move about like a ghost or a shadow. I slip quietly up spiral staircases or hide behind tapestries to avoid being seen. I overhear much, but take part in nothing. I'm still Eleanor Hungerford, daughter of Lord Walter Hungerford, but I eat my meals with the servants. I shun my father's presence.

Often my thoughts stray to the south-west tower, where sometimes I glimpse my mother's face, pale and wan, imprisoned behind the high windows. The Lady Tower, they call it now. The door to the tower is kept locked and I cannot go to her.

I'm older now. I am turned fifteen. And though I've grown sadder, I've grown wiser too.

# CHAPTER ONE

*Winter 1536 (four years earlier)*

I gripped the reins tightly in one hand and my practice lance in the other. I could sense my horse Arianna gathering herself beneath me, waiting for the moment when I let her go.

'Don't let me down this time, Arianna,' I whispered. I could see her ears pricking up as she listened to my words. She had tried every trick imaginable this morning already. If she had set out to prove herself an unsuitable mount for me, she could not have succeeded better. This was her last chance.

'We have to best Gregory's performance,' I told her fiercely, as I watched my cousin limping back up the meadow towards us, muddy and humiliated, leading his horse.

We were riding at the quintain, a target attached to a long arm that swings away as you strike it. We had used it often enough before, but today a heavy sack of meal had been tied to the other end of the arm. The sack would swing round and catch an unwary rider in the back. This is how it would be done in a real tournament. It had unhorsed my cousin twice.

1

'Good luck, Eleanor,' said my little brother Walter. At just four years old, he looked tiny on horseback. His legs did not reach to the bottom of the saddle. But like me, he had been riding since before he could walk.

'Your turn, Eleanor!' ordered the castellan.

At my slightest urging, Arianna sprang into a swift canter. She fought with me to turn our controlled charge into a headlong gallop. I held her steady and on a straight line to the quintain.

The target was looming closer. My heart was pounding with excitement. I could feel wild energy coursing through my veins like fire. I eased the reins a little more and Arianna quickened her pace. Her hooves were thundering on the meadow now, sending pieces of turf flying into the air.

I levelled the lance and raised myself a little in the stirrups, taking careful aim. As my lance struck the centre of the target, I gave a cry of triumph.

But the thud of the lance on the wood and the jolt that accompanied it brought Arianna up short. She shied, leaping wildly into the air. I kept my seat without difficulty, but the sack of meal that should have passed harmlessly behind us came flying straight at me. It all happened so fast I had time only to throw myself forward onto Arianna's neck. The sack struck me a heavy blow on one shoulder, knocking the breath from my body and sending me sliding across the saddle. I grasped my horse's mane, righting myself, but to my shame the lance slipped from my grip and tumbled to the ground.

I paused a moment before dismounting to retrieve it. I didn't want the others to think I had fallen. Arianna stepped sideways and threw up her head as I bent to collect the lance, dragging me through the muddy grass. I held on to her reins grimly, and once she had calmed down, I began to trudge back up the meadow to rejoin the others. I was bitterly disappointed.

'Bad luck, Eleanor,' said Gregory sympathetically. He was back up on his horse, but with a huge smear of mud across one cheek.

I scowled at him, knowing he felt better because I had failed.

'If you are going to insist on taking jousting lessons with the boys, Eleanor,' the castellan said severely as I reached him, 'you will have to ride a suitable horse.'

Dropping the lance at my feet, I pulled Arianna's head down and smoothed her velvety nose. Her glossy neck, normally gleaming, was dark with nervous sweat.

'She's already learned to let me ride astride,' I protested. 'And she is beautiful. The best horse in the world.'

I had only had Arianna for two months. She had been an eleventh birthday present from my father. He was surely the kindest and most generous father to bestow such a costly gift on me. Arianna was part Arab and the most graceful and elegant horse I had ever seen.

'Perhaps,' agreed the castellan unenthusiastically. 'But she's also nervous and flighty. You'll never make a tournament horse of her. She's putting you in danger with her tricks. I agreed to keep teaching you with reluctance. This is no sport for a girl. If you argue with me, I shall have to exclude you from these lessons.'

'Yes, Johnson,' I said meekly. I knew very well how

fortunate I was to have been allowed to continue riding lessons with the boys once they began training to tilt. My mother considered that it would be more appropriate for me to improve my stitching and learn to read and write better. Luckily, Father had overruled her, saying I might continue riding lessons for at least a few more months. He was proud of my riding skills and despised book learning of any kind.

But the castellan, our teacher and the head of castle security, was not a man to be argued with. I knew if he told Father I was putting myself in danger, Father would call a halt.

'You are possibly the best rider of your age I have ever seen, Eleanor,' the castellan added in a gentler tone. 'But you are not doing yourself justice. Have Beau saddled next time.'

The lesson was ended for that day. I felt dispirited as I accompanied Gregory and Walter across the river Frome and back up the hill to the castle. I had failed to avoid that sack, I had dropped my lance, and Arianna was in disgrace.

'What a long face, Eleanor,' remarked my cousin. 'If the castellan had spoken of my riding like that, I should be overjoyed. He's pretty sparse with his praise.'

I managed a small smile.

'And you still have Arianna to ride whenever we are not jousting,' added Gregory. 'I don't see the problem. In fact I think it pretty unfair that you should be the best rider of us. I mean, you are just learning for fun. You will never be allowed to ride in a tournament. It will be Walter and I who do that. So what use is it to you to be skilled with a lance?'

'Why won't Eleanor be allowed to ride in a tournament?' asked Walter.

Gregory rolled his eyes.

'Because she's a *girl*,' he sighed. 'Girls can't enter tournaments. They are men's sport.'

I frowned at being reminded of this. Riding was my favourite occupation.

We reached the stables and Tom, the stable boy, came hurrying up to us. He took hold of Arianna's reins and held her while I slid to the ground.

'How did you do, Mistress Eleanor?' he asked me eagerly.

'Not well, Tom. I'm to ride Beau next time,' I said sadly.

'I told you so,' Tom remarked.

'Damn your eyes, Tom,' I said rudely.

He laughed. 'Your cousin looks as muddy as a pig in a midden,' he added for my ears only. 'I'm guessing he took a tumble?'

'Two,' I said with some satisfaction. I was very fond of my cousin, but he had only been at Farleigh a year. He had come here as pageboy to my father. Tom, on the other hand, had been a friend and confidant all my life. He was also the best source of useful vocabulary anyone could want. My mother would have fainted on the spot if she had heard half the stable language I knew.

'Are you two laughing at me for falling off?' asked Gregory and grinned good-humouredly. He never minded me teasing him.

'Only a little,' I promised him. 'Come, Walter!' I cried, wanting to shake off my disappointment. 'Let us ride to find Mother!' I neighed and crouched down on the cobbles ready to be his steed. Tom swung Walter onto my back and I cantered him across the stable yard and over the bridge into the inner court of the castle. I snorted and whinnied as I went and Walter shrieked with delight. Gregory caught me up, neighing and pawing the ground.

'Faster, Eleanor!' shouted Walter, kicking me as if I were really his pony. 'Gallop!'

But we had reached the steps to the keep now, and I slowed as I mounted them.

'You are growing heavy, Walter,' I complained.

'Horses don't talk,' shouted Walter.

So I raced across the Great Hall and along the passageways of the castle, my skirts swishing around my ankles, and entered the family apartments in a riot of noise.

Mother covered her ears and raised her eyes heavenwards in mock anguish as we passed, but once we had taken a couple of turns about the room and returned to her, she was laughing. We collapsed in a breathless heap on the sheepskin rug before the fire, Walter's arms still twined tightly about my neck. Gregory threw himself down beside us, a huge grin on his face.

As we calmed down, I saw Mother compose her face and look serious: 'Eleanor,' she said. 'There is a grave matter about which I must speak to you.'

I untangled myself from my brother at once and stood before her, hands folded, eyes downcast.

'Yes, Mother?' She looked at me severely and I searched my mind for some transgression, but could think of none. She rarely disciplined us, and I could not imagine what I might have done wrong.

Mother fished in her workbox and lifted out a piece of embroidery. It was much crumpled and stained, with every stitch either strained tight or loose and sagging. I knew it well. Mother held it distastefully between finger and thumb and frowned mightily.

'What, may I ask, Eleanor, is this meant to be?'

'My most recent sampler, ma'am, if it please you,' I replied, sweeping her a deep curtsey, peeping through my lashes to see whether she was serious or merely teasing. I thought I could see a twinkle in her eye.

'I feared as much. It does not please me, Eleanor. In fact it offends the eye. I would expect better craftsmanship from the gong farmer.'

Little Walter, who had been looking anxiously from one to the other of us, hooted with laughter at this. 'But, Mother, he's the man who mucks out the moat below the latrines! He doesn't sew!'

'My point exactly,' agreed Mother cheerfully. 'I fear there is only one thing to be done with this, Eleanor,' she told me, and cast it into the fire. I gasped as it caught and shrivelled. I did not care about the hated sampler, but turned and stared at Mother, looking for some sign of how angry she really was. She tried to look severe, but then her dimple peeped out. I heaved a sigh of relief and grinned mischievously.

'And what is my punishment to be, ma'am?' I asked.

'You will begin a new one tomorrow. And I shall pray that we can find a husband for you who cares little for the domestic virtues, my daughter.'

'Lord, yes!' I agreed cheerfully. 'For I'll be damned if I'll ever be good at stitchery.'

'I am aware of it,' remarked Mother, a genuine frown now furrowing her brow. 'But in all seriousness, Eleanor, you must rid yourself of the language of the stables! It is one thing to be unable to sew, but quite another to swear like a groom.'

'Sorry, Mother,' I murmured, aware that I had gone too far.

She smiled, and her face lit up. 'And now that I have done my duty by you, shall we all have a game?'

We had just had time to become engrossed in a round of tables when we heard the commotion of an arrival below in the outer court. Not just one or two horses. By the sound of it there were many.

'Who can that be?' I asked Mother. 'Surely it cannot be Father?' Mother shook her head, but I could tell by the light in her eyes and the softening in her face that she thought it was.

'I dare not hope so,' she said. 'He is not due back from London for another week at the least. When last he wrote he was much taken up with business at Court. We are fortunate that he finds so much favour with the king.'

I thought as she spoke that she did not look very happy about it. I was surprised. We were all so proud of Father. But before I could say anything, my brother interrupted.

'The king is King Henry the Eighth, and he lives in London,' Walter announced importantly, showing off his knowledge. He had climbed up to one of the narrow windows, and was craning his neck to get a view of the stables. Then his voice changed abruptly. 'It is! It is Father!' he screeched. My cousin grinned, I felt a rush of excitement and saw the joy written plainly on my mother's face.

'Mother, can I run down and see if he's brought me a present from London?' begged Walter.

'No, Walter. We shall receive your father here with dignity, if you please.'

Breathlessly, we awaited the familiar tread across the main hall, and for Father's cheerful, blustering voice. He would be pleased to see us, and to be home again. He would pretend not to have presents for us, but of course he would have. He always did. He would stroke his red beard and guffaw and eventually bid us look in his saddlebags.

But today we heard only silence. For a long time. Even the usual castle bustle seemed hushed.

Then came the sound of tramping feet across the hall. Several pairs of boots, but no cheerful voices. I was still excited, but the first icy trickle of premonition ran down my back. Something was not right.

Two of my father's knights entered, their faces expressionless. I looked to my father for reassurance as he came in, but received none. His face, usually red, was pale and sickly. Another man stood beside my father. His clothes were plain, and he had not the look of a fighting man about him. As he stood there, slightly stooped with inky fingers, he seemed sinister somehow. Then I recognized him: Thomas Cromwell. He was a close friend of my father, and adviser to King Henry.

We stood in silence a moment. I felt Gregory take my hand and gripped his fingers, taking comfort from the clasp. I could feel the happiness draining out of me, leaving me hollow and sick. Something was terribly wrong. Gregory felt it too.

My father glanced at us and looked irritated at the sight of our clasped hands.

'Hungerford,' he snapped, using my cousin's surname, 'there is a gift awaiting my son in the schoolroom. Please take him there!'

Gregory cast me a frightened glance as he left the room.

Little Walter looked surprised, but went willingly enough, giving Father a hug on the way out.

'Sir Walter?' asked Mother tentatively. 'Is something amiss?'

'Amiss? Indeed it is!' he barked, with none of his usual warmth. '*You* are amiss, my *lady*!' The emphasis turned my mother's title into an insult, and she paled, grasping at a chair for support.

I stared at my father in disbelief. Where was my happy, loud, blustering father? He was transformed.

One of the men stepped forward.

'Lady Elizabeth, you are under suspicion of practising witchcraft and of infidelity,' he stated coldly. 'You are to come with us.'

I felt my insides freeze as the words sank in. Witchcraft? Not my mother. The memory of the village woman who had been burned at the stake as a witch returned painfully to my mind. I was eight when it happened. I remembered her screams, the stench of burning flesh, and the way her long hair had caught and burned like a torch.

I began shuddering, my breath coming short. I looked at my mother in disbelief. She was white about the lips.

'Walter, dearest . . . ?' she faltered. 'Is this some terrible jest?'

That's it, I thought. It's a jest. He's teasing, just like she teased me about my dreadful sewing earlier. Like he teases us about the presents. In a moment he'll laugh and they'll hug each other.

'Do you deny, ma'am, that you have lain with other men in my absence? That you have brewed potions to ensnare me anew on my return?' My father's voice was cold and hard. I gasped with shock.

'Walter, please . . . our daughter. Eleanor,' whispered my mother disjointedly.

'Do you deny the charge?' Father demanded, his voice icy, and his eyes not quite meeting hers.

'I never . . . no, I mean yes. Of course I deny it. Walter, please, what madness has come over you? I pray you, end this foolish game.'

'I'm ending it now, ma'am.' He turned to his knights. 'Seize her. Take her to the top room of the south-west tower. My chaplain has prepared it for her reception.'

'No! Walter, no!' my mother cried out. She reached out her hands to him, desperation in her face. 'God be my witness, our children have been my companions by day and my only bedfellows by night! Who has told you such lies?'

Sir Walter ignored her, merely nodding to his men.

At once they seized Mother by the arms and began dragging her away. She struggled and cried out, but then went limp, as though resigned to her fate.

Until that moment, shock and disbelief had held me frozen in passive horror. It suddenly lifted. I ran to my mother and flung my arms around her.

'No, Father!' I cried. 'You can't! It's not true . . . '

I could not believe this could be happening. What was my father thinking of? Or was it another man, a stranger, pretending to be my father?

Another guard stepped forward and tore me away from my mother. As she was taken from the room, I wrenched myself free of my captor and seized Sir Walter by the arm, shaking it urgently.

'Father! She's done nothing wrong! Tell them to let her go!'

'Be silent, girl!' He glared at me a moment, and I saw his eyes dancing madly and beads of sweat standing out on his forehead. I recoiled slightly and he shook me off in disgust, as though I were a rat or a cockroach, giving me a shove so that I fell to the floor. I was furious. My mother had often deplored my temper. It flared now. Here I was in this room which just a few moments ago had been bright with happiness. It was all gone, and in its place were swirling mists of pure rage. I got up and punched Father in the stomach. He did not flinch. I had forgotten his chain mail beneath his tunic. The pain in my hand merely fuelled my anger. I began to kick his shins and yell.

'You piece of filth!' I shouted. 'You madman! Let Mother go, at once!'

He went to push me again. This time I caught his hand and sank my teeth into it until I tasted blood.

Sir Walter's scream of pain echoed around the chamber. I heard him yell. 'You witch's spawn, you'll pay for that!'

His voice had a high-pitched, almost insane note in it.

I heard him yell an order and the next thing I knew I had been lifted bodily off the ground and was being carried out of the room. I lashed out with my feet at my captors. My foot sank into soft flesh more than once. They grunted, but didn't slacken their hold.

'Lock her in one of the top rooms,' snarled my father. 'Perhaps a couple of days with no food will tame her.'

I was dragged roughly up the spiral staircase. I fought the men every step of the way. Then, sitting on the dusty floor of an empty room with the door locked behind me, I wrapped my arms around my knees and rocked myself to and fro, shaking.

'I'll rescue you, Mother,' I vowed quietly, in a voice that sounded quite unlike my own. 'If he doesn't realize his mistake first, I'll set you free myself.'

I was young then, and did not realize that the very power and wealth I admired in my father would be turned against me. Petted and indulged as I had been up to that point in my life, I did not understand how impossible it is for a child to set herself against an adult.

# CHAPTER TWO

*Spring 1540 (four years later)*

*My dearest Eleanor,*
*Thank you for the new embroidery. It helps to pass the time, which crawls*
*by so slowly. I do believe I have counted almost every minute of the four*
*years that have passed since I was locked in here. It feels like a lifetime. A*
*nightmare that will never end.*
*I saw you out riding today and imagined I was with you.*

*Your loving mother,*
*Elizabeth*

I ran the brush vigorously along Arianna's flank, and then stroked her gleaming coat. She was a grey, but so light as to be almost white. She shone in the sun.

'I'm to be betrothed again, Tom. Have you heard?' I asked.

'Aye, Mistress Eleanor. Everyone knows it, I reckon. Why the sad face? The last one died before you could be married, and no harm done.'

Tom was tending Arianna's hooves, bending down beside me, scraping the mud away.

'Yes, and by God, I give thanks for it in my prayers every night,' I responded. 'But I can't see my luck holding a second time.'

I had been formally betrothed shortly after my mother's incarceration. My betrothed had been an elderly baronet with few teeth and the gout. I still remembered the terror and the disgust he had caused me. Luckily for me, he had died a few weeks before our wedding. But I had been left with a horror of who my father might next foist upon me. I, of course, had no say in the matter.

Tom stooped to lift Arianna's next hoof, leaning against her so she would shift her weight across to the other leg. 'You've been lucky to escape this long, if you ask me,' he commented.

I sighed and resumed steady, rhythmic brushing strokes. Arianna swished her tail and shook her head to keep the flies off. It was a warm day, and everyone moved more slowly than usual. I felt tired and listless and, in that mood, my future seemed even more daunting than usual.

'I stay out of sight,' I said. 'I doubt my father has caught sight of me in two years.'

'He's not forgot you, don't deceive yourself. It just ain't suited him to marry you off yet. But you're fifteen now; you've growed up. It's high time you was married,' remarked Tom.

'You're fifteen and you aren't married, so don't tell me I should be, you pile of horse apples.'

'I ain't the daughter of an earl, like you are. Dog droppings.' Tom grinned as he insulted me.

'Son of a gong farmer!' I threw back at him.

'That's most likely true, an' all,' he remarked wiping his nose on his sleeve. 'Don't remember much about me parents, but there weren't nothing fine about them.'

'I didn't mean . . . ' I said, colour mounting in my cheeks. Sometimes I forgot the difference in our stations enough to be unkind, and it embarrassed me. Since Gregory had left Farleigh three years ago, Tom had once more been my only friend. I had become steadily more estranged from my brother. We jousted together still, but that was the extent of our relationship.

I reverted to our previous conversation: 'Well, I cannot leave Mother. She depends on me. She's growing weaker, I'm sure of it. I don't think she ever recovered from . . . '

'Her illness?' asked Tom when I stopped.

I lowered my voice though there was no one near.

'Illness, or poison. You know that Mother is sure the chaplain poisoned her food or drink. And now she dare touch nothing that comes from him. If I didn't get food to her, she would starve.'

Tom nodded reluctantly. He knew of the secret arrangement. A woman called Alice and some of the other villagers took the food to the foot of the tower every night, where Mother hauled it to her window in a basket the village women had made for her. And throughout all this, Mother still hoped for her husband's mercy. She firmly believed the poison was the chaplain's doing, not Sir Walter's. She refused to try to escape with me.

'I know your mother depends on you,' Tom said. 'But I was thinking of you. You're not treated right here. It might be best for you to be married and have your own home.'

'Not if the marriage is of Sir Walter's making. It'll be another revolting old goat with one gout-ridden foot in the grave.'

'Eleanor!' My brother's voice broke into our conversation. I had not heard him approach. 'I need you. Would you care to joust with me?'

'Very well, Walter.' I nodded, and threw down my brush.

'You'll have to finish Arianna, Tom. But can you ready Beau for me first?'

Tom rolled his eyes.

'Yes, ma'am, you just leave it all to Tom.' He winked at me as he left to fetch the saddle and bridle.

'Desiccated dog turd!' I tossed after him cheerfully.

'Festering flea bite!' he called back.

Whilst Tom was preparing Beau, I fished a carrot out of my pocket for Arianna. As she crunched it eagerly, I stroked her cheeks and kissed her soft, velvety nose. She was a great comfort; the one precious thing my father had not taken from me. I loved her very dearly. She was at all times my favourite mount, but had never mastered the art of jousting.

I swung into Beau's saddle, adjusting the folds of my simple kirtle. My fine kirtles and gowns were all outgrown, and I dressed plainly in what clothes could be made up cheaply and easily. I looked like the servants now, except that I wore my auburn hair loose, not bound back in a veil.

I rode down to join Walter. He had shed his petticoats these two years, and was dressed now like a miniature man in doublet and hose. No expense was spared in his apparel. My brother was now a sturdy boy of eight summers, who excelled in every form of sport. He divided his waking day between riding and learning swordplay and archery. Like our father, he despised book learning of any kind. He had never learned to read and write like I had. Our affection for each other had waned over the years as he became more and more his father's son.

'Ah, Eleanor,' the castellan greeted me. He rarely allowed himself a smile. 'I'm glad you could join us. I have news for you both. There is to be a formal announcement at supper, so if you could keep it to yourselves until then. Firstly, Sir Walter will be arriving in a few days.' I groaned audibly, interrupting him. My father's arrival would mean less freedom within the castle and the end of jousting practice for me. Although it had been he that had allowed me to begin learning, I'm quite sure he would be shocked if he knew I had continued all these years.

The castellan paused in his speech and I saw his lips tighten a little. I wondered if he was annoyed at my interruption or whether he agreed with my sentiments towards my father. I had suspected for years that he continued to teach me jousting as an act of rebellion against Sir Walter and his treatment of Mother and me.

'Sir Walter will be joined,' continued the castellan, 'by a large party of noblemen and ladies. Some will reside within the castle itself, others are to pitch camp outside the castle walls. We expect that the king himself may visit.'

Both Walter and I gasped with surprise as the king was mentioned. A royal visit was not something that had happened in our lifetime.

'To celebrate the occasion and in honour of the king, Sir Walter plans to hold a tournament here at Farleigh. Lists will be constructed for the joust and there will also be other events such as archery and sword fighting.'

At this point the castellan was interrupted again as Walter fairly screamed with excitement. His pony reared up in fright, blowing and snorting in indignation, and began to bolt. Walter pulled him round in a tight circle and brought him back.

'A tournament?' Walter cried. 'A real tournament, right here?' The castellan inclined his head, allowing himself a small smile.

'I have already suggested to your father that there should be a junior event as well, Master Walter. He was disposed to agree.'

Walter whooped with delight. His pony tossed his head.

My feelings on hearing this news were more mixed. The return of my father had never yet brought me any good. Now it might mean my new betrothal was near. And although the joust would doubtless be exciting to watch, I had no chance of competing. I was nobly born, but I was female. My part would be to sit gracefully on the sidelines and watch.

'I don't suppose there will be a jousting event for ladies?' I asked the castellan bitterly.

'You know very well there will not be,' he replied quietly.

'But it is not fair that I may not compete.'

'Indeed,' nodded the castellan. 'For you have more skill than many men, and more courage too. But it would not be seemly to display yourself before the crowd. We must take the world as we find it, Mistress Eleanor.'

I did not agree. 'When the world has unjust rules, we should seek to change them,' I argued.

Walter snorted derisively. 'You'll never have women in the lists!' he mocked. 'Women sit on the sidelines and fuss about their gowns and their complexions.'

'I can defeat you,' I countered swiftly.

'Because I am a youth and you are near full grown.' He tossed his head dismissively, looking just like Father. 'In a few years I will be a strong knight, and you will be sitting with a babe in arms.'

A surge of rage swept through me and I choked on all the angry words I wanted to fling at him.

'Father would have stopped you jousting long ago if I had told on you,' Walter added.

'But you did not, and you will not, because you need me to train with,' I threw back at him.

'Pooh!' he scoffed.

We glared silently at one another for a few moments. Used to our quarrels, the castellan broke in:

'If you think the rules should be changed, perhaps you will speak to Sir Walter, Mistress,' he suggested.

I imagined the scene that would ensue, and sighed. 'Oh well, I suppose watching a tournament will be less dull than life generally is here.'

'Are we going to practise?' asked the castellan drily.

We rode hard and struck our targets accurately until humans and horses alike were blown. I felt I had proved my brother wrong with my performance, though he was not going to concede the point.

I headed back to the castle with my head full of the coming joust, and thought of little else over the following days. I wished I could enter. Nothing on the scale of this tournament had happened in years, and the whole castle buzzed with excitement. Even the servants, to whom this would bring so much extra work, walked with a new spring in their step, and could be seen bustling all over the castle, opening up little used apartments and spring cleaning. The kitchen was likewise a hive of activity, as our stores of grain and preserves were checked and counted and orders for more supplies were made out. I wandered hither and thither, without any role in the preparations, feeling wistful.

As usual, I sought refuge in the stables, and it was from here that I saw my father arrive a few days later. I was hiding in the hayloft at the time, having had another argument with Walter in which he had spoken insultingly of our mother. I could not understand that he had not more loyalty towards her. I had to remind myself that he had been only four when she was taken from us.

The stable loft was my favourite hiding place when I needed to be alone. There I could lie in the warm, sweet-smelling hay and listen to the horses breathing and moving about below. It was a place of security and comfort.

The clatter of hooves in the courtyard interrupted my thoughts. I leaned out through a window high in the wall, and looked down upon the sight of Sir Walter leading a cavalcade of about a dozen men. There were many fine horses among them, though just now they and their riders looked weary and dusty from the road.

The grooms and stable boys ran out to take the horses. There would be frantic activity in the stables from now on, as the horses were fed, watered, and rubbed down and all the tack was cleaned. From my vantage point above the yard, I saw Tom go to the head of a tall roan gelding and take his reins behind the bit, while his elderly rider struggled down from the saddle, stiff from his long ride. My insides froze, as it occurred to me that this might be the man my father intended to betroth me to. Indeed, it could be any of them, I realized with horror, looking them all over. My gaze lingered especially on the older members of the party, noting the red noses, bad teeth, and bulging paunches. I shivered.

I realized I was observed. An elegant young man, fashionably dressed, was sitting easily astride his black horse, one gloved hand resting on his hip. He was looking straight at me, a grin spreading over his face. I drew back hastily into the dim light of the loft. Before I lost sight of him, he winked at me. I was disconcerted, and hid myself in the darkest corner. There, comfortably snuggled into the hay, I contemplated the change in my circumstances these visitors might bring about. My habit was to hide from strangers. But would I now be called to eat my meals at the top table of the great hall as a daughter of the house? Time would tell.

My ears caught the sound of my father's voice in the stalls below. Cautiously, I pushed aside a pile of hay and sought a crack where the planking had shrunk with age. I pressed my eye to it. It allowed me an imperfect view of my father standing in the gloom of the stable below. I could make out the bald patch in his red hair almost directly below. He was standing close to the chaplain, and both were speaking in lowered voices. What was the chaplain doing in the stables? He almost never rode.

'Have you become squeamish of a sudden? What is wrong with you that you do not carry out my orders?' hissed Sir Walter. His voice was easy to hear; he never could speak quietly.

The chaplain's soft voice was much harder to make out. 'I can assure your lordship . . . the cordial . . . Lady Elizabeth recovered.'

'There must be other ways,' snarled Sir Walter.

The chaplain hushed him anxiously. 'Please, my lord . . . more quietly. Not without falling under suspicion . . . '

'I cannot believe how you have bungled this,' my father growled. I saw him grasp the chaplain by the front of his robe, shake him and push him back against the wall of the stable.

'Four years!' he exclaimed, his voice growing louder again. He was viciously twisting the fabric of the chaplain's garment. 'You know how important this is. You are not even trying.'

The chaplain, clearly desperate to defend himself, forgot to keep his voice low:

'Sir Walter, I have tried everything. She does not die. It must be witchcraft,' he gasped.

There was a moment's silence. I could not see their expressions from this angle. My heart was pounding in my chest. It was my mother they were discussing.

Suddenly my father released the chaplain and he fell grovelling in the straw, panting and wheezing as he recovered his breath.

'My patience wears thin,' I heard Sir Walter threaten coldly. 'Think of something.'

He left the stables. The chaplain remained, rubbing his throat. Then he too got up quietly and left.

I lay back in the hay, my heart hammering.

So Mother had indeed been poisoned, and on my father's orders. Why? Even after four years, I still did not know why he persecuted her. And now she was almost certainly in terrible danger once more. We were surrounded by enemies. I had to do something.

# CHAPTER THREE

*Mother,*
*Do not touch* **ANYTHING** *the chaplain gives you. You are*
*in grave danger.*
*Sir Walter is returned with guests. There is to be a*
*tournament.*

*Eleanor*

With fingers that shook, I took out my quill, ink bottle, and a tiny scrap of parchment and scratched a brief note to Mother. When it was done, I stared at it hopelessly. It was inadequate. I needed to do more.

As soon as the stables were quiet once more I had crept out of the hayloft and fled to my bedchamber. For the past four years a tiny room high in a remote part of the keep had served as my quarters. I had no furniture save a palliasse stuffed with straw that served as my bed, and a wooden chest that held my few possessions. It was a servant's room. No fire warmed it and no shutter shielded the narrow window from the weather. But it was mine.

I bit my lip, thinking hard. What could I do to help my mother?

I would think of something. But first it was vital that I take this note to Alice so that Mother would get it this very night. I tucked it hurriedly into my sleeve and then, snatching up my cloak, I made my way down to the kitchens where I would be able to collect Mother's daily bundle of food.

The kitchen was the busiest place in the castle. And with all the guests that had to be provided for, it was more bustling and noisy than ever. Dozens of servants were chopping vegetables, scouring pans, baking bread, and stirring cauldrons. The noise was deafening. The smells of meat roasting and gravy bubbling made my mouth water, despite my anxiety. The bundle of food Betsey, the cook, had made ready for Mother was lying neatly in its usual place.

I hunted through the steam and smoke. Seeing Betsey shouting at a lad roasting meat on a spit over the fire, I went to her.

'Keep your eyes and hands off the maids and on the spit! And if I ever catch you burning so much as a crumb again, let alone a roast for the master's dinner . . . oh, Mistress Eleanor,' she broke off distractedly.

'Can I speak with you?' I asked her urgently. Betsey was one of the few people in the castle I could trust. She was Mother's devoted retainer, and would do anything for her.

'Yes, Mistress,' she said, casting one last, dark look at the hapless lad before the fire, who was turning the spit now as though his life depended on it.

'I'll box your ears!' she threatened him. Then turning away, she hurried to the stillroom where the pickles and preserves were kept. Betsey disappeared inside, and I squeezed after her into the tiny room. It was quieter here, and we would not be overheard.

'It's Sir Walter,' I told her. 'He has ordered the chaplain to poison Mother.'

The high colour in Betsey's plump cheeks faded.

'You heard him do that?'

I nodded.

'I did. If I had not, I could never have believed that even he could be so wicked.'

'They've tried it before,' said Betsey. 'Your mother told you herself.'

I shook my head. 'No. We knew that she thought she had been poisoned. We did not know that Father himself had given the order. Mother would not have believed that. I can scarcely believe it even now.'

I realized I was shaking. The overheard conversation in the stables had come as a huge shock to me.

'My own father!' I exclaimed. 'How could he do such a thing? Surely nobody could be wicked enough to kill their own wife?'

'Oh, couldn't they indeed?' retorted Betsey swiftly. 'It wouldn't be the first time. Not even the first time in this family.'

It was as though the stone flags rocked under my feet. I was suddenly short of breath.

'What are you talking about, Betsey?' I demanded.

Betsey put her hands to her mouth and moaned.

'Oh dear. Oh dear. I'm forbidden to speak of it,' she said, her voice hushed. 'I'd lose my place if I did.'

I grasped her sleeve and shook it slightly.

'You have to tell me now,' I told her. 'Or I shall fear the worst.'

'The truth is bad enough, Miss. It don't get much worse.'

'Tell me, Betsey! You know I would never breathe a word that might harm you,' I urged her.

Betsey took a deep breath and began to speak in a low hurried voice. 'Sir Walter had a bad start in life. His mother died. And his father, Sir Edward, fell in love with one of his own servants. Agnes, she were called. But she were already married, weren't she? So what do you think she did?'

'I don't know,' I whispered.

'She had her husband murdered,' said Betsey.

I gasped.

'I have heard nothing of this,' I replied faintly.

'Of course not. None of the servants is allowed to speak of it. But his body was chopped up and burned, here in this very oven,' said the cook. She looked at me anxiously, as if wondering how I'd take the news. I gulped, feeling sick and faint. After a moment, Betsey continued:

'No one discovered it at first. She married Sir Edward, your grandfather. But then Sir Edward himself died mysteriously, leaving all his money to Agnes.

'That's when it affected your father. Sir Walter lost his inheritance and his home by the will. Well, that ain't normal. Noblemen don't leave their property away from their sons. So there was an investigation. And it all came out. She was hanged at Tyburn for the murder of her first husband. They found the men what did it. They admitted

28

it. But no one could prove Agnes had murdered Sir Edward. And your father, he was not much older than you then. Imagine that going on around you. No wonder it soured him.'

'So Father's stepmother murdered his father? My grandfather? Is that what you're saying?'

The cook shook her head. 'I'm saying nothing. They couldn't prove it.'

My head was reeling with all this information. But Betsey was still speaking.

'And then . . . your mother is not Sir Walter's first wife you know, Mistress,' she said darkly.

'I know that,' I replied. 'He was married twice before. There's no secret about that. His previous wives died . . . ' My sentence trailed into silence as I took in the significance of what I was saying. 'What are you suggesting?' I faltered. 'That my father murders his wives?'

Betsey shook her head, but the expression on her face frightened me.

'I'm just saying they died. Nothing more, nothing less. And he weren't happy with them. Treated them something terrible. But your mother was different. He did well married to her. Till these last years.'

'Why is he doing this, Betsey?' I asked, my voice choked. 'She's never done him any harm.'

'I don't know any more than you do, Mistress,' Betsey replied, shaking her head.

There was a shout and a clatter from the kitchen and we both jumped.

'I must get back to work before the supper is spoiled,'

said Betsey, her mind veering back to her duties. 'But you warn her ladyship, Mistress Eleanor.'

'I am about to, Betsy,' I told her, holding up the note I intended to lay inside the bundle of food. Betsey nodded grimly and we left the stillroom together. At once she became distracted by a dozen kitchen servants' questions. And we could both see the lad who was supposed to be minding the spit. He had his back to the fire and was leaning over the shoulder of a young kitchen maid as she kneaded dough, one hand on her slim waist. Judging by her blushes he was whispering in her ear. Betsey sallied over before he knew she was there and boxed his ears.

I grabbed the bundle of food and fled the kitchen, the spit-boy's howls ringing in my ears.

I was deeply shaken by what Betsey had told me. I had grown used to my mother being locked away now. It no longer shocked me, though I still missed her terribly. But this news had shaken me to my very bones. Suddenly, murderers lurked around every corner. I imagined phials of poison in the chaplain's hands dripping their deadly contents into Mother's mouth. As I crossed the court and walked to the gatehouse, my mind filled with images of dismembered bodies consumed in flames, I was breathing in short gasps, my limbs heavy and unresponsive as I walked.

The guards at the gatehouse let me pass without comment. They were used to my daily outings to Farleigh Hungerford village. I went sometimes to visit the poor and the sick as my mother used to do, so my regular visits to Alice went unnoticed. I walked across the wooden drawbridge, my bundle concealed beneath my cloak.

I tried to push the images of murder from my mind and focus instead on how I could reach Mother. I took several deep steadying breaths. It would not do to frighten myself so that I couldn't think.

I poured my woes out to Alice when I reached her tiny cottage. Alice had been very sick some years ago and Mother had cared for her, bringing her food and even calling a doctor. Alice had recovered from her illness, and had been devoted to Mother ever since. She would do anything for her, convinced Mother had saved her life.

Alice listened, while she rocked her tiny newborn baby in its cradle. It was crying fretfully, its face pinched and sallow.

'And so you see, I must find some way of speaking with Mother, before they . . . before anything dreadful is done to her,' I concluded, twisting my hands together in distress.

Alice laid one rough, work-worn hand on mine.

'Her ladyship will not take food from the chaplain again,' she said soothingly. 'Not as long as I and the other women take her food each night.'

'But he might find some way to trick her,' I protested.

Alice shook her head, but asked: 'There's no way you can get to speak to her, is there? They keep the Lady Tower locked.'

'Yes. The chaplain has the keys. I see them every day, Alice. He has them hanging from that cord around his waist. He grows fatter with every month that passes, eating most of the good food he pretends to take up to Mother. The keys bump against his belly at every step, but he doesn't seem to mind. I never see him without them.

He pretends to be a man of God, but in truth he is no better than a gaoler and an assassin.'

'Except that he has not killed your mother, Mistress,' said Alice. 'He must have had chances aplenty, these past four years, but he has not taken them.'

'What I don't understand,' I said, 'is why it is suddenly so urgent now? Mother has been locked up for four years. Has something happened to make Sir Walter more angry?' I shook my head, at a loss to know what to think. It made no sense to me.

'I can't help you there,' Alice said. 'I don't know nothing about the ways of noblemen.'

I got up to go, leaving the bundle of food for Mother and the precious note.

'Is there anything you need, Alice?' I asked. 'I'm sorry. I was so upset today that I forgot to pack a loaf for you.'

Alice shook her head. 'Never mind, Mistress. I've hungry mouths to feed but we can manage.'

I looked at the baby, still grizzling in its cradle. The thought of this family's poverty drew me from my own troubles for a moment. They had helped Mother without hesitation, even though, if caught, they could lose their home and their employ for defying their landlord.

'Can I bring you some milk, Alice, or some cream? I'm sure Betsey would spare some.'

'That would be most kind, if it's not too much trouble,' said Alice gratefully. 'The older children would love to have some milk to drink. They're out in the fields helping their father this morning, but they are always hungry when they come in.'

'I'll bring something tomorrow,' I promised her.

I returned to the castle deep in thought. The day was drawing to a close and it was chilly as I walked along in the shadow of the curtain wall towards the drawbridge. I had the beginnings of an idea in my mind. It was not possible to take the keys without the chaplain noticing, I knew that. But what about when he slept? Where did he put them then? The very idea of creeping into his rooms at night made me feel dizzy with fear. Did I have the courage to carry such a plan out? For Mother's sake, I thought perhaps I did.

# CHAPTER FOUR

*My dearest Eleanor,*
*Fear not. I will touch nothing. Tell me more of the tournament. Every*
*piece of news is like a breath of fresh air,*

*Elizabeth.*


I went to the chapel as darkness fell that night. I had not
gone in to supper, feeling too excited and terrified at the
thought of what I was planning to do to eat a single bite.

Selecting a secluded pew near the back of the chapel, I
sat quietly as the dusk deepened around me. A single
candle flickered at the altar, casting long dancing shadows
as the flame was caught by draughts. I murmured some
prayers for Mother's safety and another for the success of
the task ahead.

I could hear voices outside the chapel. Men were
crossing the inner court, talking and laughing. Once there
was a sound of hooves on cobbles, and I heard a horse
neigh from the stables in the distance.

When it was completely dark, I heard the rattle of the
chains from the gatehouse as the drawbridge was raised
for the night. Whenever the doors to the keep were

opened, I could hear the voices and laughter of my father and his guests from the great hall. They were merry tonight. I thought again of the conversation I had overheard this morning, and wondered how Sir Walter could plot such dreadful deeds and then sit drinking and laughing, playing the carefree host. I felt a rush of hatred towards him.

An hour passed. Perhaps more. The castle grew quiet at last. I heard the guards retire. I was beginning to feel stiff and cold. I had been certain the chaplain would come to the chapel before he went to bed, but it grew so late, I began to doubt my plan. I was just about to move, when the chapel door was pushed open. I jumped, even though I had been waiting for it.

The chaplain didn't see me, a still figure in the deep shadows. He walked to the front of the chapel and kneeled at the rail, his head bent in prayer. What a hypocrite, I thought. Did he really expect God to sanction him poisoning Mother?

After some time the chaplain heaved himself to his feet, leaning heavily on the altar rail. He had grown fatter than ever, wearing his stolen food around his middle like a roll of guilt. Then he gave a great sigh and blew the candle out.

The chapel was plunged into darkness. I heard him lumber down the aisle towards me and pause at the door. I held my breath, willing him to leave quickly. The door banged shut and he was gone. His footsteps faded.

I heard only the sound of the wind in the hour that followed, and once I was startled by a mouse scuttling across the chapel floor.

At last I thought the chaplain must be asleep. I bent and picked up my lantern, which I had darkened on three sides so I would not give myself away with too much light. I stretched and slipped out of the chapel. There was a torch guttering in the porch and I lit my candle by that. Then I crept towards the chaplain's chambers. My heart was hammering now and my mouth unpleasantly dry. I hesitated for a moment, grappling with my failing courage.

The latch was cold in my hand. I eased it slowly up, doing my best to make no noise. Then I pushed the heavy door open. If it had creaked, I would have fled at that point. But it did not. It swung soundlessly open, and so I crept forward into the dark room.

The air was thick and stale. I could hear the chaplain's grunting snores coming from the inner room. It was a disgusting but reassuring sound. There could be no doubt he was asleep.

No moonlight penetrated this first room, and so I lifted the lantern, aiming its narrow beam of light onto the chaplain's writing table. There were rolls of parchment, a couple of quills, and a bottle of ink, but no keys. I scanned the walls looking for nails they could hang upon. I felt in the wall niches, but there was nothing. My heart sank. The keys must be in the chaplain's bedchamber.

As I turned to creep into the lion's den itself, I stumbled over a chair. I grasped it and prevented it falling, but in the process it made a scraping noise against the flagstones.

The chaplain's snores stopped abruptly. I quickly shuttered the lantern and stood stock still, hardly daring to breathe. I could feel my heart knocking against my ribs.

After a long moment, I heard the chaplain sigh and roll over in bed. There was a short pause and the snores began again, more quietly and regularly this time. As I moved towards the bedchamber again, I found I was shaking. I breathed deeply and glided noiselessly forward. There was some moonlight in here, showing me the huge, blanket-muffled form of the sleeping chaplain. One flabby white arm was flung up over his face.

I shone the lantern onto the walls, taking care not to allow any light to fall upon the sleeping man.

There. Suddenly I saw them. They were lying on a small chest next to his bed. I took a step closer to him. And then another. I put out my hand and took hold of my prize. There was a faint clinking as I picked them up. It sounded loud in my ears but the chaplain did not stir.

I crept backwards out of the room, crossed the outer chamber and then I was out in the fresh air, flying across the inner court. Abandoning my lantern at the foot of the Lady Tower, I fumbled with the bunch of keys, searching for the right one. It was the biggest and the newest key and it turned easily in the lock. I tore up the spiral staircase, heedless now of noise, and hammered on the topmost door.

'Mother!' I cried. 'Mother, it is I, Eleanor!'

This key was harder to find and fit to the lock in the deep darkness of the stairway. But at last the lock clicked back and I flung open the door.

I could see Mother like a deeper shadow in the darkness.

'Eleanor, is that really you?' I heard her voice utter faintly.

I dropped to my knees beside her and threw my arms around her.

I hugged her tight in the darkness, noticing how thin and frail she felt.

'Eleanor, it's the middle of the night,' protested Mother, half crying, half laughing. We clung to one another, and Mother was kissing me on the cheek, and stroking my hair. It was comforting.

'What are you doing here?' Mother asked.

'Mother, you are in such danger. I am so afraid for you,' I said. 'Did you get my note?'

'I did, an hour since, and I penned a reply by candlelight. You must not fear. I shall eat or drink nothing that does not come from you, my dear one.'

I pulled back, trying to look at her face, but I could not see it in the darkness. The window was closely shuttered. I got up and threw open the shutters to let in what little light there was. It turned the room a ghostly grey, but I could still not see the expression on Mother's face.

'Does the chaplain not wonder that you eat and drink nothing?' I asked her.

'Eleanor, my dearest girl, I am not stupid. I throw the food and drink he brings into the moat.'

'Mother, leave Farleigh with me,' I begged her. 'Right now, while I have the key.'

'In the middle of the night?' asked my mother gently. 'How would we get out?'

'We cannot, but we could hide in the stables and leave at first light, when they let down the drawbridge,' I urged her. 'Before they discover you are missing. Please. I cannot bear being parted from you like this. I cannot live with the dread of what they might do to you.'

'Eleanor.' Mother stroked my hair back from my face. 'Do you really think the guards would let me pass? And if they did, where would we go? Do you have money? For I have none.'

I shook my head despairingly.

'Not a single coin.'

Mother hugged me again, and rocked me a little in her arms.

'We must pray that your father relents, my dear daughter,' she whispered. She took my face in her hands and they were thin and dry like birds' feet. 'Are you well, at least, Eleanor? Does he treat you properly?'

'I am well enough,' I replied. 'But I am to be betrothed again. I dread to think who my husband will be. If he is half as old and repulsive as the last one, I would rather die than marry him. And if I am forced to wed him and leave Farleigh, who will take care of you?'

'Perhaps,' said Mother, 'he may be a good man. You could tell him of my situation. He may be able to help. To speak to the king or to Thomas Cromwell.'

'I could try,' I replied doubtfully. 'But, Mother, Cromwell will not help you. He is Sir Walter's closest friend. And I overheard him the other day, ordering the chaplain to . . . '

'Hush . . . ' said Mother suddenly, clutching my arm. 'I hear something.'

The words had barely left her when the door behind me swung open. There was the click of a lantern being unshuttered and a light shone into my eyes. From somewhere behind the light a male voice spoke.

'Well, well. What a nice surprise, Mistress Eleanor.'

# CHAPTER FIVE

I jumped to my feet. I could not see who the speaker was, but I knew his voice. The chaplain was standing in the room with us, and I could well imagine his malicious glee. But there was another man with him. A second lantern moved into the small room, and lit up the angry face of my father, a tunic and leggings hastily pulled over his nightshirt by the look of him. His hair was tousled and his eyes were wild. He had none of the chaplain's calm enjoyment of the situation.

'Father?' I faltered. My lips felt numb with shock as I tried to speak. I realized my hands were shaking and took hold of the folds of my gown to steady them.

The chaplain stepped forward and stopped right in front of me.

'Did you really think we were so easy to fool? That I did not hear you sneaking into my room like some shameless wanton? Like a thief in the night?'

His breath was in my face, smelling of wine and meat.

I turned away from the chaplain. It was useless to appeal to his finer feelings. He had none.

'Father,' I begged. 'I miss Mother. Is it so very bad to want to see her?'

'Address me as Sir Walter, if you please,' he snapped.

'And don't pretend you had no motive in coming here. We have been at the door long enough to hear what you are planning.'

My heart jumped into my mouth as I remembered urging my mother to flee.

'Bring her,' ordered Sir Walter abruptly. The chaplain nodded. He grasped my arm in a painfully tight grip. I resisted, twisting around to look at Mother. But she sat huddled on the bed, hugging her knees, moaning softly. I wondered what they had done to her to break her spirit so.

The chaplain marched me out through the door which Sir Walter held open. I gave one last anguished backwards glance. The banging of the door echoed round the tower, and I heard the stolen keys rattle in the lock.

I was pushed and pulled all the way to my father's great chamber, my arm twisted painfully behind me. The chaplain left us alone. My father locked the door behind him and pocketed the key. I felt fear beginning to rise in me. The father I had once loved was long gone. In his place stood a wild animal. Unpredictable and dangerous. He might do anything.

Sir Walter leaned back against the wall and folded his arms.

'So you sneak around the stables eavesdropping on private conversations, do you?' he asked.

'No, Sir Walter,' I said, forcing my voice to be meek and casting my eyes down in what I hoped was an apologetic, submissive way. I had discovered over the years that it was the way to provoke the least anger from him. 'I overheard you quite by chance that day.'

And how much had Sir Walter heard of our

conversation, I wondered, casting my mind back over what had been said. Had he overheard that I smuggled food and notes to Mother? If he had, we were in very serious trouble. Surely he could not have followed me up the staircase in time to have heard that?

Sir Walter stepped forward, took hold of a handful of my hair and twisted it so that I cried out and was forced to my knees.

'Don't even think about talking to your future husband about me or my business,' he hissed in my ear. 'He knows everything. He is deep in my confidence. And you breathe one word to him, or to anyone else, about your mother, I will know at once. Do you understand me?'

'How can I, when I don't even know who he is?' I cried angrily.

'You'll know soon enough. I asked you if you understand me!'

'Yes, Sir Walter,' I gasped, the pain of my twisted hair making my eyes water.

'You went to Doctor Horde at the priory once. Do you remember? I found out the very same day.'

'I remember,' I said bitterly. Dr Horde was the prior of the monastery at Henton Charterhouse. I had gone to him for help years ago, but my father had somehow found out. I had been locked up without food for days. I wondered what my punishment would be this time.

Abruptly, I was released, and got to my feet panting with relief. Sir Walter was looking at his hand, with the strangest expression on his face. I saw several long auburn hairs lying across his palm. The same colour his own hair had been before it was touched with grey.

He spoke again and his tone was changed.

'Why, Eleanor?' he asked. Sir Walter was now gazing at me with such intensity that it made me uncomfortable. 'Remember you are my daughter,' he said softly. 'Why don't you forget that evil witch, and you and I can be friends? We can be allies.'

'She's not an evil witch,' I cried. 'She's Mother. And you are wrong to lock her up.'

'How dare you question my actions?' roared Sir Walter, making me jump. 'I'll teach you some manners! And I'll teach you what will happen to you if you dare to defy me.'

He stepped back from me and began to unbuckle his belt. There was a look of hard anger on his face. I felt my legs give way in fear and I fell once more to my knees. I had never been thrashed. Surely he would not do so?

'Father, please. Sir Walter, I mean. I'm sorry if I've angered you.'

He took hold of the buckle end of the belt and twisted it firmly around his right hand, drawing the leather through his left hand in a menacing way. Cold terror gripped me.

'Please, please, don't hit me,' I begged him, despising myself even as I spoke the words.

My father said not a word. As the blows began to rain down on me I could not help crying out, though I stifled my cries as much as possible, gritting my teeth together and clenching my fists. I tried to turn from him, to evade the lashes, but he pursued me relentlessly, delivering blow after blow. He struck me hard on my back, my arms, and my legs—I had never felt such pain. The stinging leather struck every part of me except my face. Even at the time I noticed that he avoided my face.

Eventually I lay curled in a tight ball on the floor, my arms over my head, whimpering like a baby. I am ashamed to admit it, but I fear it's the truth. At last the blows ceased and I dared look up. Sir Walter was leaning against his desk, panting and sweating, his face a contorted mask of hate and rage. The disgust I felt for him gave me a little strength.

'Get up!' he snarled. I struggled to my feet, hurting and smarting all over. The floor swayed under me and my legs felt unsteady.

Sir Walter passed a hand over his face, and his mood changed abruptly once more.

'Do you understand now, Eleanor?' he asked, and his tone was haunted. 'I did not want to hurt you. But I cannot have you turning out like your mother.' Sir Walter's tone was pleading, like a small child who had been naughty. I felt a wave of sickness sweep over me, and recoiled from him. My father approached me closer and took my hand. My skin crawled at his touch. I forced myself to remain still and neither flinch nor look at him. When he got no response, he flung me from him. Sir Walter unlocked the door and threw it open. 'Go,' he snarled, his voice surly.

I did not need telling twice.

# CHAPTER SIX

*My dearest Eleanor,*
*I hope you have not been punished for what you did last night. I shall*
*not be easy until I have heard you are well. It was wonderful to see you*
*and I shall pass many days enjoying the memory of holding my dear*
*daughter in my arms once more. But please, Eleanor. Never take such a*
*risk again.*

*Elizabeth*

I lay face down on my palliasse for two days after that
fateful night. My body was bruised and cut and I could
not move without grievous pain. No one knew what had
occurred and so no one came to tend me.

Eventually, thirst and my fear for Mother drove me
downstairs.

'Mercy, Mistress, whatever happened to you?' cried
Betsey as she saw me limping, stooped and faint, into the
kitchen. I knew I must look a sight. I had not washed nor
even put a brush to my hair in two days. My mouth and
skin felt parched from lack of water.

As briefly as possible I told Betsey what had occurred
and she threw her hands up in horror. She made me sit

down on a footstool and drink some milk, fussing over me like a mother hen.

'What about Mother?' I asked. 'She's had nothing for two days either.'

Betsey looked concerned, but said, 'Perhaps that's just as well, Mistress, if they're watching her at the moment. You could have put her in real danger with that jaunt of yours.'

'I was trying to help,' I murmured.

'I knows that,' said Betsey, grasping my shoulder. I winced and she released me.

'Perhaps I can take something to Alice today,' offered Betsey.

'No,' I cried. 'Do not! If I am caught leaving the castle with food, it is alms for the poor. If you are caught, it would be stealing.'

Betsey acknowledged this with a reluctant nod.

'But you're not well enough, Mistress,' she said anxiously.

'I will be in a few moments,' I said firmly. 'This milk is giving me new strength already. Oh, and Betsey, I promised Alice some milk. Her baby is ailing and her other children are suffering hunger.'

Betsey nodded and bustled away to get the provisions together.

It was a struggle to walk to the village, but I was well rewarded by Alice's joy in seeing me safe and in receiving the gifts of bread and milk for her family. She also tended some of my cuts with vinegar. It stung greatly, but gave some relief.

'We wondered what in the world could have happened to you, Mistress,' Alice said. 'I knew you'd never stay away on purpose. We took your mother some water last night, but we had no food to spare but a crust of bread.'

'Bless you for your help,' I told her gratefully.


Sir Walter sent a message to me that very night: one of the kitchen maids knocked on the door of my attic room.

'Begging your pardon, Mistress Eleanor, but master says you're to dine in the hall with the guests tonight,' she said nervously, bobbing a quick curtsey.

I heard her with dismay, and merely nodded a silent dismissal. I did not want to set eyes on my father. It was repugnant to have to show him smiles and obedience. Moreover, I was still so sore, it was hard for me to move about. But I knew I had little choice.

So I was ordered to dine with the guests. I was to be a part of the Hungerford family once more, no longer banished to the servants' table. I felt anxious about this, quite apart from my bodily hurts. I no longer felt sure I knew how to dine in polite company. I also feared it meant my betrothal was approaching. Perhaps my future husband was already in the castle.

Moreover I had a practical difficulty. What was I to wear? While my brother had had clothes and gifts aplenty from Sir Walter, I had had nothing in four years.

I pulled all my old clothes from my linen chest and searched through them for a kirtle or a gown that might still fit me. One by one, I pulled them on, wincing as they chafed my maltreated body. I shook my head in despair. Here was nothing that would not shame me before visitors. No fifteen year old can look presentable in dresses made for an eleven year old, and to make things worse, I had grown tall for my age. My skirts did not cover my ankles, my sleeves were strangers to my wrists, and my breasts pushed uncomfortably against the too-tight fabric of the kirtles. Finally, and with great reluctance, I pulled on the green kirtle and cloth of gold gown I had worn for my previous betrothal, covered it with a shawl, and sought my father. He was in his office, giving audience to a long line of tenants who doubtless had many complaints and requests to make of their landlord. He had been little enough at Farleigh over the last four years.

I went to the front of the queue. The steward stopped me at the door.

'Mistress Eleanor?' he asked, a questioning lift to his brows.

'I must see Sir Walter about an urgent matter,' I explained in a low voice. He nodded and soon ushered me into my father's presence. I was met with a hefty frown.

'What is it, girl? I have much business to conduct today.' He shifted impatiently in his seat. I dropped a curtsey and kept my eyes lowered. This was the room where I had been beaten so recently. It was not pleasant to be here again.

'Sir Walter. I am sorry to intrude. I received your message about dinner tonight and I find myself in a sad difficulty.'

I did not wish to argue or provoke him today either. I was safer if he believed me to be compliant.

'What?' he barked. 'Spit it out!'

I lifted my eyes briefly to his face to gauge his mood then cast them humbly down once more. 'I have nothing to wear that will not shame you, my lord,' I said apologetically. You mean, traitorous dog, I added silently.

I lifted my arms to show him the shortness of my sleeves and saw his eyes wander over my ill-fitting bodice.

'Damnation,' he swore loudly. 'This should have been thought of.' He banged his fist down on the table suddenly. I jumped, but held my ground. 'More expense to deck you out in finery,' he muttered. There was silence for a few moments except for the impatient drumming of his fingertips on the desktop. Then he rose suddenly to his feet and kicked a chair brutally across the floor.

'A curse on your head, you little witch!' he shouted. 'Stay in your room for a few days until you can be suitably dressed. Eat your meals in the kitchen. None of your sneaking about. I'll give out that you are indisposed.'

I was trembling with fright, praying that he would not let his anger loose on me again. I managed to curtsey and was leaving as quickly as I could, when my eye fell on a Bible lying on Sir Walter's table. I paused, without realizing what I did, and stared at it. It was bound in leather and I could see it was printed, not scribed.

'What are you staring at, girl?' demanded Sir Walter irascibly. 'Oh, the new Coverdale Bible. That cost me more than my three best tournament horses. Aye, I can see you are dying to look at it. Well, you may borrow it, if it will keep you in your room. It's no use to me. I bought it to please the king.'

Hardly able to believe that my father was giving me so valuable a book to read, I picked it up and hugging it close I made for the door.

'Eleanor!' came a shout behind me. I turned anxiously.

'Don't damage that!' Sir Walter warned me.

'I won't,' I promised and fled.

I had accomplished my aim and much more.

The Bible was in English, the new translation approved by the king. I had learned to read from portions of the New Testament copied out by scribes. This would be better by far.

I did not stay in my room, of course. Dressed as a servant, as I was, there was little danger that any of the guests would recognize me later as Mistress Hungerford. Servants were well nigh invisible to fine folk, I knew that well enough. With just a few precautions, I could continue to roam the castle as I pleased.

# CHAPTER SEVEN

*Dearest Mother,*
*I am well enough. Sir Walter did not punish me. It is you I*
*fear for.*

*Eleanor*

The building work had begun on the tournament ground. From the old schoolroom window, I watched several large trees being felled. An army of craftsmen—joiners, carpenters, and labourers—were busy in the field across the river. The lists were taking shape and the seating was under construction.

Sir Walter must be spending a fortune, I thought. How I will laugh if the king does not come after all.

I had seen the king once before. I was only seven when we last visited London. We stayed at Hungerford House, but I went with my parents to Windsor. I saw him in the gardens. He was very tall. I had never seen such a tall man. Fair of face and fine of figure. All England loved him. Later, people began to mutter against him. They did not like the break with Rome or the new Protestant priests.

I never heard such gossip within the castle, for Cromwell

and my father were the king's advisers. Here everyone was loyal. But when I rode out to the villages around the estate, I heard a different story. They disapproved of Henry's many marriages. He was now on his fourth marriage, to Anne of Cleves, and the gossip told me it was not going well. That had to be dangerous for my father. I knew he and Cromwell had proposed and arranged the match. Perhaps this tournament was an attempt to placate the king.

My musings were interrupted by a rustle of skirts behind me. I jumped and looked round. A lady stood in the doorway. I could not help but stare. She was dressed so very grandly in velvets and silks. There were jewels winking at her throat and on her arms, and her fingers were laden with heavy rings. She wore a headdress, but it was not the English hood I had once hated to wear. It was a new fashion I did not recognize.

'You must be Mistress Eleanor?' she asked. I recollected myself and hurriedly smoothed my shabby kirtle. Sir Walter's instructions had been to stay in my room, so I made to leave, but she remained in the doorway, blocking my exit and smiling. 'I'm so pleased to meet you! And to see that you are recovered from your indisposition, of course.' She stepped forward and embraced me, kissing me on both cheeks. I felt myself stiff and resistant. I did not like being hugged by strangers. In fact I wasn't used to being touched by anyone at all.

The lady looked out at the building work and smiled slyly at me.

'Ah! You have been dreaming of the knight who will ride into the lists wearing your favour. Of watching him ride to victory. I see it in your eyes.'

I cast my eyes down hurriedly. I was thinking of no such thing, I thought indignantly. If I were to think of the tournament at all, I would dream of riding in it myself.

'So shy?' laughed the lady, and put her arm about my shoulders. She reeked of perfume and hair paste and I pulled away. There was a large pomander swinging from her girdle giving off a sickly scent.

'You do not know me, Eleanor. But we shall be better acquainted hereafter. I am Maria Sheldon. I have been looking for you. Can you guess why?' She looked at me archly, her brows raised, a determined smile pinned to her lips. I shook my head mutely.

'The merchant has arrived with cloths and silks. Your dear father has asked me to choose something suitable for you. And I can see you are sorely in need of new clothes.' She cast a doubtful look at my attire. 'Will that not be exciting?' she asked.

She treats me like a small child, I thought. But I suppose I must go along with it, at least a little, if I do not wish to anger Sir Walter. I can be as false as she.

'Indeed, ma'am,' I said drily as I curtseyed. 'That will be vastly entertaining. Do I accompany you at once?'

She seemed to notice nothing amiss in my tone, for she smiled once more and led me down to the former family apartment. There, a sharp-faced merchant awaited us, his bolts of cloth laid out for us to view.

I must confess that after wearing worn-out dresses for so long, the prospect of new ones was appealing. Mistress Maria quickly totted up what I would need on her fingers, and the list made me reel with shock.

'Four chemises, two kirtles for day wear, with matching

gowns. Two evening gowns. Matching girdles for each outfit. And red flannel for underclothes—it's the warmest. A cloak for riding. Do you ride? You do? Yes, very well then, a cloak. And headdresses . . . do you favour the English hood, my dear?'

'No, certainly not,' I began, but I was not allowed to continue.

'You are quite right. *So* out of style. The French hood is far more becoming. We will need several ells of black velvet for French hoods.' This last was spoken to the merchant, whose small eyes were lighting up with glee at the length of Mistress Maria's list.

I almost forgot my hostility towards my companion as we examined and selected fabrics. Mistress Maria was some years older than I and far more experienced in the ways of the world. She chose and directed with great confidence, and drove a hard bargain with the merchant.

The cloth cut and the price agreed, she grandly waved him away, telling him to present his bill to Sir Walter. The shoemaker and hatter followed and my hoods were ordered and my shoes chosen. It had become the fashion, it appeared, to wear shoes with a square toe, and I would need one pair for each outfit, as the leather was slashed and the coloured lining arranged to show through and match the gown.

Maria threw herself back into my mother's chair and sighed.

'I declare there is nothing more exhausting than the choosing of clothes,' she remarked languidly.

I could have agreed, but I refrained. Instead, I wondered

to see her so at home here where Mother had once lived. She cannot be aware that this is Mother's room, I thought.

'I think we have chosen well, Eleanor. Will it not be delightful to have new clothes?' Without waiting for a reply, Maria continued, lowering her voice confidentially: 'I have heard how shamefully your mother has neglected you of late, you poor child.' Maria leaned forward and squeezed my hand. I whipped it away.

'What do you mean?' I demanded abruptly.

'We must forgive her, though,' she said, ignoring my question and nodding compassionately. 'I see it is a painful subject for you, but your mother cannot help being sick, you know. It is very tragic.'

'Mother is not sick,' I uttered in a choked voice. 'Unless being deprived of her freedom, being locked in a tower, can make her so.'

Miss Maria looked startled for a moment, but then smiled again. 'But it is for her own safety. And it is natural that you should wish her to be well. It is hard to lose your mother. But she is not likely to live much longer, Sir Walter tells me.' She leaned forward to stroke my cheek. I thought there was a look of greedy anticipation on her face. I leapt to my feet to avoid her and walked away across the room.

'It is my father who is sick,' I exclaimed indignantly. 'He goes mad and locks people up or beats them!'

The look of shock on Maria's face gave me pause. I bit back the next words I had been about to utter. This was clearly a friend of my father's. She might repeat anything I said. He would flay me alive.

The servant entered at that moment with wine and cakes, and his entrance gave me time to gather my scattered wits and put on an act.

'Indeed you do not know what you are saying,' uttered Mistress Maria gently once the servant had left us. 'You are upset and it has unbalanced your mind. Perhaps your father should send for a doctor for you too?' She spoke with false concern, and took a step towards me. 'Perhaps I should tell your father how wildly you speak?'

My stomach tightened with fear and I realized how stupid I had been. To retrieve the situation, I stepped back away from her, and put a trembling hand up to shield my eyes. I swayed a little, feigning dizziness.

'No indeed. There is no need. You are quite right: I am greatly distressed for Mother. I sometimes think it will drive me quite mad. I am so frightened for her.' I gave a stifled sob. I hoped it sounded realistic.

'Of course,' came the honeyed tone. I could smell her overpowering perfume once more: the awful woman had come closer and might hug me again at any moment. 'Sit down and take a glass of wine, my dear Eleanor,' her voice purred in my ear. 'You will feel better for it.'

'No, I need to lie down,' I gasped and turned and fled the room.

'That's a good idea,' I heard her say as I left. 'I will look in on you presently.'

I must be more careful, I thought as I took the spiral steps to my room two at a time. No one is on my side. They are all my father's spies.

# CHAPTER EIGHT

*Dear Eleanor,*
*Your note has relieved my mind. The castle sounds much busier than*
*usual. Even in my seclusion I hear the change. Tell me the news!*

*Your loving Mother*

Guests continued to arrive at Farleigh. Noblemen and
men of power and influence were quartered within the
castle. Lesser men pitched camp in the fields beyond the
lists. All of them made merry whilst awaiting the arrival
of the king and the start of the tournament.

From the castle windows, I could see how the camp
soon filled with gaily coloured tents topped with
fluttering pennants. By night I could see the numerous
campfires. The sound of voices and laughter drifted up to
the castle. My home was become a bustling hive of
activity, the formerly silent, empty corridors transformed
into busy thoroughfares for guests and servants. I did not
like the change. I risked being recognized every time I left
my room. I borrowed a servant's veil from Betsey and tied
my distinctive hair up in it. I kept my head down.

'Why will you dress yourself like that, Mistress

Eleanor?' cried Betsey. 'Do you *want* to be taken for a servant?'

'Yes, Betsey. It's the easiest way to get about.' I grinned.

She shook her head disapprovingly as she wrapped a clean cloth around a soft loaf, some sweetmeats, and two apples, supplies for Mother.

'There, I hope that's enough for the poor dear,' fussed Betsey, opening the bundle again to add a leg of chicken. 'It's little enough to sustain her. Here—take this loaf for Alice too.'

'I will, Betsey, though it's hard to conceal so much.'

As I wrapped the provisions in my shawl, Betsey tutted over my apparel once more.

'Whatever be the world coming to when young ladies have to dress as servants in their own homes?' Betsey grumbled. 'Is the master going to get you nothing new at all for the king's visit?'

'Oh yes, some very grand clothes are being made for me. But they aren't yet ready. Meanwhile I have to get out to the village.'

She nodded. 'To think, that we shall see the king in a few days.' She stopped what she was doing and hugged herself, her face lit up with excitement. 'Is he as handsome as they say, Mistress?' When I nodded, she shivered with sheer pleasure. 'Ooh, I shall be all of a twitter worriting about serving food to royalty,' she exclaimed. 'And will his new queen be accompanying him?'

'Anne of Cleves?' I asked. 'I do not know.' I leaned forward conspiratorially: 'I have heard that he travels into the west country to escape her,' I whispered. 'There is talk of divorce.'

'Surely not?' She gasped. 'They are not five months wed!'

'Well, that's what I heard,' I told her.

I left her to her work, and headed out of the kitchens and up a staircase to the next floor. I skirted the great hall, not wanting to risk my disguise too far. I slipped down a narrow, little-used corridor.

It was very early and most of the guests were still abed. I was disappointed therefore to see a smartly dressed young man coming down a stairway towards me. It was too late to turn back; he had already seen me. I glanced swiftly and recognized him. He was the man who had spotted me peeping from the hayloft the day my father returned.

I kept my eyes down and hurried up the stairs. He was looking at me. I turned my face away, but to my great annoyance, I caught my foot on the step just as I was level with him. I fell onto the stone stairs, striking my shin painfully on the edge of a step, and the bundle flew out of my hands. I cursed myself. Before I could scramble up again, strong hands took hold of my arms, and pulled me to my feet.

'Are you hurt?' he asked.

'Not at all,' I assured him mendaciously, looking anxiously for my bundle. He let me go and went to gather it up for me. I saw it had come unwrapped and my heart jumped into my mouth. An apple had rolled out onto the stairway and I could see my folded note lying loose. I rushed to grasp the note before he could, stuffing it into my sleeve.

'Please, do not trouble yourself,' I begged him, trying to pick up the other things myself as well.

'It's no trouble,' he replied.

Fortunately, he gathered my bundle without curiosity or comment and handed it to me. I almost snatched it from him in my eagerness to hide it and be gone. Before I could make my escape, he took hold of my arm again.

'May I not know your name?' he asked in a light-hearted voice. I panicked for a moment, but then remembered I was supposed to be playing the servant. I had quite forgotten.

'It's Jane, *if* you please, sir.' I told him, bobbing a curtsey, eyes down. 'Please, may I pass, sir?' I imitated the west-country burr with which all the servants spoke and was pardonably pleased with the result. I hoped he would not notice the inconsistency with my former speech.

'Why, what's the hurry?' he asked. 'Let me see your face first.'

I wished to avoid his close scrutiny at all costs. He must not know me when I made my appearance as Mistress Eleanor Hungerford. 'Please let me pass,' I repeated, my voice less calm.

He chuckled. 'You may,' he said, 'if you give me a kiss first. It is the penalty for help so early in the morning.'

My stomach plummeted. I had never been in such a situation before, and I did not know what to do.

'This is most ungentlemanly of you, sir,' I reproached him. He had his hand under my chin, pushing it up. I resisted a moment, then thought better of it and yielded, at the same time taking a firm grip on the stair rail behind my back.

He looked into my eyes a moment, a triumphant smile curling his lips. Then, as he bent forwards to kiss me,

I stamped on his foot. He swore and I twisted out of his slackened grasp. I ran up the stairs as fast as I could. I crossed the inner court at a run, fearing pursuit, but all was quiet. I slowed to a walk as I crossed the bridge and made my way to the gatehouse. I was filled with glee at the manner of my escape, and grinned cheerfully at the guard who stood aside on the drawbridge to let me pass. However, by the time I reached the village, I had had time to question the wisdom of angering one of my father's guests. I was also uneasily aware that he might well recognize me when I was introduced to him as the daughter of the house.

# CHAPTER NINE

*Dear Mother,*
*The castle is very crowded and noisy. Father has a*
*lady called Mistress Maria to be hostess. I cannot bear*
*her. People know you are in the tower, but Sir Walter*
*has given out that you are very sick. Everyone is sorry for*
*you.*

*My best love,*
*Eleanor.*

I underestimated Maria. I did not expect to see her again, but she visited me in my attic several times over the next few days, always at unexpected times.

'Such a small chamber, and so poorly furnished!' she exclaimed in surprise, the first time the servant brought her to my room and bowed her in.

I was sitting on my shabby palliasse, with my bedclothes unmade, scribbling a note to Mother. I hastily hid it between the leaves of Sir Walter's Bible. Scrambling hurriedly to my feet, I endured her scented embrace.

'Ah, I understand!' she said, as I offered no explanation as to the poverty of my room. 'You have been moved here to make way for all the visitors. How generous of you! It must be dreadfully inconvenient?'

'I manage,' I said stiffly. 'But I'm afraid I cannot offer you a seat.'

If I hoped that would make her go away, I was wrong. She was made of sterner stuff than that. She seated herself upon my mattress, arranging her skirts gracefully, and patted the place next to her invitingly.

'I shall speak to your dear father about some more suitable furnishings. Even a temporary apartment should be comfortable, should it not?'

I remained standing, scowling. Maria appeared not to notice, and picked up my precious Bible. 'Ah! So pious,' she commented, laying it aside. 'But of course you cannot actually read it?'

I snatched it up and tucked it away in my box.

'Yes, why not? My mother taught me to read. Did yours not teach you?'

Maria shot me an unloving look and avoided my question.

'How original! A girl scholar,' she sneered.

'You would be surprised how many uses I find for the skill,' I said cordially, thinking of the secret notes exchanged with Mother.

'Indeed? Come, Eleanor, sit by me and talk to me,' Maria invited me once more.

'About what?' I asked suspiciously. I regarded her warily.

'Oh, anything you like. You could start with what you have been doing these last two days since we saw one another last.'

Her tone was honeyed. I quickly reviewed my activities

of the last two days and discarded all of them as possible topics for conversation. I remained stubbornly silent. Maria sighed.

'I see I shall have to win your friendship, Eleanor. And indeed, you have no reason to trust me that I know of.' She sounded wistful, and I felt almost guilty for a moment. I allowed her to take my hand and draw me down next to her.

'Shall we begin with a gift?' asked Maria unexpectedly. With a smile, she drew a slim box from her reticule and offered it to me. I hesitated. She sighed again and opened it. Inside lay an intricately wrought gold chain. 'It's for you,' said Maria simply.

'Why would you give me this?'

'Because I thought you might like to wear it with your new clothes when they are ready,' Maria explained patiently.

'Yes, but why are *you* giving me an expensive gift?' I asked. 'I hardly know you.'

'I told you already. I desire to be your friend.' She drew the chain from the box and fastened it around my neck. 'There, is that not charming?'

I touched it uncertainly. It felt cold and unfamiliar against my skin. I had never worn a necklace before.

'Thank you, I suppose,' I said. I sounded ungracious. I still did not trust her.

Maria brought other gifts over the next few days. An ivory comb, a silk scarf, an embroidered cushion. I stuffed them all in my linen chest as soon as she left.

With the gifts came gentle questions. Where did I disappear to all day? Who were my particular friends in the castle? Neither my taciturnity nor my open dislike could keep her away from me.

I took to seeking refuge in the stables even more frequently than before to escape Maria's company. I stroked Arianna and apologized for not being able to ride her. 'All these grand people are everywhere, Arianna, and they would stare to see a serving girl upon so fine a palfrey as you,' I whispered.

I kept Tom company in the harness room, even helping him clean the mountains of stained leather the guests created, until the head groom caught me and sent me away.

''Tain't fitting, Mistress, for you to be working like a stable girl, whatever your mother's misfortunes may be,' he said firmly, shooing me out.

Deprived even of this pastime, I climbed up to the hayloft and buried myself in the hay, lying there for hours on end with nothing but my own thoughts for company.

One day, upon my return to my room, I entered and stopped dead, thinking I had gone into the wrong room in error. A bedstead hung with curtains stood in the place of my old palliasse and there was a washstand and two comfortable wooden chairs which had not been there before. Maria's doing, no doubt. I ought to have been grateful to her, but I was not. A scented pomander lay upon the bed. Another gift from Maria. It reminded me of Maria's sickly scent, and turned my stomach. That could not even be banished to my linen chest; it would make everything else stink. I went to the window and dropped it out into the moat.

No doubt Maria would be sniffing out where I had been today like a bloodhound. It seemed she had been set to spy on me. No doubt my father wanted me watched. Why else would a fashionable, grown-up lady trouble herself with me?

And indeed, Maria sent her maid for me later that afternoon to escort me to her room. It was a grand chamber, close to the great hall and had clearly been recently refurbished. I was glad not to see her in my mother's room this time. She had no business usurping Mother's position.

The seamstress was awaiting me, and with Maria's sharp eye on her she fitted my new clothes and made some last-minute adjustments. Stomachers were laced and unlaced around me. I was pushed and pulled out of the various kirtles and gowns. The clothes were heavy and strange.

I looked down at myself in my new pale yellow evening gown. I thought I must look years older—quite grown-up. And very grand. Only my unruly auburn hair still felt untamed and familiar. The kirtle beneath the gown was shimmering gold and caught the afternoon sunlight when I moved. The chemise was cream with fine lace edging, and looked beautiful against my pale skin.

'I feel quite different,' I said nervously.

'Indeed you do. This is the real you.' Maria considered me, her head on one side. 'And I do believe you will break hearts in that dress. If only I were as pale as you. My, I feel quite envious!'

I turned from her with barely concealed disgust. Her insincerity was nauseous.

'And is that my cloak?' I asked of the seamstress. 'May I try it?' She placed the black velvet cloak reverently around my shoulders and fastened it in front. I swept the heavy fabric around me and paraded a little, my excitement returning. Until I tried to turn my head.

'Why, I cannot see a thing!' I exclaimed. 'This stupid stiff collar is in the way.'

I saw Maria and the seamstress exchange looks. 'It's the latest fashion, Mistress,' the seamstress assured me timidly.

'Well, it's no good for riding,' I argued. It would be like wearing blinkers. 'Can you not remove it, please?' Lady Maria shook her head decisively. 'Certainly not! Whatever would your father say if he saw you in an outmoded cloak?'

I hunched an impatient shoulder. 'The devil take Sir Walter,' I retorted. Immediately I bit my lip wishing I could take my words back.

Both the women gasped. Maria shook her head at me repressively. 'You do not know what you are saying,' she chided. 'Why, he has just paid for all these fine clothes for you! Your father should limit the time you spend in the stables, it seems.' And she then turned the subject at once, picking up the shoes that had been made for me and begging me to try them.

I was as quiet and acquiescent as a doll for the rest of the fitting, understanding that I had disgraced myself. Not that I cared a jot for that, but I must think of Mother's safety and behave myself. I even allowed them to comb the tangles out of my hair, part it and paste it down flat ready for the French hood. I hated the hood very nearly as much as the

English style. It was heavy and pressed on my head, and I could not imagine how ladies could bear to wear all that black velvet hanging down their backs in the hot weather.

I looked an entirely different person when I made my first official appearance amongst the guests. The great hall had undergone as many changes as I had. Many more tables had been set up and all were full. I wondered how the king and his attendants would fit in. The hall was ablaze with candlelight and lit the colourful clothes and jewels of the many guests. There were ladies in sumptuous gowns and men scarcely less finely dressed. At each end of the hall, huge fires blazed, despite the mildness of the early summer weather.

There was a jester in brightly coloured clothes dancing around and making a nuisance of himself. I saw him trip a hapless manservant, who fell headlong onto the rushes, smashing the plate he was carrying. The men at the table nearest to him set up a shout of laughter.

Maria took my arm and led me forwards. There was a sudden hush as Sir Walter came forward to greet me before the assembled visitors. He took my hand and saluted my cheek, just as though I really were his beloved daughter who dined with him every evening. I felt a rush of anger, but I repressed it sternly. He's acting, you fool, I told myself fiercely. Just acting, and you must act too. And so I curtseyed before him and smiled. You need not think I've forgiven you, you disease-infested dung beetle, I thought, as he offered me his arm in exchange for Maria's. I placed my fingertips lightly upon it and he led me forth to be introduced to some of the guests.

Lady this and Lord that, it seemed my father had only

to lift a finger and the rich and powerful flocked to his halls. The names meant little or nothing to me. I simply kept smiling and curtseying. My brother was seated at the top table, of course, drinking his wine like a miniature man. I gave him a smile as I passed him and he nodded casually. Beside him was a handsome young man with a vaguely familiar face.

'You will remember your cousin, Gregory Hungerford,' said my father.

I gasped.

'Cousin Gregory? It is indeed you?' I asked in delighted surprise, examining his face to find the boy I had known four years ago. He stood up at once and bowed gracefully over my hand.

'Enchanted, Mistress Hungerford,' he said formally. Then he grinned and added: 'Goodness, Cousin Ella, how you have grown up!'

'So have you. You were eleven years old when you left Farleigh! You were called home because your mother was ill. Did she recover?'

'She did, thank you, Eleanor. Though her health is not strong.'

I couldn't stop beaming at him. Sir Walter made an impatient sound in his throat. Recalled to my surroundings, I smiled at Gregory and moved on. I was delighted to see him again. It made the ordeal of meeting so many new people bearable.

The introductions were almost done now. Cromwell was present, and I curtseyed to him, haughty and unsmiling. I was introduced to a small, weedy man with a nervous twitch who I had not seen before.

'Father Bird, vicar of Bradford,' my father said. I wondered what he was doing here. He did not strike me as a man likely to be interested in the joust.

There was a young man beside the vicar, and when he stood up unhurriedly to bow to me, I saw with a small shock that it was the man who had asked for a kiss on the stairs. Did he recognize me too? I could not tell for sure, but as he bowed over my hand, he sent me a swift look under his lashes and I thought I saw amusement gleaming in his eyes.

'*This*, my dear Eleanor, is Viscount Stanton,' Sir Walter said with emphasis, as though revealing a treat. I sent him a puzzled glance as I curtseyed. What was he to me? Obviously someone important, by my father's tone.

'I hope you are recovered from your indisposition,' murmured Stanton languidly. He didn't sound as though he hoped any such thing.

'I am quite well now, I thank you, my lord,' I replied, and then stood awkwardly silent, realizing that if he did recognize me he must know very well I had not been ill. I wished my father would move on, but he stood frowning at us, clearly expecting more.

'Fresh air is beneficial to the health,' remarked Stanton blandly. 'You should try taking a walk each day. To the village and back, perhaps.' There was no hint of a smile as he said this, but now I was certain he had recognized me. My heart beat quickly and I threw Sir Walter a frightened glance.

'Thank you, but I prefer to ride,' I said, flustered. Stanton merely bowed in response and turned away.

At last my father showed me to a seat and I sank into

it. I had a headache drumming at my temples where the wires of my new hood were pressing. I closed my eyes, breathing as deeply as my stomacher would allow, waiting for the giddiness to pass.

'Are you ill, Cousin Eleanor?' asked a solicitous voice. I looked up and found that Gregory had exchanged seats to sit by me.

'Oh, it is only meeting so many new people.' I smiled a little wanly. A thought struck me. 'Cousin,' I asked, 'do you ride in the joust?'

'But of course!' he replied.

'That is excellent,' I told him. All at once the joust was something to be looked forward to after all. I could not ride myself, but I would be able to cheer my cousin on.

# CHAPTER TEN

*Dear Eleanor,*
*Thank you for the fruit and sweetmeats. Such a treat! Time passes so*
*slowly, I sometimes feel I shall indeed run mad. Your notes and gifts are*
*my only solace.*

*Your loving Mother*

I struck a flame, set light to Mother's note and watched it
curl and blacken. With my father in residence at Farleigh
and Maria snooping in my room, I was careful never to
leave any evidence of our correspondence lying about.
I dropped the ash into the grate and left the room,
making my way down the stairs. I was to ride with
Gregory.

My greatest worry now was the whirl of gaiety into
which I had been drawn. There were plays and concerts as
well as endless banquets. My father required my presence
at all of them, and Maria ensured that I attended.
Sometimes I felt she was a sheepdog worrying at my heels
rather than the friend she pretended to be.

Renewing my acquaintance with my cousin, on the
other hand, was a comfort to me. I found his company

most agreeable. I must confess though, he was not quite the happy-go-lucky youth of my memory.

'You do not ride astride, Mistress Eleanor?' he demanded when he saw me swing onto Arianna's back. His face was a very picture of shock and disapproval. I laughed out loud.

'Indeed, I do!' I cried. I caught Tom's equally disapproving look and scowled at him. We had already had a whispered argument on the subject of my saddle in the privacy of the loose box. I was not willing to revert to side-saddle because guests were come to stay. I was no longer even sure I could ride on one. Unless Sir Walter himself forbade it, I would ride as I liked. 'And I'll wager I can outdistance you on that showy chestnut any day,' I taunted.

'I would not take a wager from a lady,' he said primly, averting his eyes from the sight of me on my horse. My temper flared.

'Do I offend your sense of decorum, cousin?' I asked.

'It is not seemly,' he muttered.

Tom sent me a look that said clearly 'I told you so'. I clicked my tongue in exasperation at them both. Their disapproval made me all the more determined to flout convention. I turned Arianna towards the gatehouse and urged her to step out smartly, leaving Gregory to follow or not as he chose. After a few moments I heard the sound of hooves behind me and guessed he was going to accompany me despite my offensive saddle.

I had not been able to ride whilst I awaited my new clothes, and Arianna was fresh. She shied at the sight of the guard and cavorted sideways across the drawbridge, pretending to be frightened of the echoing sound of her own hooves on the wooden bridge.

'That is surely not a gentle enough palfrey for a lady,' ventured my cousin behind me. He sounded anxious.

I laughed. 'You must remember Arianna!' I exclaimed. 'I had her when you were here last. This is nothing but playfulness. Come, shall we ride out Iford way? Once we pass the encampment, there's a great place for a gallop through the meadow along the river.'

Gregory smiled.

'Indeed, I do remember that stretch. But do you gallop? Surely . . . ' His voice trailed off as he met my incredulous gaze.

'Do I gallop?' I demanded in blank astonishment. 'Will the sun rise tomorrow? Of course I do.' It was on the tip of my tongue to remind him I jousted also, but I bit it back. He had become tiresomely conventional, it seemed, and I did not want to spoil the ride by hearing his reaction to *that* piece of information.

By the time Gregory had insisted on holding three gates open for me and had begged me to take care over rough ground twice, my temper was at boiling point. As we emerged from the trees by the river, a pheasant flew up, startling Arianna, who half reared, whinnying with fright. Quite used to her sudden frights, I kept my seat easily; ready to let her have her head if she wished to gallop. But before her front legs touched the ground, my cousin had grasped her reins just above the bit, bringing her to a complete halt.

'Let my horse go *at once*,' I ordered him through clenched teeth.

'But, Mistress . . . '

'Don't Mistress Eleanor me and don't interfere with my riding.' My voice was quiet but shook with anger. Gregory looked taken aback and released the reins. I urged Arianna forward and she responded by breaking into a canter and soon lengthened her stride into a gallop. The ground was soft but not wet enough to make the going heavy. I leaned low over her neck, calling encouragement to her, until she was almost flying over the grass. I could hear Gregory's horse gaining on us and urged her still faster.

Once we reached the stream at Iford, the two horses were side by side. I slowed Arianna to wade through the clear water, glad of the shade the overhanging trees offered. I heard my cousin's laughter over the splashing of the water, and looked round to see what amused him.

'By God, Cousin Eleanor, you would ride the devil out of hell!' he said and this time there was a note of admiration in his voice that made me flush with pleasure. I leaned forward and patted Arianna's sweating neck to hide the colour in my cheeks.

'Thank you, cousin.' Then I grinned at him. 'You know, we would get along a good deal better if you treated me as you were used to do, and not like some helpless lapdog. For indeed, I am no such thing.'

'But you are no longer a little girl. And I am no longer a heedless youth,' Gregory argued.

'You are not so very old,' I said. 'I see no stubble upon your cheek.' But he was barely listening, his brow furrowed with unease.

'I am a man and you are a beautiful young woman,' he tried to explain. 'You should be worshipped and served. You need to be protected from danger.'

'Stuff and nonsense!' I exclaimed indignantly. 'Where

did you get such ideas? You have become so very bound by silly conventions.'

My cousin mumbled something about the code of chivalry. I didn't quite catch it and shrugged impatiently.

'That's not the sort of protection I need,' I told him. 'Not help through gates and mounting my horse and suchlike.' I gave my cousin a sidelong glance as our horses walked side by side. I was in need of protection in much more serious matters than my cousin meant. I wondered how much he remembered of the events that had taken place just before he left Farleigh.

'Tell me, cousin,' I asked. 'Does Sir Walter believe in the code of chivalry?'

'Of course!' exclaimed Gregory. 'What gentleman does not? Sir Walter is a powerful and highly-respected man. He is a fine gentleman and most gallant to the ladies.'

'Oh, to the *ladies*! I'm sure he is,' I retorted drily. 'But not to his wife. He does not use my mother as he ought.'

'But, Eleanor, you are mistaken. Indeed you must be. Your poor dear mother is sick and he takes the greatest care of her. Everyone says so.'

'You know that is not true!' I retorted bitterly. 'Have you forgotten how he arrived home suddenly and locked her up for no reason?' My cousin was silent.

I leaned across and grasped his sleeve. 'Cousin, can I trust you?' I asked earnestly.

'You sound so dramatic, Eleanor,' Gregory protested. 'Like a play.'

'This is not a joke, but if that is all it is to you, let us drop the subject. Shall we canter?' So saying I urged Arianna faster.

My cousin cantered beside me until we reached Freshford and we slowed to a walk once more. Gregory looked thoughtful, but I ignored his sober looks and merely remarked upon the fine weather. He did not respond, but a few moments later he said: 'Tell me what is upon your mind. I am your servant to command.'

I chuckled. 'Now who sounds like a play?' I asked. But then I grew serious and told him something of Mother's situation over the last four years. And then, saving the climax for last, I revealed how I had heard Sir Walter and the chaplain planning to poison my mother again. 'She needs someone to help her,' I told him passionately. 'Someone must make Sir Walter see sense!'

'But, Eleanor,' objected Gregory, 'why would Sir Walter wish to harm your mother? It makes no sense to me.'

'I do not know why,' I said in a low voice. It always came down to this endless why, and I was no closer to answering it than I had been four years ago. 'I suspect he is not sane.'

Gregory shook his head, but did not argue.

'I can see that you are sincere, cousin,' he said at last. 'And that you believe all this to be true. But could it not be some kind of misunderstanding? Everyone has such respect for my uncle Walter. Why even the king trusts him and takes his advice!'

I made an impatient noise in my throat, but Gregory ignored it. He sat very straight on his horse, his brow furrowed in thought. I looked at him anxiously, realizing that I minded whether or not he believed me. I wanted him to be my friend as he once had been.

'Eleanor, what is it you wish me to do exactly?' he asked abruptly.

'I'm not sure, to tell you the truth,' I admitted. 'I hoped you might be able to help.'

'Do you wish me to speak to Sir Walter?'

'Good God, no! That would merely get me into trouble.' As I said this, I thought he looked relieved. No doubt the prospect of speaking to his formidable and powerful uncle on such a subject was unthinkable. 'In fact,' I continued, 'I do not want you to repeat what I have said to anyone; unless you are quite sure they might be of use.'

Gregory sighed and shook his head. 'I will think about this,' he promised. 'But really, I do not see what I can do.'

I was not sure whether I had convinced him of the truth. Neither did he actually promise me any support. But we returned to the castle much better friends than we had left it. It was a relief to have been able to talk to him.

Lord Stanton was in the stable yard when we returned. He had just dismounted from his own horse, and stood watching us as we rode in. Seeing me ride with a man's saddle made him lift his brows in surprise. He sent me a quizzical look, but I met his eyes as briefly as possible.

'Mistress Eleanor,' he bowed, 'and Hungerford!' He nodded casually to my cousin in a way that suggested they were acquainted. 'You will like to know that the king's herald arrived scarce an hour ago. The king himself is expected at any moment.'

I was taken aback. I had not expected the royal visit so soon—or indeed at all, truth be told. Stanton interrupted my thoughts.

'Mistress Eleanor, I would urge you to hurry. You would not wish the king to see you in such a guise.' As he spoke, he looked pointedly at my saddle. 'He may get *quite* the wrong impression of you.'

'I do not seek to find favour with the king, sir,' I said as haughtily as I could.

'More fool you,' he retorted. 'Better people than you have lost their heads on King Henry's orders. But it was the possibility that you might find *more* favour than you expected and of quite the wrong sort that was on my mind, Mistress.'

I felt my face flush hot, and slid off Arianna's back with more haste than elegance. Stanton stepped up to me and held out his hand for Arianna's reins. I was vexed at his interference.

'I can manage myself,' I said swiftly. Stanton shot me an amused look and bowed again.

'I did not know you numbered stable skills among your accomplishments,' he replied insultingly.

I glared at him, cursing myself silently for my awkwardness. I was beginning to think him a hard man to get the better of. I took Arianna to her stable to escape him. I found Tom there, looking harassed and anxious.

'I'll see to Arianna for you, Mistress,' he said. 'There's not going to be enough stable room. She may have to go out to pasture.' I nodded my understanding, and hurried out into the courtyard again. My cousin was waiting for me and accompanied me back to the inner court. We parted on the stairway to the great hall. 'We'd both best hurry and make ready,' he said ruefully, looking at his muddy clothes. Then he took me by surprise by taking my hand and bowing over it. 'Thank you for this morning, cousin. I shall think on what you said.'

# CHAPTER ELEVEN

*Dearest Mama,*
*You did not wave to me this morning when I passed the*
*tower. Did you not see me?*

*With love*
*Eleanor*

Upon reaching my room, I washed and dressed. I selected a kirtle of dark green and a gown of paler green woven with silver thread to go over it. Maria had insisted that yellows and greens were the best colours for me, so most of my new garments were shades of these. I picked out a pair of soft leather slippers slashed with green satin and pulled them onto my feet. They were more comfortable than anything I had worn in years, but would not last five minutes outside the castle. A rich girl's shoes, I thought. For someone who doesn't have to walk. But a part of me felt a guilty pleasure in wearing them all the same.

I could not fix my hood, having no maid of my own. So, carrying the offending article, I was obliged to make my way reluctantly to Maria's apartments.

'Ah, Eleanor, there you are at last. You are tardy, the

king will be here any minute,' she scolded. Then turning to her maid, she snapped: 'I am ready now. See to Mistress Eleanor's hair, and be quick about it.'

The maid bobbed an apologetic curtsey and drew me into a chair. But no sooner had she picked up the pot of hair paste, than we heard a bugle blown from the gatehouse.

'The king approaches!' we heard the herald cry.

'Quick, quick!' cried Maria, quite distracted. 'We must be in the great hall before he comes! No time for the paste.' She snatched the hood from the maid and hastily placed it onto my head herself, pinning it into place. I winced as the pins stabbed at my scalp. 'Let us just hope that keeps it in place for the evening. Come, we must go.'

'The king will only just be riding into the stables now,' I protested. 'What's the hurry?'

'You have much to learn, Eleanor,' Maria told me sternly. 'The king may keep us waiting for as long as he chooses, but we must not be even five seconds late for him.'

'He's not going to care about me,' I grumbled under my breath. 'I shouldn't think he'll even notice I'm there.'

With my headdress in place and my dress adjusted, I felt prepared to meet a dozen kings if need be. We hurried to the great hall, our skirts hushing as we walked.

'For pity's sake, do not hold up your skirts like that, Eleanor,' said Maria.

'But the floor is dirty. They might become soiled.'

'That is your maid's business, not yours. At least *try* to act like a lady.'

I pulled a face behind her back.

We were not the first to arrive in the great hall by any

means. There was a large crowd already gathered to greet their monarch and more people arriving. The ladies glittered with gold or silver cloth and jewels, the men were equally grand in their extravagantly padded doublets and their tight hose.

When the king entered at last, my father at his side, everyone bowed or curtseyed low. It was a fine sight, and I was just a split second late dropping into my own deep curtsey. I peeped up at King Henry and experienced a shock. Gone was the tall, handsome man of my memory. Gone was the carefree smile and glow of health and happiness. Instead, an immensely fat old man waddled into view, leaning heavily on a stick. His cheeks drooped and his once merry mouth pouted discontentedly. His eyes, formerly full of energy and joy, now gazed on the world with suspicion and cynicism.

He was approaching, and Maria nudged me to curtsey deeper. I knew I should not gaze upon the king thus, and I dropped my head lower, watching his feet approach, noting the swollen ankles and also the terrible smell that hung about him. The feet stopped right in front of me.

'My daughter, Your Majesty,' I heard Sir Walter say. I peeped up again, and my father motioned me to rise. I straightened up and found the king gazing intently at me. There was something other than world-weariness in the eyes that lingered on my face and figure.

'Charming. Quite charming, Hungerford,' he said. I felt my face grow hot under the royal scrutiny, and was glad when he nodded and walked on.

'You have caught the notice of the king, Mistress Eleanor,' hissed Maria, wasp-like in my ear. 'That is fortunate but also dangerous. He has always an eye for the young and pretty.'

I glanced at her and saw envy. He had passed her by without a look. Could she not be content with her conquest of my father? I considered her dispassionately. She was young, though not as young as I, but was she beautiful? I thought perhaps she was, in a strong-featured way that I did not admire.

'I do not want the king's notice,' I said shortly.

'Oh, I doubt you need fear greatly,' she sneered. 'I hear he is much taken with one of the young Howard girls. Catherine, I think she's called.'

'But he's not divorced yet.'

Maria regarded me coldly. 'My, what a child you are, Eleanor.' Then obviously feeling she had been too harsh, she slipped her arm through mine, gave it a squeeze and smiled. 'He is the king. He can choose another wife, or take mistresses as he pleases.'

I shuddered at the thought.

The banquet that night was splendid in its extravagance. There were tables all the way round the hall and every seat was full. There were deer roasted on a spit, swans and peacocks dressed again in their splendid plumage. A sucking pig roasted whole in the kitchens, and carried in on a huge tray decorated with fruit. I had never seen such a selection of pies and pastries and the array of sweetmeats and fruits made my mouth water.

The king presided over all this, one leg laid tenderly upon a footstool, eating steadily. He ate for over an hour. When at last he sighed and pushed his plate away, everyone in the great hall stopped eating at once. I regretfully relinquished the dish of sweetmeats, from which I had been about to select another marchpane confection, to one of the many servants who hurried forward to clear the tables. Never mind, I comforted myself. I could always visit Betsey in the kitchen on the morrow.

Dishes were cleared from the top tables. At the lower tables, where the guests had made do with trenchers instead of plates, crusts and bones were thrown to the dogs. An unlucky servant tripped and fell while removing the king's dishes. There was a huge crash that caused a sudden hush in conversation at the top of the hall. The incident would have been soon forgotten but for my father's conduct. He leapt to his feet and began beating the unfortunate man with a tall wooden candlestick he had snatched from the table.

'You clumsy oaf!' he screamed. 'What do you think you are doing causing such a commotion before His Majesty?'

The man cried out apologies, but he was ignored. Sir Walter continued to strike him and berate him at the top of his voice.

'Lord Hungerford,' rumbled the king into the shocked silence. His voice brought my father up short. He looked around him, as though dazed, and let the candlestick fall.

'Your Majesty,' he said with a deep bow. 'I could not watch the clumsy fool insult you so without becoming enraged.'

'It is well,' nodded the king, and waved dismissal to the servant, who fled at once.

The king invited my father to sit beside him, and engaged him in conversation. I watched them for a moment, Sir Walter inclining his head respectfully.

It had been a dangerous moment, but it had passed. I wondered yet again whether my father really was insane. I blushed at what the other guests must think.

Gradually the noise of conversation increased once more, until there was a lively buzz around the hall. The guests appeared to have put the incident out of their minds for the time being.

Sir Walter rose to his feet and hammered on the table. My heart jumped into my mouth, but he seemed quite controlled again.

'My lords, ladies, and gentlemen,' called Sir Walter. 'In a few moments a play will be performed for His Majesty's entertainment. But first of all, His Majesty has graciously agreed to bestow his approval on the formal betrothal of my daughter, Eleanor.'

My knees turned to water. No, please, no, not here in front of all these people. Not in front of the king.

I became aware of an excited whispering in the background. Sir Walter had paused, no doubt for dramatic effect. He was looking around at his guests, obviously enjoying being the centre of attention. Maria prodded me in the side.

'Go on,' she hissed in my ear. 'He's waiting for you. Hurry!'

I wasn't sure that Sir Walter was waiting for me, but as I was about to argue with Maria, my father turned and held out his hand to me. An affectionate gesture, hardly suited to our feelings for each other. I pushed myself unsteadily to my feet. I was trembling uncontrollably and could scarcely summon either the courage or the strength to walk across the front of the hall. I could feel all the eyes of the guests boring into me, and felt my face flame.

As I reached Sir Walter, he took my hand and patted it, as though he really was a loving father. I felt too numb to feel angry. My hands were cold as ice.

I curtseyed deeply to the king, and then faced the hall, careful not to turn my back on His Majesty. I looked out over the assembled faces before me. Which old fright have you chosen for me this time? Will he be older and fatter than the king? The defiant thoughts gave me some courage, and stilled my trembling for a moment.

'My precious daughter, Eleanor, is to be pledged to a member of one of our oldest and most respected families,' announced Sir Walter. 'The betrothal will unite the Hungerford and the Ashington families with even closer ties of friendship and alliance.'

There was a murmur of interest from the guests at this point. They knew more than I, for the name meant nothing to me. I was not acquainted with any of that family to my knowledge. Who could it be?

'Lord Stanton.' My father bowed and a familiar figure rose from a nearby bench, stepped forward and bowed.

My heart sank into my fashionable new shoes. I could hear applause around us, but I felt nothing but dread. Lord Stanton was standing before me. The very same man who had asked me for a kiss on the stairs. It was almost a greater shock than if it really had been some octogenarian with the gout and a wooden leg.

I had heard only his title, not his family name, before. He was young and handsome, true enough. But I had already such a dislike for him. What was worse, I knew him to be scheming with my father against Mother. To become betrothed to him was insufferable. I fear I was glaring at him, because I saw an amused smile creep into his eyes. I averted my own hurriedly.

Sir Walter was speaking. I heard nothing, my mind a turmoil of anger and fear.

'Eleanor Hungerford,' I heard the king say, and I struggled to gather my scattered wits. 'Do you plight yourself to Philip Ashington, Viscount Stanton, and are you ready and willing to marry him in accordance with your father's wishes?'

What choice did I have?

'Yes, Your Majesty,' I murmured, dropping a respectful curtsey. I heard Stanton make some similar response. It was done. We were betrothed.

'And when does the wedding take place?' asked the king.

Sir Walter bowed. 'In a month, sire, if it pleases you.'

The king nodded his approval.

So soon, I thought, panic rising in me again.

The entire hall rose to toast us and wish us health and happiness. My heart was hammering with fear. It was like being married already. And if the wedding was planned for just a month away, I might almost as well be.

Sir Walter put my hand in Lord Stanton's, but Stanton dropped it almost immediately. It was the first thing he'd done since I met him that I was glad of.

Worst of all we were seated side-by-side at the king's table after the betrothal. We sat in silence, avoiding each other's gaze, as the hall was rearranged for the play. I was painfully aware of his presence throughout the performance. I did not follow a word of the entertainment, though usually I would have been greatly amused by such a thing.

A month. I had a month to somehow persuade Mother to run away with me. We had to escape from Farleigh, before I could be married off. I could see no other solution.

# CHAPTER TWELVE

*Dearest Mother,*
*I am betrothed again, to a scheming demon of a man. We*
*are to be married in a month. I am afraid. Mother, will you*
*consider running away with me, if I can free you? I long to*
*be with you.*
*Alice tells me you did not let down your basket again last*
*night. So they could not deliver my note or the food I sent.*
*What is wrong? I will ride past the window every day till I*
*see you. I pray you get this note.*

*Eleanor x*

The inner court was crowded with men, horses, and dogs.
I had saddled Arianna myself and hidden in a stable. I was
waiting to join the hunt at the very last minute. My main
reason was to avoid Lord Stanton who I had managed to
ignore since our betrothal two days ago. But I also wanted
to prevent my father catching sight of me just yet.

It had been my original intention to stay behind, and
see whether I could get to Mother somehow. I was
worried sick about her. She had only once before failed to
wave to me or accept notes. That was the time she had

been poisoned. But that could not be the case now. Not when we sent her food. Surely she had not been foolish enough to accept anything from the chaplain? My stomach tied itself in a knot of fear at the thought. I longed to speak to her.

Maria had foiled that plan.

'Eleanor, do you not hunt? Strange! I've heard you are such a fearless horsewoman. Never mind,' she said, slipping her arm through mine. 'Let us go to my room and have a cosy chat while we sew. Then perhaps later we can take a little walk together in the garden.'

Horrified, I cast around in my mind for an excuse. 'No indeed, Maria, that will not do. For I fear I have the headache, and mean to lie down in my room.'

'Oh, you poor child!' she cried at once, all tender concern. 'I'll send my maid to you at once to lay a cool flannel on your brow and burn feathers in your room. That is the best cure for a headache, trust me!'

'No really, please, I could not put her to so much trouble. And I do not like a fuss made. Perhaps I should hunt after all. The fresh air might clear my head.'

So saying I made off in the direction of the stables at once. I could achieve nothing by staying behind.

I watched the king get into his saddle. It took the united efforts of several strong men to hoist him on to his poor horse. I wondered whether he would turn back with the ladies after the first few fields. I myself had every intention of staying the pace and seeing the kill. We were to hunt deer so that the king could eat venison that night.

It was not the season for stag hunting in May, but who

was to argue with His Majesty? Why should he not hunt the king's own deer when he chose?

A horn sounded. The hounds were baying. With a clatter of hooves and some shouts, the yard began to empty. I could hear the hollow clumping of many horses crossing the drawbridge.

I led Arianna out and swung myself into the saddle. Unfortunately Tom chose that moment to cross the yard. At the sight of me he dropped the broom he was carrying with a clatter.

'Mistress Eleanor! You'll never—' But he did not get to scold. Gregory's voice broke in and rescued me.

'Ah, cousin! I thought you would not miss this sport. I've been looking for you. Come, let us not be left behind!'

I followed Gregory from the yard, leaving Tom behind, standing shocked and anxious.

'Don't worry, Tom,' I called out softly. 'I'll come to no harm.'

I had a fair idea it was not my safety he was concerned about, but my etiquette.

We followed the last of the horses out through the gatehouse. More horses and riders were joining the hunt from the encampment. I used my cousin as a shield to stay out of sight of Sir Walter and his friends. I stayed close beside Gregory as the hounds took up a scent and led us up the hill away from the village.

'We shall have some sport today!' exclaimed my cousin as we swiftly crossed the first field. His eyes were alight with anticipation. 'Though I suppose you will be turning back with the other ladies in a while?'

I threw him a look of deep reproach. 'Turn back? There

is little chance of that. I'll wager I can ride as far and as hard as you can.'

'I wouldn't take you. I'd be sure to lose,' Gregory laughed. 'But will Sir Walter allow it?'

'Of course,' I replied. 'As long as he doesn't see me.'

The hunt was thrilling. I knew every inch of countryside, but I had never experienced the excitement of the chase before. I rode mostly beside my cousin, following his lead in matters such as how closely to follow the hounds. But I frequently showed him a better line across streams and through thickets. All my senses were trained on the dogs and the distant stag. I did not notice when the other women turned back, or when the king no longer rode with us. My brother Walter must have been sent home, too. I forgot to look out for Sir Walter as the hunt thinned, but perhaps he was as intent as I, for if he noticed my presence, he did not object. Once I saw Stanton looking at me. I ignored him.

We pulled up in the lee of some trees, while the hounds cast for the scent. There were fewer than twenty horses left. I was too excited to be tired, but the horses were glad of the respite. The weather was growing warmer, and many of them were lathered with sweat.

Sir Walter's eye fell upon me at last. I saw his brow crease with annoyance, but he refrained from speaking to me. We were surrounded by his friends, and he did not choose to quarrel. We were also many miles from Farleigh, and he could not send me home without accompanying me, or requesting someone else to do so. It was what I had relied upon. He did, however, cast a look of outrage at my saddle, and I feared I might hear more upon that subject later.

The hounds picked up the scent at last and gave tongue. We wheeled about and pursued them, skirting the copse and crossing the next two fields. I thought I had my cousin beside me and called out to him: 'Do you think we are close now?'

'Drawing closer,' the wrong voice shouted back. I saw with a shock it was not Gregory who rode next to me, it was Stanton. I bit my lip, furious with myself for having appeared so friendly to him. 'Do you always ride astride, Mistress Eleanor?' he asked.

'Yes.'

I urged Arianna on faster, hoping to outpace him. But his black gelding kept pace with my palfrey easily. Slowly, he began to draw ahead. I could have fallen back, and have avoided him that way. But something inside me urged me onwards.

Arianna was galloping flat out, she could do no more. Our way forward was over a stream not far ahead. I could remember it. It had steep banks and there was only one point where it could be crossed with any degree of safety. The only other option was a shallower spot at the far end of the meadow.

As the other horses slowed and their riders began to cast about for a safe crossing, I steadied Arianna and headed her for the place we had crossed once before. She remembered it too. I could feel her gathering herself for the scramble down the steep bank. We shot past Stanton and dropped down the slope. My stomach lurched suddenly, but not with the descent. To my horror, a fallen tree that had not been there before lay at an angle across the stream.

It was too late to stop. I held Arianna grimly on course,

shouting encouragement. She managed to steady herself in the water and cat-leap the tree. I felt her hind hooves catch on the trunk, and she stumbled, lurching and floundering. I thought we were going down. In those few dreadful seconds, I saw Arianna with a broken leg, needing to be put out of her misery. The world darkened around me.

And then we were up. Arianna had got us both over and regained her balance. She paused a second and then heaved us both up the bank. I slowed her to a gentle walk on the far side of the stream and patted her soothingly. We were both trembling with shock.

'Well done, girl,' I praised her. 'Brave Arianna. That was close.'

The sounds of the other riders were falling behind us. Luckily no one had tried to follow me. They would find the crossing place soon, but meanwhile we had a few moments to recover. Stanton was the first to reach me.

'Rash, Eleanor,' he commented. 'Very rash.' He fell into step beside me once more, and Arianna quickened her pace.

'I knew the stream,' I answered him, more defiantly than I felt. We broke into a trot. One of the huntsmen was blowing a horn.

'But not the fallen tree. Do you not even know the phrase "look before you leap"?'

'Yes, and the phrase "all's well that ends well",' I retorted angrily.

There was no time for more, the hunt was pressing on, but Stanton called over his shoulder: 'That's a fine palfrey you have there. Too fine to risk her legs with reckless riding and showing off.'

'I was not!' I gasped. I was speaking to myself, however, for he could no longer hear me. He was galloping now, mud flying from his horse's hooves. Arianna was fretting to keep up, but I was holding her back, gripping the reins tightly, my knuckles white. I was furious with Stanton, because he was right. The knowledge was humiliating. For a moment, I considered turning back. I could find my own way home easily. I won't give him the satisfaction, I thought angrily, and gave Arianna her head once more. She was tired, but broke into a canter, and we followed the hunt more soberly than before.

It was soon after that we finally cornered the stag. The hounds surrounded the exhausted beast. He shook his antlers fiercely at them, courageous to the last. He tried to charge the dogs, but they quickly brought him down. Sir Walter rode forward to be in at the kill, but at the last minute I found I did not want to see the noble beast die, and averted my eyes.

The ride home was long. At first everyone discussed the chase in eager, excited voices, reliving the excitement of the last few hours. Gradually, however, weariness came upon us all, and we fell silent. Horses and riders alike were spent.

I brought Arianna alongside Gregory's horse.

'You did well today, Eleanor,' he said. He had not seen the incident at the stream.

'Thank you, cousin. You are a skilled rider yourself,' I responded.

I could not take much pleasure from his praise. I was still smarting from Stanton's reprimand. My cousin's voice broke into my thoughts.

'That's a fine hunter Stanton has there. I wish I had one half as good. And he has at least one mount I envy for the joust as well.'

'He has?' I asked curiously. 'He must be wealthy.'

'Oh, very. He has a good estate in Hampshire. Well, you will see it soon, as you are to marry him.'

I cast a quick glance around but there was no one near.

'Not if I can avoid it,' I confided in him. He turned a startled face towards me.

'What can you mean?' he asked. 'You are betrothed! Do you not like Stanton? He is considered a good match.'

'I dislike him intensely,' I replied fiercely.

Gregory frowned. 'I thought all the ladies ran mad over him. He is a handsome fellow and rich. He's only a viscount now, but he will inherit the earldom from his father. He is the eldest son.'

'For all that, he is intolerable,' I retorted.

I would have said more, in fact I would have liked to vent my feelings by enumerating all Stanton's many faults to my cousin, but there was one point that could not be argued with. I lowered my voice:

'I know him to be involved in the plot to do away with my mother,' I said.

Gregory turned a shocked face towards me.

'Eleanor, that cannot be. What would he have to gain from such a crime?'

I shrugged.

'I have no idea. But Sir Walter told me so himself.'

My cousin opened his mouth to reply, but at that moment he was called from my side by Sir Walter who wished to speak with him.

Arianna and I jogged on steadily. My good mood was gone. I told myself I cared not for Stanton's opinion of my riding. He was nothing but a low, murdering villain. But I did care, for I had been in the wrong, and I was furious with him for pointing it out.

My thoughts were interrupted by a voice at my side.

'Your skills in the saddle command admiration, Mistress Eleanor. Especially in such a saddle.'

I scowled at Stanton, who was riding beside me once more, his face the picture of bland good humour.

'Oh, no. It is all *showing off*,' I snapped. I watched resentfully as his eyes creased with amusement.

'You are too reckless, it's true,' he replied. 'But you did not panic when faced with danger. That is a skill in itself.'

'I don't want your compliments.' I was becoming angrier at every word he said, convinced he was taunting me. I risked a brief glance at him. He wasn't actually smiling, but I was sure he was making fun of me.

'But, Mistress Eleanor,' he said, and now there was no mistaking the teasing note in his voice, 'you are my bride-to-be. If I may not both scold and compliment you, who may?'

'I don't wish to marry you,' I blurted out. 'I should prefer never to have set eyes on you.'

'Dear me, you have taken me in dislike, haven't you? What can I have done to deserve that?'

'I do not wish to be married at all. And certainly not to the sort of man who kisses servant girls in corridors.'

To my fury, Stanton threw back his head and laughed.

'Have you not yet forgiven me that?' he asked. 'I believe I was the one who came off worst, you little vixen.'

'Your behaviour was disgraceful. Is that how you treat serving girls?'

'No, only ladies dressed up as servants,' he responded cheerfully.

I was infuriated, and urged my tired mount to walk faster. To my annoyance, my unwanted companion kept pace with me, riding so close that from time to time our feet touched. I could not move further away without riding into the hedge.

'You crowd me, sir,' I commented. Stanton grinned but did not move further away.

'I did not kiss you, and you were not a servant girl,' he pointed out at last. 'I shall consider that kiss owed to me.'

'It is no such thing!' I cried. 'You insulted me. You should be ashamed of yourself.'

'Not at all. I was expressing my admiration for your fine looks and figure.'

To my annoyance, I felt the colour flaming into my face. I tried another tack:

'Why do you wish to marry me anyway?' I asked. 'Is there not some girl of your acquaintance you would prefer to a stranger such as me?'

'Mistress Eleanor, I did not wish to marry you at all. It was my esteemed father's notion. Truth to tell, I was most reluctant.'

I looked at him in astonishment. 'But then surely—' I began. He interrupted me by holding up a hand.

'But I can assure you I am becoming hourly more reconciled to the prospect. Your obvious dislike enhances the betrothal no end.' The laughter was back in his voice, and my surprise turned to anger once more.

'You are no gentleman,' I said, my voice shaking. 'I'll never marry you.'

'It is rather late for that, Mistress,' he remarked. 'The whole hall heard you plight your troth to me two nights ago. I'm afraid you'll just have to grow accustomed to the idea. I believe I improve upon acquaintance.'

'You think you're so clever,' I said in a low voice that shook with passion. 'But I've wiped cleverer shit off my horse's arse.'

I saw Stanton blink with shock, and felt a tiny stab of satisfaction, but he recovered swiftly. He bowed ironically—as far as he could in the saddle.

'Mistress Eleanor, allow me to tell you that my horse's arse is cleaner than your mouth.'

I had had enough.

I turned Arianna and rode off in a different direction to find my own route home. There were hot tears of anger and humiliation stinging my eyes. I would not give Stanton the satisfaction of seeing them.

# CHAPTER THIRTEEN

*Mother,*
*I am so afraid something has happened to you. Just let me*
*have one word to reassure me that you are well! And*
*please—agree to flee this place with me. For your safety and*
*mine. Mother, I tell you, I am betrothed to a monster.*

*Your*
*Eleanor*

The next morning, I begged a few pieces of fruit, some
pie, and some more sweetmeats from Betsey to send to
Mother. I did not give up hope that she would be at her
window again soon. I wrapped the food in a napkin, in
which I also laid the note I had written to her.

I headed for the gatehouse. I avoided the stairway where
I had run into Lord Stanton once before, using a servants'
stairway instead. But as I stepped out into the hallway at
the bottom of the stairs, Stanton came in through the
doorway from the inner court. I could not believe my ill
luck. I acknowledged his presence with a brief nod and
tried to walk past him, my bundle concealed behind my
back. He stopped me by stepping into my path.

'In such a hurry, my gentle bride?' he asked. 'After deserting me so abruptly on our ride yesterday, I thought you might be eager to bandy words with me again.'

I frowned. The memory of our conversation yesterday was still painful. Looking up at him, I saw a mocking smile curling his lips. I felt anger rise in me.

'Why would I wish to bandy words with you, ox-brain?' I asked.

Stanton laughed, the mocking smile gone from his face. He looked genuinely amused. I wasn't sure how to feel about that. I had been trying to offend him.

'No, indeed. I cannot allow ox-brain to be appropriate,' he replied. 'Do I not give as good as I get? An ox would merely stand and low.'

'Let me pass, please.'

'You are always in such a hurry to escape my company,' Stanton complained, pretending to look hurt. 'Tarry a moment, for I have a matter of great importance to discuss with you. I wish to hurry forward our wedding. I cannot possibly wait a month to be wed to such a charming bride. Shall I speak to your father?'

'No indeed,' I cried in horror. Then, when I saw Stanton laughing softly, I understood he had merely been taunting me again. I struggled to regain my composure.

'Your lordship chooses to amuse himself at my expense. Allow me to assure you that nothing could be further from my wishes than a hasty marriage. I fear I should make you a sad wife.'

'You will certainly be an unusual one,' he commented, and tweaked one of my curls. I pulled away crossly. 'I feel sure you would keep me entertained,' he added.

'I thank you, but I have no desire to be your jester,' I responded swiftly, dropping him a small curtsey. My breath was short and I could feel my heart beating uncomfortably inside the tight lacing of my stomacher. I made an attempt to push past Stanton, to get out through the door behind him, but he leaned back against it, his hand on the latch.

'That door opens outwards,' I told him. 'I really hope someone opens it. I should dearly love to see you fall in the dirt.'

Stanton bowed slightly.

'Charmed, Eleanor,' he remarked.

Exasperated, I spun round and made off for a different door. But before I was more than two steps away, Stanton caught hold of my arm. I clutched my bundle in alarm.

'Another parcel! What are you so busy carrying out of the castle every day?' he demanded.

'I am not yet answerable to you for my actions!' I cried. 'But if you must know, it is food for the poor of the village.'

Stanton held out his hand. 'Show me!' he asked. It was more of an order than a request.

'It is none of your business what alms Sir Walter chooses to give his tenants!'

'That is true,' he agreed solemnly. 'But I have an insatiable curiosity about you, you see. So when I see you leaving the castle every day with a bundle—there's no point denying it—I have to know what you are doing. You are always so busy, Eleanor, so rarely to be found with the other ladies. One cannot pay court to you in the usual manner.'

'I do not want you to pay court to me,' I replied angrily. 'I just want you to let me alone.'

'So you keep telling me.'

In one swift movement, he caught me round the waist, deftly twitched the bundle out of my hand and shook it open.

'You must not! Truly!' I cried in alarm, as my mother's precious provisions rolled onto the dirty stone floor.

'How interesting.' I heard Stanton's voice above me as I scrabbled on the floor attempting to salvage the food. 'Such luxury items for the poor of the village! Pie, sweet-meats, and apples. It must be a most valued tenant.'

I blushed and didn't look up.

'How unlikely, Eleanor. And how very shocking that you are such an accomplished liar. Do you have any other surprising talents that I should know about before we are wed?'

I did not reply, but my face was burning with fury as much as with shame. As I stood up, I stamped hard, aiming for his foot, but he moved it just in time, and my foot thudded painfully on to the stone floor instead.

'You cannot catch me out with that one twice, dearest,' he said provocatively.

Stanton was still holding the napkin that my bundle had been wrapped in. With a sickening jolt of fear, I saw my note to Mother flutter out of it. I dropped the food I was holding and dived for it, but Stanton snatched it away and my fingers closed on air. He straightened and waved it tantalizingly out of reach.

'A love letter, Eleanor?' he asked, brows raised. 'That would certainly explain why my suit is so repugnant to you. You have a rustic lover in the village. A rustic who can read, no less. Tell me it's not the blacksmith's son!'

'No, the blacksmith has no son,' I replied, confused and flustered. 'I have no lover.'

Stanton thought he was merely teasing me, having fun, but if he read that note, all would be at an end. What had I written? Dear God, I had urged Mother to flee, and described Stanton as a monster. I quailed at the thought of him reading it. If he could read, that is. I had no way of knowing. He would take it to Sir Walter . . . I dared not think further.

'You have no chivalry in you, my lord, to use me like this. Please, will you not give it back to me and let me go my way?' My voice wanted to tremble, but I governed it. I would show him no weakness.

'Indeed, I cannot, Eleanor,' Stanton replied. His voice was serious now, the smile gone from his face. He took a step towards me, and I felt suddenly breathless and afraid. I backed away. The tension was unbearable.

'Will you give me back my letter?' I pleaded.

Stanton smiled again. 'I will, but only upon certain terms.'

'Terms? What do you mean?'

'I wish to ride into the tournament with your favour upon my lance. And you will bestow it publicly. With the appearance, at least, of goodwill. That pretty scarf you are wearing would be most suitable.'

He reached out and touched the scarf. I flinched with annoyance. To bestow my favour before all our guests, to appear to acknowledge openly my feelings for Stanton, would be intolerable. But I had no choice.

'Agreed,' I said reluctantly, my eye on the note in Stanton's hand.

'I wasn't finished.' Stanton bowed slightly to acknowledge my agreement. 'When I win the tournament, I also win a kiss from you, fair Eleanor. The kiss that you owe me.'

'I owe you nothing. I'd as soon kiss a dung beetle. Sooner, in fact,' I flung at him.

'I'm sure I could find you one,' Stanton responded without a flicker of a smile. 'But do you not think you would prefer to kiss me when it came to it? I am not generally considered ill-looking.'

'Your horse looks better from behind,' I remarked.

'I have a very fine horse,' Stanton responded gravely.

'You are certainly arrogant. What if you do not win the tournament?'

'Oh, in that case, I shall relinquish the note to you without a kiss,' he grinned.

'And if I refuse your terms?' I asked. I could feel the net closing in. I saw I would have to agree, but if there was an alternative, I would find it.

'I would be most loath to read your private correspondence. I fear I should have to lay it before Sir Walter. He, as your father, would not scruple to read it.'

'He cannot read,' I retorted, trembling with fear at the thought.

'A detail, Eleanor. There are people in the castle who would read it for him.'

I stood before him, fists clenched, breathing hard. I considered the options. I could try and snatch the note now, and perhaps bite him as I once bit Sir Walter. But as

I glanced at the note again, Stanton tucked it inside his doublet, as though he had read my intention. He patted it, a satisfied smile playing about his lips.

I had no choice. I had only the hope that he would keep the note to himself and I would be gone before the tournament was over.

'Very well,' I agreed ungraciously. 'As long as I have your word that you will not pass the note to Sir Walter.'

'Word of a gentleman,' he nodded, and handed me back the napkin. I snorted derisively.

'A gentleman? No, indeed. You are only a nobleman,' I told him. He chuckled appreciatively.

I quickly picked up the food, even though most of it was spoiled now, and bundled it into the napkin. This time Stanton let me go. For the rest of the day I trembled with fear at the thought of the note in Stanton's possession. What if he read it after all? What if he took it to Sir Walter? I could not be easy now until I either had the letter safe once more, or was gone from the castle.

# CHAPTER FOURTEEN

*I am alive still, but very sick. Poison.*

*Mother*

I felt such relief when I reached the village and Alice handed me a note from Mother. I opened it at once, fumbling with eagerness. The shock of her few scrawled words in a hand that clearly shook as it wrote, almost undid me.

'Sit down, Mistress Eleanor! You've gone white as a sheet!' exclaimed Alice. She helped me into a chair and I sank into it gratefully.

'Oh, Alice! They have poisoned her again! How is that possible?' I cried, my breath coming short. 'She would not touch the food the chaplain takes her, I'm sure of it.'

I don't know, Mistress,' said Alice shaking her head. One of her many children tugged at her skirts, whining, and Alice turned and picked him up. She hushed him, her tired face gentle with care. Then she turned to me again.

'Are you sure?' she asked, a worried crease on her brow.

I nodded. 'It says so here. *Poison*. In her very own hand.'

Alice did not even glance at the parchment. She could not read, of course. But her expression was concerned.

'Who has poisoned her? The poor angel that was so good to us. Is there not something we can do?'

I took a deep breath, trying to steady myself after this shock. The fear for Mother's life, never far from me, flooded through me. What if she died? I could not bear to imagine it.

'I suppose it was the chaplain,' I said. 'I must free her somehow, Alice. But I am beset by enemies. Why, just now on my way here, my note to Mother was taken from me and the food I was bringing her dashed on the ground.'

Alice gasped. 'We are discovered?'

'No, not yet. You are not. It's . . . complicated.' I felt anger with Stanton surge through me again. How dared he take that note?

'If only I had some poison, I'd put it in the chaplain's cup,' I said bitterly. 'It is he that holds the keys to Mother's room.'

'You don't mean that, Mistress!' exclaimed Alice. 'You'd never do something so wicked!'

'How else am I to get the key?' I asked, a note of desperation in my voice. 'I need to have him out of the way somehow.'

Alice stared at the floor for a moment. Her son, perched upon her hip, and no doubt bored by our talk, grabbed her hair with one hand, and tried to push his other grubby hand into her mouth. She disengaged herself absent-mindedly.

'I wonder . . . ' she began. 'Could you make use of a sleeping draught? That would not be so bad as poison.'

'Yes, indeed, if I could procure such a thing.'

'Joan might be able to help,' said Alice tentatively.

'Joan?' I asked. The name was not familiar to me.

'The wise woman. Would it help you free her ladyship?' asked Alice.

'Oh, it would!' I breathed. All sorts of possibilities floated through my mind. If I could drug the chaplain, I was sure I might be able to free Mother.

'Joan's at the end of the street, Mistress. In the last house, with the chickens in the front garden. But she'll want paying. Food or goods.'

I thought of the unwanted gifts from Maria, lying in my chest. 'I have no money, but perhaps I can trade something. Thank you, Alice. I'll go to her now.'

'Yes, Mistress. Oh, and, Mistress? Be careful. They say she's a witch.'

Her words sent a brief shiver down my spine. A witch! Here in the village. Mother had never mentioned a witch since the last one was burned.

I walked between the rows of cottages, past the church, until I reached the last dwelling of the village. The garden was a profusion of colourful plants. There was nothing eerie about it, but still my skin prickled as I pushed open the broken gate and went to the front door. It opened at my first knock, taking me by surprise. A young woman not much older than myself stood at the door.

'I am looking for . . . Joan?' I asked, embarrassed.

'That's me. You'd better come in,' the woman said.

She did not look remotely like a witch, I thought, as I stepped over the threshold. I found myself in a small room, with straw upon the floor, and a few sticks of shabby furniture. It was neither clean nor dirty, neither comfortable, nor yet destitute. There were no signs of witchcraft as I understood it. But there was an intriguing and not unpleasant smell of herbs pervading the room.

'What can I help you with?' Joan asked abruptly. 'It's usually babies with girls of your age. You're not with child, are you?'

'No!' I exclaimed, embarrassed. 'Certainly not.'

'Good. Cos I don't hold with getting rid of babies,' continued the unnerving young woman.

'I'm . . . I'm Eleanor Hungerford,' I began by way of explanation.

'I know that,' interrupted Joan.

'Oh.' I was finding this surprisingly difficult. 'Then you'll know that my mother, Lady Elizabeth, is imprisoned in the castle?'

Joan nodded.

'Alice sent me. She thought you might be able to make me up a sleeping potion or some such thing, that I can give to the chaplain who guards her. I want to help her escape.'

'I can do that,' she said. 'What will you pay me?'

'I have . . . an ivory comb, or some embroidered cushion covers . . . ' I began uncertainly.

She sighed.

'Do I looks like I needs an ivory comb?' she demanded. 'Food'd be more useful.'

'But much more difficult for me to bring out of the castle,' I explained. 'I already bring some food out for my mother and it's risky. Can you not trade the goods?'

She looked at me for a moment and nodded. 'As it's for her ladyship. Come back in two days, and I'll have it ready.'

'Thank you.' I stood up to go, and at the door I paused, remembering Alice's warning.

'It won't kill him, will it?' I asked.

'No. But he'll have a head fit to bust next day,' she said caustically.

'Good.' I gave a satisfied nod and made my way back to the castle. My fear for my mother, a few moments ago all-consuming, was now tempered with hope.

# CHAPTER FIFTEEN

*Dearest Mother,*
*I am so afraid for you!*
*How did this happen?*
*Are you well enough to flee Farleigh? Betsey sends her best*
*foods to make you well again.*
*I love you,*

*Eleanor.*

I sought out Gregory at breakfast the next day.

'Good morrow, Ella,' he greeted me cheerfully. 'And so—the tournament begins!'

'Indeed,' I answered distractedly. 'And do you ride?'

'Nay, cousin. It is the junior event today. Shall we cheer on your brother Walter? I hear he is a true Hungerford and talented in the lists.'

'Yes, he is very skilled for his age,' I answered. I lowered my voice. 'And what of Lord Stanton. How good is he?'

'He will not be riding today either, cousin,' replied Gregory, a twinkle in his eye.

'I know that,' I sighed impatiently. 'But is there any danger he will win the tournament?'

To my dismay, Gregory nodded. 'He's nigh unbeatable,' he replied simply. My jaw dropped. I had not expected that.

'Truly?'

'Most truly. He has won almost every event he entered in years.'

I sagged a little against the table. Then I straightened and said briskly: 'No one is unbeatable. Who has the greatest chance of defeating him?'

My cousin became suddenly preoccupied with his goblet, twirling it in his hand. Then, a little colour in his usually pale cheeks, he replied hesitatingly: 'Well, I am generally considered . . . that is to say, I have come second to him a number of times. But Sir Peter is also . . . ' He stopped and grinned. 'What must I sound like, boasting of my own prowess?'

'You sound very modest,' I assured him at once. 'You do *not* boast, and you are not arrogant like Stanton.'

'Has he been boasting?' asked Gregory, his brows lifting in surprise.

'Yes, indeed. From what he said to me, I believe he expects to win. And I would dearly love to see him lose.'

'How I wish I *could* beat him!' exclaimed Gregory.

'Is he always so arrogant?' I asked.

'I am not one of his cronies,' shrugged Gregory. 'But I believe him to be generally liked. His sporting prowess makes him popular and his manners and temper are generally considered good. I've never heard ill of him. At least not until you—' He broke off uncomfortably, not wanting to refer to the conversation we had had the day of the hunt.

'Well, I think ill of him, as you know,' I said. 'And I should like it very much if you were to win this tournament. In fact it is vital that you do so.'

'I shall do my best, for your sake,' bowed my cousin. 'But tell me. Is it because you dislike him so much, or do you have a wager?'

'Both,' I replied promptly. 'I'm relying on you, cousin!'

As the guests left the breakfast table and made their way out to the lists, I was caught by Mistress Maria.

'I expect the pleasure of your company at the lists, Eleanor.'

I felt annoyed and suppressed it with an effort. I could see Sir Walter standing within earshot, a frown upon his brow. I curtseyed politely.

'Of course,' I said meekly. 'I am quite ready to accompany you.'

The event was entertaining. There was a large crowd, and many of the youngsters rode well.

I could not help but feel excited when my brother's herald announced him. Walter looked splendid on his sturdy mount, his legs reaching barely halfway down its sides. His horse bore the Hungerford coat of arms on his cloth: a griffin and a long-beaked bird. The Hungerford device of the sickle was emblazoned on Walter's tunic.

As usual, Walter rode fearlessly and defeated his first opponent easily. I was less sure how he would do against the other contenders, especially as some of the boys were a few years older than him. But I need not have feared. Walter won round after round to resounding cheers and applause.

There was a break for refreshments at midday, and

then the event continued, with more youngsters trying their skills. The standard was high, and I cheered my brother on each time he rode.

My cousin came by briefly in a pause between contestants.

'So Walter is in the final round,' he said excitedly. 'A great day for the Hungerfords. He rides against the winner of the next round.'

'I hope you will be as fortunate,' I told him warmly. Gregory smiled, pleased.

'Well, someone needs to defend the family name,' he said. 'It is a shame Sir Walter is not riding, for he was a great champion in his youth.'

'Indeed, he still is,' objected Maria, beside me. 'The only reason he is not competing this week is because he is hosting the event. It would scarcely be fair to win it. Nor is he so very old!' she chided. Gregory and I exchanged grins as soon as she looked to the lists once more.

Walter rode to victory, of course. I felt jealous watching him showing off his skills. I was much better than he, and yet must sit watching, trammelled by my petticoats as he had so unkindly predicted.

My father was glowing with pride as the king presented Walter with his prize, nicknaming him 'Knight of Farleigh'.

'Well done, Walter my boy,' roared Sir Walter, slapping his son on the back. 'I did the same at your age. You do our name honour.'

Honour. Do you dare to speak of honour, I thought resentfully. I imagined my mother waiting patiently in the tower, sick from her recent poisoning. There is no honour in you. I bit my lip and glowered at my father as he continued to speak.

'We will have dancing tonight, if it pleases Your Majesty,' Sir Walter declared, bowing low to the king. 'To celebrate my son's victory!' The king nodded his gracious consent, and my father hurried away to make the arrangements.

The evening was a splendid affair. My father had hired musicians and the guests had surpassed themselves and dressed even more lavishly than usual. The hall was so crowded it was difficult to move about. The king sat upon Sir Walter's carved chair on the dais and surveyed the crowd, ogling the pretty women and greeting friends. My brother had a place of honour near him and looked as though he might burst with pride and excitement. He caught my eye and gave me a lofty look, which said as plain as could be 'I told you so.'

When it was time to begin the dancing, my father bowed low before his liege and offered him the honour of opening the dance. We all knew the king's leg was troubling him, so no one expected him to dance, but to my surprise he nodded and spoke a few quiet words to my father. Heaving himself to his feet, he was supported down from the platform by two of his courtiers. To my horror, I found I was to have the honour of leading the first dance with the king.

I had danced so little in my life and I could feel all eyes upon me. My body became stiff and clumsy and I found it difficult to move. The king offered his arm and I laid my hand upon it, whereupon he led me to the top of the hall. Couples formed all the way down the hall behind us while we stood and waited. I kept my eyes mostly on the floor, but I could feel King Henry's eyes upon me. They seemed to burn into me. I felt hot and had trouble breathing in my tight clothes.

The music began. The king bowed. I curtseyed, and almost lost my balance. Then we were dancing. I had to mind my steps so carefully that my fierce concentration almost overcame my fear. But then every time we came together in the dance, the king and I, he squeezed my hand with his podgy paw, and I could feel his smelly breath on me. Twice he farted and the stench almost overwhelmed me. We all had to pretend we had not heard him, though it had been as loud as a trumpet. I began to fear I would faint long before the two first dances were over. But somehow I survived.

The king bowed over my hand and went off to dance with a duchess. I found Gregory at my side and clung to his arm with relief, my limbs trembling.

'Would you like to dance?' he asked.

'Never again!' I said, breathless and dizzy. 'I need some air.'

Gregory cast his eyes over the room, looking for the best way out. But then I felt a light touch on my shoulder and turned to see my betrothed standing behind me.

'Mistress Eleanor,' he bowed. 'Is it too much to hope that after your royal partner, you will condescend to dance with a mere viscount?'

'I regret to inform you that the lady is already promised to me,' said Gregory swiftly, taking my hand.

'Ah. I was under the impression it was me she was promised to,' returned Stanton ironically.

'In marriage, yes.' Gregory bowed courteously. 'But the next two dances are mine.' So saying, he pulled me through the crowd and onto the dance floor. As soon as we were out of earshot, we both giggled like children.

'Well done, Gregory,' I praised my cousin. 'That left him without a word to say. No small achievement!'

'I was under the impression . . . ' Gregory mimicked Stanton's lazy voice, and we laughed again. 'And we did not even give him the chance to engage you for the next two dances,' he added.

'For which I thank heaven, fasting!' I responded. 'But look, cousin, he repines not. He is dancing with Maria! I don't think much of his taste.'

'Nor I, indeed. She's handsome enough, I grant you, but her temper would turn the milk sour.'

I could feel myself beginning to relax after my ordeal of dancing with the king. I was breathing more freely and with my cousin I was not ashamed to make a wrong step now and again.

'So what kind of women do you admire, Gregory, if not Maria?' I asked.

'Angelic,' he said at once. 'Golden haired and delicate.'

'Oh.' I was taken aback, and a little hurt. I had asked the question light heartedly, but his answer was serious. I thought of my hair, which was more red than golden, and of my body, muscled and strong from hours in the saddle and the lists. 'Nothing like me then.' The words were out of my mouth before I could stop them. Gregory's dreamy eyes came back into focus.

'No, indeed,' he agreed, a little too decidedly for my vanity. 'Not that you are not a very pretty girl, Eleanor,' he added hurriedly, perhaps reading my feelings in my face. 'But I admire the ethereal qualities, you understand. And you are so very—'

'You do not need to explain,' I said, piqued. 'Cousin, I have the headache a little, would you mind if I retired? Perhaps you could help me escape the hall without Lord Stanton seeing me?'

'Of course,' replied Gregory, at once. 'Eleanor, this doesn't have anything to do with our conversation, does it? You are not offended? After all, you are betrothed.' He looked concerned.

'No,' I assured him, not entirely truthfully. 'But I have a long day tomorrow and I am very tired.'

'A long day? Watching the joust do you mean?' he asked with a grin. Then as I hesitated, he asked sharply, 'Eleanor, what are you up to?'

'Not here,' I whispered urgently. Gregory ushered me from the great hall as quickly as the crowds of dancers and spectators would allow. There was a worried crease in his brow, as he hunted for an empty chamber near the hall where we could talk privately. Several rooms were brightly lit with candles and contained guests playing at games of chance. In one room, we came across a couple locked in each others arms in the darkness. We withdrew hurriedly before they became aware of our presence. At last we found a deserted chamber overlooking the garden. There were no candles, only a gleam of moonlight shining through the narrow window. Gregory pulled me into the room, and shut the door behind us.

'What scheme are you hatching?' he asked. 'Is it something to do with your mother?'

'Mother has been poisoned,' I explained. 'I do not yet know how. I need to get into the village to see whether there is a message from her. Only—I am so closely guarded during the day. It has to be before anyone else is up in the morning.'

'I had forgotten you both could read and write,' Gregory remarked. 'How do you obtain messages from your mother?'

I hesitated, reluctant to confide in him any further. But he meant well, I was sure.

'Mother lowers a basket from her window late at night. I am not allowed to be out at night. But the village women retrieve the note and send the food I take.'

'But . . . ' Gregory looked puzzled. 'The moat. How do they cross the moat?'

I grinned. 'They do not. They have a long pole with a hook at one end. Alice's husband made it.'

'Do not tell me more,' my cousin begged. 'And, Eleanor, promise me you will do nothing more than exchange notes. Promise you will do nothing foolhardy.'

'What do you care?' I said fiercely. 'Go back and dance with the ethereal angel you are so in love with and let me deal with the dangerous stuff.'

'So you *are* offended by what I said,' exclaimed Gregory. 'Eleanor, you are my friend. Of course I care what happens to you. You know that. I have been in love with Mistress Phoebe since before I met you again, and it has nothing to do with my cousinly care for you.'

'Mistress *Phoebe*?' I repeated incredulously. I knew

exactly who she was. 'I wouldn't have described her as ethereal myself. Sickly perhaps.'

My cousin looked deeply offended. 'Don't insult the queen of my heart,' he told me.

'Don't make me puke,' I told him. We regarded each other in great hostility for a few moments, our good understanding in danger of vanishing for ever. Then we both became aware of footsteps outside the door. Instinctively, I grasped my cousin's hand and dragged him to the window niche. He did not resist, and once there, I pulled the heavy curtain across. It reached right down to the floor to exclude draughts in winter, so we were completely hidden. I'm not quite sure why I felt the need to hide. Perhaps it was the habit of concealment that I had practised for years or perhaps I was reluctant to be discovered conversing alone in a dark room with my cousin.

We heard the door open and close again on the other side of the room. Whoever had entered was carrying a candle, for there was suddenly more light. I did not dare peep out to see who it could be. Indeed, there was no need, for as soon as I heard their voices, I knew them.

'Are you certain of this plan, my lord?' came my father's voice, lowered conspiratorially.

'Not certain, but desperate, Sir Walter.' The voice was Cromwell's; I could recognize his measured tones. He sounded less calm than usual though.

'The king intends to divorce Anne as soon as possible,' Cromwell continued. 'The marriage has been a disaster. And I risked my career for it.'

'We both did. If you fall, do you think my life will be

safe? Henry does not offer honourable retirement to his counsellors when they fail him. It will be the scaffold for both of us.' Sir Walter's voice was hoarse with fear. 'Do you consider our danger imminent?' he asked.

'I do not know. I thought, when I was awarded the earldom, that the danger was past,' Cromwell muttered. 'But Henry grows ever more capricious and dangerous, and my enemies have been busy against me.'

'And yet he agreed to come here,' argued Sir Walter. 'He shows us great favour by so doing. Especially when all know he longs to be by the side of Catherine Howard. And she would be reason enough to throw aside the marriage with Anne, and us with it.'

'Is there a chance you can interest him in your daughter instead of Catherine Howard?' Cromwell asked. 'He seems mightily taken with her. That would be a triumph indeed, and would secure us the king's favour for some time to come.'

There was a long pause. My hand found my cousin's and gripped it hard. He returned the pressure, trying to comfort me.

'I fear it is a slim hope,' sighed Sir Walter at last. 'There was not that look in the royal eye that I observed when it fell upon Catherine last. I do not believe Eleanor could hold him.'

I did not want the king's notice. The very thought made me sick to the stomach.

'Your daughter has grown into a beautiful young woman,' argued Cromwell. 'It is worth a try.'

'A try, yes. And a new marriage of my own into the right family might help matters also. But we still may need to revert to your plan, dangerous though it undoubtedly is. A boy king on the throne would be so much easier to control,' Sir Walter murmured. 'We know that Henry will live for some years yet.'

'Hush, do not speak of that horoscope. You took a great risk there. If even a breath of that comes to the king's ear, we are dead men, and that pitiful vicar of Bradford with us.'

'We had to know,' hissed my father.

His voice made me shiver. My heart was beating so loudly, I was afraid they would hear it.

'I believe we will have little choice,' Cromwell whispered. 'Did you not hear, yesterday, how—'

There were more footsteps approaching the room. The door opened, more light came into the room. There was a sudden burst of female laughter.

'Ladies,' cried my father in an unsteady voice. I could only imagine the shock he must feel to be disturbed during *such* a conversation. 'Forgive us! We are dull old men, discussing business!'

It seemed that this was not an excuse, however. We heard the women cajole and plead. With much drunken laughter and many vulgar shrieks they eventually succeeded in drawing the two men from the room and back to the hall. The door banged shut behind them, and we were left in darkness and silence.

My cousin let go of my hand and let out a long, unsteady sigh of relief.

'Business?' he whispered. 'Treason, more like. Dear God, cousin, what evil have we just overheard?'

'That they should dare . . . ' I breathed. 'Plotting against my mother is bad enough, but this is the king of England. They put themselves in mortal danger.'

'And us,' said Gregory quietly. 'Good God, they have been casting a *horoscope*. They must be mad.'

'What is so bad about that?' I asked. 'Surely it cannot be worse than planning to overthrow the king?'

'It is as bad,' replied my cousin. 'Henry has expressly forbidden the casting of horoscopes or any other means of predicting his death. It is high treason and the penalty is death. Come, Eleanor. We must leave this room. Is there another door? They must not suspect we overheard them.'

I nodded, and cautiously led the way out of a second door which gave onto another empty chamber. We crept thence into a corridor in the servants' quarters, swiftly descended two flights of stairs and then emerged into the castle garden. The evening air was balmy, and I could smell the roses. The moonlight was bright and cast sharp shadows along the walkways.

Gregory and I walked in the garden a few minutes in silence, each busy with thoughts of what we had overheard.

'I think this explains why it is suddenly so urgent for Sir Walter to be rid of Mother,' I said hesitantly. 'He is relying on a new marriage to shield him from the wrath of the king.'

'Perhaps,' replied Gregory absently. There was a pause and then he continued. 'Eleanor, if you are planning to leave the castle, I can only advise you now to do so,' Gregory whispered. 'I have changed my mind. You will be far safer away from here. Do you need any help?'

'I may do. I have yet to gain Mother's consent or to

hear whether she is well enough to flee. Cousin: thank you. I'm sorry I spoke ill of Mistress Phoebe. I'm sure she's very . . . that you'll be very . . . '

I couldn't think what to say, but my cousin gave me a rather strained grin. 'That's all right. Lord Cromwell clearly thinks you a beauty, if that is any comfort.'

'None at all. Good night, cousin.'

Gregory took my hand in his and raised it briefly to his lips.

'Good night, and good luck, Eleanor.'

# CHAPTER SIXTEEN

*My Eleanor,*
*I am ready to leave as soon as you can contrive it. But I am still very weak.*
*The chaplain forced a poisoned glass of wine down my throat. I fear he*
*may do so again.*
*All my love*

*Mother*

I collected Mother's note and the sleeping powder from
the village at dawn the next morning. Joan accepted my
comb and my cushion covers, and I gave her some
sweetmeats I had saved from the banquet besides.

On my walk back to the castle, my head was busy
with schemes to obtain the key. I knew the chaplain
drank the wine Betsey poured out for Mother morning
and evening. It should be possible to drug it. And then,
once I had the key, I needed to get Mother out when
the castle was quiet. The servants were unlikely to
prevent me, but I needed Sir Walter, Mistress Maria, and
Lord Stanton and as many others as possible out of
the way. During the joust seemed to me to be an ideal
time.

On my return, I went straight to the stables. There I found Tom grooming one of Sir Walter's horses in the yard. The early morning sunshine was gleaming on his coat as Tom brushed him.

'Good morning, Tom!' I greeted him. 'Have you been promoted from cleaning tack? Sir Walter's Thunder—that's an honour.'

'Aye, Miss Eleanor, that it is,' responded Tom.

'No one else in the stables can equal you in caring for horses,' I told him warmly.

'Are you feeling all right, Mistress?' asked Tom, looking surprised. 'I thought I was a pile of horse apples.'

I laughed. 'I can be nice sometimes.'

'And how're you liking all the gaiety?' asked Tom gruffly. 'You be fine as a new-minted coin. Dressed up proper like you should be.'

I sighed. 'Yes, I'm in favour all of a sudden. But I find I miss the freedoms of my old life after all.'

'We miss you in the stables,' said Tom.

I stepped closer. 'You'll have to do without me altogether shortly, I'm afraid, Tom,' I said quietly. 'I need Beau and Arianna saddled and ready to go within the hour. I know there's precious little stable room, but can you do that for me?'

Tom stopped brushing and stared at me.

'I knowed there be summat wrong soon as you started sweet talking me instead o' the usual stuff,' he remarked. He glanced around to see if anyone was nearby and then lowered his voice further. 'Be you going away with your mother?'

'If I can arrange it.'

Tom stared at me. His hand was gripping the brush so hard his knuckles gleamed white.

'Take me with you,' he urged.

I felt a tug on my heartstrings. Tom was my oldest friend. It was hard to abandon him. For his own sake, I hardened my heart.

'You know I can't,' I whispered. 'We don't know where we are going. We have no money to pay you, nor even to buy food. You have a good place here. In any case, you are Sir Walter's servant. I can't just take you.' To my embarrassment, I could see tears gleaming in Tom's eyes.

'You'll be a-needing someone to protect you, like,' he muttered. 'What do two females know of travellin' alone?' He wiped his nose on the back of his hand, and stood looking down at me. It struck me he knew I was going to say no, so forlorn was his expression. I squeezed his shoulder briefly.

'I'll send for you as soon as ever I have a safe home somewhere,' I promised.

'You could do worse than marry that lord o' yours,' said Tom unexpectedly. 'He might help get your mother freed.'

I looked at him in blank astonishment.

'Are you joking? I hate him. And he would no sooner help me than fly to the moon!'

'I've reason to believe he's a good man, Mistress Eleanor.'

'What makes you say so?' I asked.

'His servants and his horses love him,' stated Tom.

I snorted. 'Am I a servant or a horse?' I demanded. 'Anyway, I've every reason to know he's no gentleman.'

I left Tom rather abruptly. I was taken aback by what

he had said, but soon dismissed it. 'Let a man be good with horses,' I said to myself, 'and Tom will be certain they have every imaginable virtue.'

Back in my room, I tucked my twist of paper containing Joan's powder into my reticule and deliberately left my scarf lying on my bed so that I had an excuse to come back for it. Then I made my way down to breakfast.

I sat nervously, fidgeting with my food, unable to swallow a mouthful. The bread was too dry, the ale too bitter to swallow. My stomach was tying itself in knots at the thought of what I had to do. I could see Sir Walter conversing with the king, Maria sitting nearby, listening avidly. My cousin Gregory was seated with friends, eagerly discussing today's jousting tactics, no doubt, and I could see Walter reliving yesterday's triumph, re-enacting his tilts, a knife serving as his lance. I whispered a silent goodbye to them all. However I felt about them, they had been in my life for many years.

Just as I was about to get up and leave the hall as unobtrusively as possible, Maria arrived at my side. 'Eleanor!' she greeted me enthusiastically, enveloping me in her usual scented embrace.

'Are you dying to see the joust? I can hardly breathe with excitement! Your father says you simply must be seated with us to watch.'

I forced myself to smile.

'Of course I shall do so,' I promised.

'And on whom do you bestow your favour?' Maria asked slyly. 'On your betrothed, no doubt. He is expected to win, you know. Or do you perhaps favour your cousin?' she asked with an arch look. 'He seems to be quite a favourite with you, I've noticed.'

I could feel her watching me closely and tried to keep my face blank.

'Oh, I really haven't decided yet,' I replied carelessly. 'Jousting doesn't interest me much.' I still hoped to get away before I was forced to bestow my favour on Stanton. 'And what about you, Maria?' I asked, trying to be polite.

Maria simpered.

'Well, the king does not ride—his leg is paining him, you know, after the dancing last night. He told me this morning that he would be forced to withdraw from the tournament.' Maria spoke loudly, and looked around her, to make sure everyone at our table heard that she had spoken to the king. She then sighed theatrically. 'And our dear host, your father, chooses not to ride also . . . so I scarce know *whom* I shall bestow my favour on.'

My goodness, did she really think anyone was interested? I had noticed no queues of eager suitors languishing for her favour.

With a flourish, Maria unfastened her silk scarf and called a serving boy to her side. She whispered to him and pointed. He went scuttling across the hall with the scarf and presented it, with a bow, to Lord Stanton, who looked mildly surprised when the boy told him who it was from. He bowed politely in Maria's direction and she pretended to blush and hide her face. Then Stanton caught my eye. He indicated my lack of scarf with a questioning lift of his brows.

'Oh dear, I've forgotten my scarf,' I said to Maria,

feigning surprise. 'How vexatious. I shall have to run and fetch it. Please excuse me, Maria.'

'Oh, my dear Eleanor, I declare, I cannot eat another bite. I shall accompany you. Then we can go to the lists together.'

'No, please, there's no need to trouble yourself. I'll be back in a moment.' I was beginning to panic, thinking my carefully planned ruse was going to fail completely.

'It's no trouble, for you shall tell me on the way who your favour is destined for,' said Maria, taking a firm hold on my arm and propelling me from the hall. At the doorway, she paused. 'Oh, look, Eleanor! Mistress Phoebe favours Gregory. Well, that's no surprise.'

I looked round and saw my cousin kissing a pale pink silk scarf and bowing across the hall. Mistress Phoebe was blushing. It suits her to blush, I thought. It puts some colour in her complexion. Poor Phoebe. Feeble Phoebe. I felt annoyed with my cousin for bestowing his affections on such a dull girl. Then my father caught my eye.

'Maria, Sir Walter wants you,' I said, relief flooding through me. And indeed, my father was attempting to catch her attention.

'Very well,' said Maria, releasing me. 'Wait for me a moment.'

'I will,' I lied, and as soon as her back was turned, I fled.

# CHAPTER SEVENTEEN

*Dear Mother,*
*I am coming for you as soon as possible.*
*With love*

*Eleanor*

I found a harassed Betsey in the kitchen, struggling to keep up with the demands of serving meals to so many. She was gutting and preparing chickens for the evening banquet. As each one was done, she threw it onto a pile on a freshly-scrubbed table. Watching her made me realize how much extra work the guests were causing. There was a whole army of servants working in the kitchen, already preparing the midday and evening meals. Others were carrying breakfast things into the scullery to be washed. They worked as though every minute was precious, as though their very lives depended on it. Betsey had laid out a tray for Mother, but had not yet put any food upon it.

'Betsey, can I make the tray up for Mother? For you have so much to do with all these guests,' I asked her.

'That I have, Mistress,' she replied. 'I'd give anything to

see the men riding today meself, given half a chance, but I'm stuck in here gutting birds for their suppers, ain't I?' The next carcass went the same way as the last. 'So I'll thank you kindly for any help, my dear.'

I laid out some bread and some meats on the tray and added a slice of plum pudding. Betsey, poor dear, had to do this every day, knowing full well the chaplain, that hog, stuffed most of it in his own belly, and Mother dared not touch the rest for fear of poison.

I reached up to the shelf where the tankards were kept, and selected a pewter goblet for Mother's wine. I carried it over to the barrel, stumbling in my eagerness. Crouching down, my back to the kitchen, pretending to be filling the goblet with wine, I shook the twist of paper out of my sleeve. My fingers shook so much I couldn't undo it. As I fumbled with it, a most unwelcome voice sounded in my ears:

'*There* you are, Eleanor. I have been looking for you all over.'

I jumped so guiltily that both the goblet and the paper fell from my hands. The goblet clattered loudly on the flagstones, and a little of the precious sleeping powder spilled from the paper. I bent hurriedly to retrieve them both, stuffing the paper back into my sleeve, and then straightened up, my heart thumping.

'Why, Maria,' I managed to say, 'what . . . what brings you to the kitchen?'

'You, of course,' said Maria impatiently. 'I asked you to wait for me! Hurry now, or we shall miss the opening of the joust.'

'I was helping Betsey prepare my mother's tray,' I

stammered. As I spoke, the chaplain entered the kitchen, his keys jangling at his waist. I filled the goblet with wine and almost screamed out loud with frustration. I could not add the powder with both of them watching. I placed the wine on the tray with the food. Looking up briefly, I met the chaplain's eyes.

'How very touching,' he sneered softly, before picking up the tray and departing. Maria looked around the kitchen disdainfully. She called me to her side, and led me off to my room, where she fussed over some last minute adjustments to our apparel.

'Eleanor, you are about to forget your scarf again!' she said coyly as we left the room. I was obliged to turn back and pick it up off the bed.

I ground my teeth as we walked. Maria had foiled me. There would be no escape for Mother and me this morning. A minor setback, I comforted myself as I took my seat in the stands overlooking the lists. Mother had told me that she was still very weak. Perhaps another few hours rest would see her more restored. I would try again this evening. I fretted that Arianna and Beau would stand saddled and bridled in their stalls all day without riders, but there was no way of getting a message to Tom.

The king was seated in a great chair with an awning over it to protect him from the sun. My father, Cromwell, and a few other favourites were seated around him. The rest of us were seated according to rank in the open stands. From my seat beside Maria, I had an excellent view of the lists.

Maria nudged me.

'Eleanor, you are wanted,' she said, far too loud.

Lord Stanton was before us, sitting his splendid black horse with ease. He had not yet donned his helmet and his dark hair gleamed in the sun. As I met his eyes, he bowed and my heart sank. I had not even managed to escape this. Stanton smiled his lazy smile at me.

'Will Mistress Eleanor honour me with her favour?' he asked softly.

Most unwillingly, I thought. But there were many pairs of eyes on us, including my father's, and I dared not refuse. Nor did I quite dare fling it ungraciously in his face, as I longed to do. Instead, I pulled it from my neck, knotted it loosely, and dropped it over the tip of the lance that he held up to me. A cheer went up from the spectators around us, and I flushed with annoyance. Stanton raised the scarf ostentatiously to his lips and kissed it for all to see. Then he tied it beside the half a dozen others that were already secured to his lance.

'Among so many, my poor offering can have little significance, I fear,' I remarked.

'On the contrary, madam. Your favour carries a most particular honour,' he responded.

I sat back and folded my arms. He had managed to best me yet again. Go ahead and triumph over me, I thought to myself. I'll pray I see you flat on your back before this tournament is done.

A blast on the horn, and the knights left the ground to make way for the first competitors. Stanton rode to the far end of the lists and donned his helmet. He was due to ride in the opening tilt. I watched him calmly sitting his restless horse until the flag was dropped. Then he rode forward, apparently effortlessly, horse and rider moving fluidly together. He knocked his opponent to the ground in the first run, and a great cheer went up from the crowd. He had not only won that heat, but by unhorsing his opponent, he had won his steed as well. I had to admit—with the greatest reluctance—that the man had consummate skill on a horse. It only made me hate him more. But surely he must have a weakness? As I was forced to stay and watch, I would observe him and report my findings to my cousin.

Despite the weightier matters on my mind, I became deeply engrossed in the tournament. There were many riders engaged to joust, and the thunder of hooves and the clash of lance upon armour filled me with excitement. The crowd cheered and screamed, and I found myself cheering with them. I longed to pit myself against the competitors. I was sure I had more skill than many of them.

I observed my cousin and my betrothed closely as they rode their several heats. Gregory was a courageous and a dashing rider and defeated his opponents with style. But he had weaknesses. He took risks, and in my opinion he aimed consistently too high, which gave a skilled jouster the possibility of rolling back from the blow. He also rode fast and furiously down the lists. While this was intimidating to his opponent, and gave him greater power in his blows, it also gave him less time to aim accurately or respond to his opponents' tactics.

Stanton, on the other hand, I could not fault. I watched him closely and had to concede him a grudging admiration. He was unpredictable, riding and striking differently each time. He seemed to know each opponent's weak points and use them. This was explained when I saw him on the benches between his own heats, observing each rider as closely as I. His pose was negligent; he sat at ease, but his eyes did not leave the combatants as they rode. He was watching them, deciding the best way to defeat them. And defeat them he did. In every bout he rode throughout the morning, he was victorious.

The sun rose higher in the sky and the day grew warm. The familiar smell of horses and harness grew stronger in the sun. Ladies were fanning themselves and complaining of the heat when the gong was sounded for the midday break.

Sir Walter had caused huge tables to be set up in the shade of some large oak trees, loaded with refreshments of every kind. Competitors and spectators alike drifted over to select pastries, meats, and cooling drinks. I sought out Gregory and drew him apart from his friends.

'Cousin,' I said urgently. 'If you ride against Stanton this afternoon, you must alter your tactics. Do something he doesn't expect. He has been watching you, and knows how you ride.'

My cousin regarded me, a bemused look on his face. 'Since when have you been an expert in the joust?' he asked mildly.

'I . . . I have watched and advised my brother Walter for years,' I said, slightly hesitantly. 'And I learned with you both, four years ago. Don't you remember?'

'That was long ago, Eleanor,' Gregory said dismissively.

I was tempted to tell him the truth, but for the fear that I might be overheard. 'Walter takes my advice,' I said instead. 'And he did well, did he not?'

'True. In the junior event,' replied Gregory.

'Trust me,' I urged him. 'Ride slower and aim lower if you face him.'

Gregory smiled. 'No, cousin. He would flatten me.'

'He'll flatten you if you ride as you usually do,' I assured him. Gregory's face closed, and I could tell I had gone too far. 'I'm only trying to help,' I said softly, putting one hand on his arm. He looked as though he would like to have shaken my hand off, but restrained himself.

'Cousin,' he said stiffly, 'I cannot allow a lady to be the judge of how I joust. Not even so redoubtable a lady as yourself.' He bowed slightly and walked away. I stood alone feeling both hurt and annoyed.

'If only you would direct such a heartfelt look at me, Mistress Eleanor,' said a hated voice in my ear. I drew myself up stiffly, but did not look round. 'In fact,' continued the voice, 'I am beginning to think that I shall have to challenge your cousin Hungerford to a duel to remind him whose bride you are intended to be.'

'There is no need, I assure you, sir,' I responded. 'And no danger at all of you allowing me to forget our promises.' I turned as I spoke and saw to my great annoyance that Stanton had shed his armour and was wearing my scarf, loosely knotted in his belt. He saw me looking at it and touched it lightly, smiling.

'I'm honoured that you treasure my poor favour so highly,' I said, attempting to imitate his own sarcasm.

'Oh, I do,' he assured me. 'And I am looking forward to returning it to you later.'

I was furious at being reminded of the wager he had forced upon me. And I was furious with my cousin for not listening to me. Was I to be doomed to be humiliated by Lord Stanton? He would win the joust, that much was clear. I glared at him, wondering whether he would claim the kiss in public or whether he would catch me alone somewhere. I was not sure which would be worse, and felt a spasm of dread.

Stanton was smiling his insufferable smile. I turned on my heel, and walked away. It seemed he had always the power to enrage me. No doubt he had had much practice in fencing with clever words. I imagined Stanton at the king's court, flirting with all the ladies there, and the picture added to my anger.

I felt a strong determination not to let him worst me. Was there nothing I could do to prevent his victory? I could not bear to harm his beautiful horse, but I mulled over the possibilities of putting Stanton himself out of action for the afternoon. The visions gave me great pleasure, but none of them were realistic. Not even putting the sleeping potion in his goblet. No, I must keep my eyes on my true goal, and save it to free Mother.

Nonetheless, I longed to be revenged on Stanton for his persecution of me. I reflected the best humiliation I could inflict on him was to escape and leave him without a bride on our wedding day. That would make him look such a fool. The disadvantage was that I would not be here to see his discomfiture.

Maria was at my side. I scowled.

'Oh, my dear Eleanor!' she cried when she saw my angry face. She came forward to put her arms about me. I pulled away crossly.

'What is the matter?' she asked, gently enough. When I didn't answer, she continued: 'Well, whatever is wrong,

I have just the news to cheer you up. First of all, everyone is sure that Stanton will win this afternoon. He carries your favour, remember? I'm sure you will be happy to see his victory.' I was silent. Maria continued undaunted. 'There will be more dancing tonight to celebrate, and then tomorrow the seamstress is coming to measure you for your bride clothes. You will be married in a fortnight! There! I knew that would cheer you!'

I was certainly shocked. A fortnight! How close it was. I had to succeed with our escape tonight. Mother could not stay in that tower a day longer, and I could not stay here to be married.

# CHAPTER EIGHTEEN

The sound of the gong drew the ladies and other non-competitors back to the lists and the men back to their armour and their horses. I trailed after Maria. The king was already in his seat and the first horses were lining up at the ends of the lists.

'Eleanor, you seem out of sorts. Are you unwell?' Maria asked. I could see her observing me closely, and I tried to pull myself together.

'Oh no, indeed! The heat is a little tiring, that's all,' I assured her.

'Good, for Lord Stanton rides now—see! We must cheer for him, he jousts for our favour, remember!' Maria smirked and looked sideways at me. I pretended not to notice.

'Stanton rides against Sir Percy,' I commented. 'He has come thus far by luck, not skill. I certainly cannot imagine him successfully challenging Stanton.'

'You are severe,' replied Maria amused. 'And very certain of your lord's prowess!'

'Oh—as to that . . . ' I shrugged. 'I still believe my cousin may defeat him.' I was not sure I did believe it any longer, but I said it anyway.

'You surely do not *wish* for your cousin to defeat your betrothed?' exclaimed Maria. 'No, I cannot believe it.'

I didn't reply. It was nothing to me what Maria believed.

I was right about Sir Percy. Stanton bore him to the ground in their first run, thus winning his second horse of the tournament. I sighed. Maria took it to be a sigh of pleasure and nudged me with a sly smile.

Gradually the number of competitors was reduced until only a few skilled riders were left.

My cousin rode his penultimate bout against one Sir Peter. I rather thought he was the man my cousin had named as a contender to win, but from what I could see, my cousin had a better chance of defeating Stanton himself.

I found it hard to stay in my seat, so desperate was I for Gregory to succeed. My hands were balled into fists and I was holding my breath as the two riders approached one another. Gregory struck his opponent successfully once, and then twice. But as they rode towards each other for the third time, I could see at once that something was wrong. Gregory was sitting less straight and his aim went wide. His opponent struck him hard on his left side. Time slowed. I watched my cousin drop his lance and sway in the saddle. He crumpled forward over his horse's neck.

'Stay on,' I muttered, and then I shouted it: 'Hold on, cousin!' I no longer felt detached and tired. I passionately wanted my cousin to win. My voice was joined by a sea of shouts, as the excitement mounted. If my cousin fell, he would lose his horse and he would not be riding in the last round.

Somehow Gregory hung on. Crooked and clinging to his saddle, he reached the end of the lists. The result was announced, and Gregory had won the bout on points. He slid off his horse rather than dismounting. I saw his squire catch and support him as they left the lists. I jumped to my feet. I had to know at once how badly hurt Gregory was.

'Maria, I must go and see my cousin,' I said. 'He is injured.'

Maria looked taken aback. 'But, Eleanor, they will be tending to him. You cannot . . . '

I did not wait to hear her objections. I left the stands and ran to the end of the lists. It was some moments before I could locate his tent among the sea of competitors' tents beyond the stands.

When I found it, I burst in unceremoniously and was confronted with the sight of Gregory stripped to the waist, having a nasty gash in his side tended to. Around the wound, bruising was already evident. The doctor, the squire, and Gregory himself all looked horrified at the sight of me. I cared not.

'Madam, you intrude,' the doctor pointed out politely. I ignored him and stepped forward.

'How do you fare, cousin?' I asked him.

'Not dead this time, Eleanor,' he said with a wry grin, and I could hear he was steadying his voice against the pain.

'I have just been telling Hungerford that he cannot ride again today,' the doctor explained, as he resumed examining the wound. 'There is at least one rib broken here, and some severe contusions. I could not answer for the consequences.'

'Withdraw?' I gasped, horrified. 'Gregory, no!' My cousin grimaced as the doctor dusted his wound with some powder and began bandaging it. I could see how white his face was. Even his lips seemed drained of colour. 'You've come so far . . . ' I said hopelessly.

He shook his head sadly at me.

'Shall I go and announce the withdrawal, sir?' asked Gregory's squire.

His words brought me to life. 'No!' I said firmly. 'Not until I've spoken to Gregory. In private.'

My cousin didn't countermand my order, and the doctor continued bandaging, muttering dire warnings against the wiles of females under his breath. The doctor left at last, and my cousin lay carefully down, his breathing coming in short gasps. He was clearly in considerable pain.

'Wait outside would you, Matthew,' he ordered his squire. Then he closed his eyes. 'Eleanor, I'm sorry to disappoint you. But I can scarce hold onto consciousness lying here, let alone mount my horse,' he whispered. 'And I could not lift my lance if my life depended on it.'

I knelt beside him and clasped his hand in both mine. 'I have a better idea,' I murmured low. 'Is your servant trustworthy? Does he keep your secrets?'

'Of course,' muttered Gregory. 'Why?'

'I'll ride in your place.'

Gregory's eyes flew open at that. 'What? Tell me I misheard you.'

'You did not mishear me. I'll don your armour and ride. We're near the same height. No one will ever know.'

'They'll know soon enough,' exclaimed my cousin scornfully, and I was pleased to see a little colour return to his cheeks. 'Good God, Eleanor. You won't even be able to mount my horse in full armour! Or hold the lance!'

'I will,' I promised him. 'I've jousted every day for the last four years. I train with Walter, and he cannot touch me.'

Gregory groaned. 'You think because you can defeat an eight year old, that qualifies you to ride against Lord Stanton, do you? For it is him I face in the final bout. You're mad. Go away and leave me in peace.'

'I won't,' I said stubbornly.

'Why do you wish to do this? Is this just the stupid bet you told me of?'

'It is that and more,' I told him fiercely. 'The bet was conceived to humiliate me. If Stanton wins, I must kiss him!' I hoped my voice conveyed the disgust I felt.

Gregory laughed weakly and then grimaced with pain. 'Eleanor, you are about to *marry* him. You'll have to do more than just kiss him then!'

'I will be gone before the wedding. In any case, it's about more than that. He gets the better of me every time we meet. He is so arrogant and sure he will win. And also . . . ' I hesitated, unsure whether to continue. Gregory opened his eyes.

'Yes?'

'Also I have dreamed for years of riding in a tournament such as this.'

My cousin groaned.

'Eleanor,' he pleaded, eyes shut again. 'If you are wounded, there'll be no hiding it. It's deception. Cheating. Imagine the shame for us both.' Gregory was white about the mouth again. He needed to rest. I had a momentary twinge of guilt, but I didn't let it stop me.

'Just lie quietly and get some sleep,' I told him. 'And don't worry. All you need to do is get well.'

So saying, I called in his squire. 'Matthew, your name is? Good. I am to secretly ride in your master's place in the final,' I informed the astonished youth. 'Time is short. Please help me find some suitable clothing and assist me in donning your master's armour.'

Matthew gawped at me open-mouthed. Then he turned to Gregory.

'Sir, you'll never let her . . .' he managed to gasp at last.

'He's in no position to prevent me,' I replied quickly, removing my hood and flinging it aside. I stripped off my gown and threw it down on the ground and my kirtle followed it. I did not even stop to consider the need for modesty. Excitement was coursing through me. I bundled my clothes under Gregory's things. 'Come, Matthew! A shirt. Some hose. Look lively!'

Matthew looked at Gregory lying helplessly on his palliasse. He was as pale as death and made no move to stop me. I wondered if he had fainted.

Bemused, Matthew handed me spare hose. He blushed and averted his eyes as I rolled them onto my legs.

'There's no shirt, Mistress,' he stammered. 'Only this one.' So saying he held up the sweaty, bloody, and torn shirt that Gregory had recently shed. I grimaced.

'Oh well. So be it.' Gingerly I pulled it on. I also tied back my hair and stuffed it down the back of my shirt. 'Now, my armour.' I clicked my fingers at the bemused Matthew and then turned to my cousin. 'Is he always this slow?' Gregory did not reply.

As Matthew began buckling my cousin's armour on to me, I felt a wild joy. I was going to ride! It felt so good to be doing something at last after so many days of frustration. That this would not help free Mother, I did not pause to think.

I needed to surprise Stanton. He was expecting Gregory Hungerford, not Eleanor Hungerford. That might be surprise enough. I had also the advantage of being completely fresh, while Stanton had ridden many bouts already today.

Gregory was right. A serious injury would mean my unmasking. It was a risk, but I relished it.

'Now, Matthew,' I ordered the hapless squire once my armour was in place, and I had pulled on my cousin's tunic, bearing the Hungerford device of the sickle. 'You must accompany me and speak for me if anyone tries to talk to me, otherwise we'll be undone. I'll pretend to be injured, you'll be supporting me. Let's go. Did you say something, cousin?' I turned to Gregory, who had been muttering something about deception and dishonour again. 'No doubt you wished me good luck?' I asked him. Gregory lay silent, eyes shut. I grinned, pulled down my visor and limped from the tent, leaning heavily on my faithful squire. 'Close the tent after us,' I muttered. 'We don't want anyone finding Gregory.'

Fellow knights slapped me on the back, making me stagger, and wished me luck as I reached the lists. Matthew helped me onto my cousin's horse. The horse sidled and fretted, snorting and pawing the ground nervously. He knew he had a strange rider on his back. The crowd saw only Gregory Hungerford, however, the Hungerford coat of arms on my horse's cloth, and the device on my tunic. The spectators set up a great cheer, which I acknowledged by raising my armoured right hand. I could see Stanton at the other end of the lists and my excitement steadied into a fierce concentration. I felt serious now.

I bent forward as though in pain, hoping Stanton was watching and triumphing. I could hear the crowd murmuring uneasily, and grinned to myself. I knew as sure as if he'd told me where Stanton would aim. That gave me a huge advantage.

I patted my steed. 'Good boy, Damien,' I whispered. 'You can trust me.' Damien wasn't reassured, and backed up anxiously, arching his neck. I gathered the reins and drove him forward to the starting point. Our heralds announced us and we saluted one another. I could hear the crowd cheering, and it was thrilling. Though I had jousted so many times before, I had never known the excitement of a tournament.

Damien skittered sideways and I realized I was nervous. But then the flag dropped and there was no more time to think about it. Damien plunged forward into his usual wild gallop. As we thundered down the lists, I lifted my lance high as I had watched my cousin do, and aimed for Stanton's shoulder. I tried to steady my steed so that I could aim more carefully, but he fought the bit, careering on in the uncontrolled way he was used to.

I could see Stanton aiming low, and I guessed he would go for what he thought was my wounded left side. All my concentration was focused on getting Damien under control. There was nothing I could do to avoid Stanton's lance. I gritted my teeth and braced myself to take the impact. As his blow struck me, his lance shattered, and knocked the wind out of me. I felt no pain at first. My own blow glanced off his shoulder with my lance intact. No points for me.

I fought for breath and hauled on Damien's reins, bringing him almost onto his haunches. I needed air, but I dared not lift my visor. Matthew was at my side, muttering something.

'What?' I gasped, irritated, once I had succeeded in drawing air into my lungs once more.

'Withdraw,' he was saying in a low undertone. 'You cannot take another blow like that one.'

'I will not let him strike me again,' I replied, still breathless.

He was right. Another blow like the last could put me in real danger. Perhaps I had been out of my mind to pit myself against so skilled a rider. It was done, however, and I would see it through.

I wheeled Damien about and faced my opponent once more. I could feel pain spreading through my side, where Stanton's lance had struck me. 'It is only bruising,' I told myself inside the darkness of the helmet. 'I have suffered worse during training.'

I could already feel Gregory's horse gathering himself beneath me for a second charge. I took a firmer grip on the reins and fought to gain mastery over him. I wished above all else that I was riding Beau and not this brute. He had no finesse.

The flag dropped and we surged forward once more. Damien's hooves thundered on the turf and the crowd was going wild. I rode him hard up to the bit, not allowing him to get his head. Then I focused on Stanton.

He was powering towards me, aiming for my left side again. I expected that.

I took careful aim at the very centre of Stanton's breastplate. It would have been a fine hit, but at the last minute, Damien, fighting the bit, veered to one side, and my lance went wide. Stanton, deprived of the body blow he had been aiming for, thrust his lance as I passed, shattering it on my arm instead. It snagged in a joint of the armour, penetrating it, and ripped my sleeve underneath. I felt a red-hot, searing pain and gasped. I brought Damien to a halt at the end of the lists. Gritting my teeth, I pulled the splinter from my arm. It was red with my blood.

'Are you all right, my la . . . sir?' asked Matthew, appearing beside me. I nodded, afraid to speak in case anyone but him heard my voice. There was blood oozing from my arm and the injury throbbed unpleasantly. I guessed it would hurt far more later on. For now it was a question of keeping going.

I could see people standing up in the stands, shouting and clapping, and I sensed that excitement was running high. Stanton was now in the lead, two points to none. I imagined the whole crowd was now expecting him to be victorious. I was angry at my failure. It was unlikely now that I could defeat him. But I could try.

It was time for the final gallop. And this time Damien was going to obey me.

'Do you understand that, horse?' I hissed at him. 'This time you do as I tell you.'

I pulled him round to face the lists once more. I could see Stanton waiting, watching me from the far end. I imagined how he must already be counting the tournament his own. Perhaps he was even already planning when to take his 'reward' from me.

I felt simultaneously a soaring confidence and a nervous dread. They were so blended I scarce knew where one ended and the other began. I faced Stanton once more, and this time I allowed myself to feel the exhilaration of confronting him. I was so much better with a lance than with words. It was time to put all those hours of practice to the test.

The flag dropped. Stanton thundered towards me. I urged Damien forward, but held him under control with all my strength. He fretted as I kept him firmly to a steady canter, but this time he obeyed me.

I took my aim carefully as Stanton approached. I ignored his lance and lowered my own a fraction. At the last moment I spurred Damien onwards. He leapt forwards suddenly. It took Stanton by surprise. His aim wavered fractionally and his lance glanced harmlessly off my shoulder, remaining intact. I barely felt it.

I held my aim with all my strength and concentration. It caught Stanton square in the stomach. So central was the blow that he could not roll away from it. The impact on my injured arm was tremendous, but I held on grimly, and Stanton was knocked back, clean out of the saddle.

I did not see him fall, for I was past him in a thundering of hoof beats and flying turf, but as I turned at the top of the lists and looked back, I saw him, one foot caught in the stirrup, being dragged along the ground, his attendants running to him.

I raised my lance in triumph and shook it at the

screaming crowd. People were standing up, applauding and shouting. I rode a lap of honour—I could not resist it. This was my moment of glory. I bowed to the king and to the stands. I waved to the crowd. I even singled out Feeble Phoebe for a special bow. I spared a swift glance for my opponent. I could see him being helped to his feet, so clearly he was alive.

Well-wishers were running towards me to help me from my horse. Abruptly, I was forced to leave the field and make for my cousin's tent. Matthew was waiting at the far end of the lists and ran beside me to the tent. I flung Damien's reins into his hands and crashed down to the ground, the weight of the armour making me land heavily. I was surprised how weak my legs felt. They shook uncontrollably beneath me.

'Let no one come in!' I ordered Matthew, and ducked under the flap into my cousin's tent. Gregory tried to raise himself on one elbow, a look of painful enquiry on his pale face.

'You are tournament champion, cousin,' I announced triumphantly, flinging down my gauntlets and tearing off my helmet. I took a gulp of cooler air and beamed down at Gregory. 'And you win Stanton's horse into the bargain.'

'No,' breathed my cousin, and fell back. There was no joy in his face.

'Are you not delighted?' I cried. 'You should be. You rode brilliantly. In the final run in any case. Cousin, why do you ride such a brute?'

As I spoke, I removed my tunic and began stripping off my armour. I fumbled frantically with the straps and cast each piece into an untidy pile as I freed myself from it. 'Everyone's going to be rushing here to congratulate you,' I explained. 'I need to make myself scarce.' I removed my breastplate and chain shirt, and had just bent over to undo my leg straps when we heard raised voices outside.

'You will let me in *at once*,' I heard Maria order Matthew in a voice of cold fury. 'I know she's in there.' In defiance of his anguished protests, the tent flap lifted and Maria stepped inside. I straightened up, horribly aware of my leg armour and bloodied shirt. From the corner of my eye, I saw Gregory cover his face with his hands.

Maria looked around, taking in the scene, and I could see comprehension dawning fast.

'*Well*,' she cried in scandalized tones, which had none of her usual insincerity. 'This *is* unexpected.'

# CHAPTER NINETEEN

Both Gregory and I froze, appalled. Our deception had been discovered.

As Maria stood there staring at us, a triumphant smile curling her lips, the cheering continuing in the distance, I heard Sir Walter's voice approaching the tent. He was loudly praising his nephew's skills to some unseen companion. Any second now, he would walk in here and all hell would break loose.

Maria seemed to have heard him too, and the sound of his voice seemed to bring her to a decision.

'Put your clothes back on if you have them,' she ordered me brusquely. 'And make all look right. I'll delay Sir Walter if I can.' So saying, she turned and ducked back out of the tent. Outside, we heard her rap out an order to Gregory's squire in a fierce undertone and then greet Sir Walter in her usual voice.

'Eleanor, move!' Gregory urged me. I realized I was still standing frozen with shock, struggling to grasp what had happened. Surely Maria was not *helping* us? I came to my senses when Gregory threw my gown at me and then winced in pain at the movement. I hurriedly stripped off the rest of my armour and borrowed raiment, before binding my injured arm in a clean handkerchief.

My arm was throbbing with pain and hampered my movements. Ignoring it, I began to drag my kirtle and gown back on. Meanwhile, Matthew ducked into the tent and helped Gregory to sit up and put his shirt back on.

'Here,' I said, falling on my knees beside Gregory and winding a bloodied cloth, from the pile the doctor had used, around his right arm.

'What are you doing?' he asked weakly.

'You have a wounded arm, you fool,' I muttered. 'Gregory, listen. You scored no points in the first two runs. Stanton broke his lance on your body and then your arm. Then you unhorsed him in the final round. Do you understand?' Gregory nodded. He was pale, and his brow glistened with sweat from the effort of sitting up. I doubted he could play the part.

I was replacing my French hood when the tent flap opened and my father and three companions entered. Maria followed, and gave me a relieved glance as she saw that all appeared well.

'By God, Hungerford, that was the best I've ever seen you ride!' roared Sir Walter. 'We thought Stanton had you for sure until that final run. Well done!'

He grasped Gregory awkwardly by his left hand and pumped his arm up and down. Gregory gasped, and Sir Walter released him at once.

'Has a surgeon been to you?' he asked. 'How bad is it?' He indicated Gregory's injuries with a sweep of his arm. I held my breath, praying that Gregory would not give anything away.

'Not since the last bout, Uncle,' said Gregory, with an

effort. 'My left side was struck afresh and troubles me somewhat.'

'And your arm? I saw you took a nasty blow to that.' Sir Walter pointed at my clumsily tied bandage on my cousin's arm. Gregory blushed.

'Oh, it's less than nothing, sir,' he responded truthfully.

I let out an involuntary sigh of relief. It drew my father's eye upon me at once.

'What are you doing here, girl?' he asked sharply. Maria intervened swiftly:

'Poor Eleanor was so concerned for her cousin that she rushed to tend him at the first opportunity,' she said.

'Well, well,' responded my father impatiently. 'Very touching I'm sure. But it is hardly proper for you to be here. You'll kindly remember who you are betrothed to, madam. Not that you are to go running to *his* tent either,' he added hastily. 'Maria, take her off, will you?'

'Perhaps we should all leave Hungerford to the care of his squire,' suggested Maria tactfully.

'Yes, very well,' agreed Sir Walter. He turned back to Gregory. 'Well done. You've made it a Hungerford victory all round, damn me, so you have. I couldn't be prouder if I'd won it myself. Get yourself dressed for the prize giving now, there's a good lad. We can't keep the king waiting.' So saying, he strode out of the tent. We followed. As I ducked out of the tent, I looked back and gave my cousin a quick wink. The look he gave me in return was anything but friendly. Outside the tent, Maria quickly straightened my hood and adjusted my gown slightly.

'That went well enough, did it not?' she asked lightly. 'I believe they suspected nothing.'

I raised my eyes to hers.

'Thank you, Maria,' I said. 'I don't know why you chose to help us, but . . . '

'Hush, child,' said Maria, giving me a quick hug. 'Think nothing of it. If only you could bring yourself to trust me more, you would not be so surprised. I desire only to be your friend.' She patted my cheek, and then tucked her arm in mine and guided me back towards the lists. I walked beside her feeling thoroughly confused. It seemed Maria was most truly kind after all. Perhaps I had wronged her all along. I had been blinded by her unfortunate manner and the affectations which hid her good heart. I reproached myself as we walked, but Maria interrupted me.

'As for what you just did, child, I think the less you tell me the better. But was it truly you we all watched on Hungerford's horse? I would never have guessed it.'

'I learned jousting with my brother Walter, ma'am.' I felt I owed her this confidence at least.

'How . . . shocking,' was her comment. 'Please do take care that no one but me discovers your secret. You can trust me, of course. But others would take a very dim view of it, I fear.'

'I shall not boast,' I replied.

'And how is your arm?' Maria asked. 'It must be very painful?'

'I don't mind the pain,' I told her. 'But it is still bleeding and I'm afraid that the blood might soak into my sleeve and show.'

'You will let me bind it for you properly soon,' said Maria, giving my good arm a squeeze. 'It would be better not to see the surgeon. And now, we must attend the ceremony as if nothing had happened.'

My cousin managed to dress himself and appear before the crowd to be awarded his prize, a gleaming golden statue. I thought he looked deeply embarrassed as he received it from the king, but I hoped everyone else believed him to be much moved. I heard people around me praise his modesty, and I smiled to myself.

If I had hoped to see that Lord Stanton was a bad loser, I was disappointed. He too was on his feet again, though moving with less than his usual grace after his fall. I saw him shake my cousin by the hand and clap him on the shoulder. He praised Gregory's skill and courage for all to hear. Gregory looked awkward and when Stanton offered to hand over his horse, Gregory tried to refuse.

'No, really, Stanton,' I heard him say, low. 'Not Caesar. That horse means so much to you. I could not accept him.'

'You won him fair and square, did you not?' asked Stanton, embarrassing my cousin still further. I was standing near enough to hear the low-voiced negotiations that followed, which ended in Gregory accepting a horse that Stanton had won earlier in the tournament in place of his own. I felt very annoyed with Gregory for being such a gentleman. Maria overheard this exchange too, and whispered in my ear:

'Did you ride for love of your cousin, Eleanor?'

'No, certainly not,' I snapped back.

Despite Maria's promise to bind my arm, she became engaged in conversation with the king. I managed to slip away. I went, not to my bedchamber, where she would quickly find me again, but to my old haunt above the hayloft. There I hoped to be safe from discovery for a while. I looked for Tom as I passed through the stables, but he was nowhere in sight.

I lay on my back in the sweet-smelling hay and relived the joust for a while. The cheers and screams of the crowd, the deep satisfaction of victory. Once again I pictured Stanton, on his back on the grass, one foot still caught in his stirrup, and a delighted smile spread over my face. The pain that now throbbed and burned in my arm was a small price to have paid for such revenge. It was almost a pity he would never know it was me, not Gregory Hungerford, who had put him there. If he could have known, it might make him regret having taunted and persecuted me. It might even make him regret having plotted against my mother.

This reminded me of my anxieties for my mother. It struck me for the first time how foolish, how thoughtless had been my conduct this afternoon. I could have been seriously injured. Then Mother would have been entirely at the mercy of our enemies. I shivered guiltily, and reminded myself that my injuries were trifling. I had been fortunate.

As I lay thinking everything over, a new plan stole into my mind. I lay turning it over, fear churning my insides. Could I possibly free my mother this very night? The castle would be far busier than during the joust, of course. But on the other hand, there was to be more dancing. That, surely, would keep everyone occupied. If I could drug the chaplain's evening wine instead of his morning wine, it could . . . perhaps . . . be done.

My plan was almost ready when my thoughts were

interrupted in the most unexpected way. I could hear someone coming up the ladder to the hayloft. I remained where I was, assuming it was merely a groom coming to fetch some hay. The grooms all knew I hid here, and they kept my secret.

But the figure that emerged was not the roughly-clad figure of a stable hand. Elegantly dressed and apparently recovered from his close acquaintance with the turf of the tournament ground, Lord Stanton stepped off the top of the ladder into the hayloft. He saw me at once, smiled slightly, and came to sit on a pile of hay beside me. Quickly, I pushed myself up, wincing as I inadvertently rested my weight on my injured right arm. I nervously brushed wisps of hay from my hair and clothes with my uninjured hand.

'Please do not,' he said, lifting a hand. 'You present a charmingly rural picture, I assure you. Ah . . . you are not awaiting a tryst with the blacksmith's son, I trust?'

I scowled at him without replying, straightening my gown so that my feet and ankles were covered.

'Your friend Maria is searching for you,' he informed me after a short silence.

'Oh.'

'She obviously does not know you as well as she thinks she does, for she is searching in your bedchamber and in the kitchens.'

'And how did you know where to find me?' I asked suspiciously.

'I saw you here the day I arrived, do you not remember?' he asked.

I did remember, but I had not been aware that he saw me clearly enough to recognize me.

'No,' I lied. 'But I'm honoured that you do, sir'

'Liar,' he responded appreciatively, and I could not help a small smile. 'You are annoyed to be discovered in your secret hiding place, and by me of all people.'

'Perhaps.' I noticed that Stanton held himself straighter than usual and seemed to have a little difficulty breathing. I wondered whether he was merely bruised, or whether he had broken a rib or two in his fall.

'Are you not concerned about my possible injuries?' Stanton asked. 'I heard you were most concerned about my opponent's.'

I frowned. 'You look remarkably well, my lord. I see no cause for concern. But tell me: how did the lists look from the ground. Muddy?'

To my surprise, Stanton laughed. 'It was a most unfamiliar perspective,' he conceded. 'I am used to win.'

'So you told me,' I agreed affably. I took enormous pleasure in his defeat and my own role in it. I was enjoying this exchange and I fear my delight showed.

'I therefore owe you your letter,' Stanton continued without rancour. He held out my precious note. I gave a gasp of surprise and reached out for it with my left hand. I could see my seal was still intact. He had not read the note, nor had he shown the contents to Sir Walter. I took the note and crumpled it tightly in my hand. I might still be trapped at Farleigh, but at least my plans were not uncovered.

'And so, your gallant cousin has deprived me of my kiss!' commented Stanton. His tone was still light, but I blushed and could not meet his eyes. 'Unless of course you choose to bestow it willingly on a defeated knight?'

he asked hopefully. That surprised a small laugh from me. I shook my head, but also wondered what it might be like to kiss him. I stole a look at his face. He was certainly handsome. Would he put his arms around me if he kissed me? I shivered slightly, and I wasn't quite sure why. Stanton was looking at me closely, his expression hard to read.

'Ah well, I thought not,' he said at last. 'But you will shake hands at least?' His eyes didn't waver from my face. I hesitated. I could not decently refuse, and yet my right arm was so very painful now. I gritted my teeth and held out my hand to him, somewhat stiffly, hoping he would not shake it too vigorously. He did not shake it at all. Instead, taking it firmly in one hand, he used his free hand to push my sleeve back in one deft movement, revealing the bloodstained handkerchief still bound tightly over the injury.

I cried out, partly with the pain, and partly in shock and fear.

'An accident, Mistress Eleanor?' asked Stanton, sardonically. 'What did you do? Fall up this ladder?'

'I . . . no, one of the horses bit me.'

Stanton untied the knot, ignoring my attempt to pull away, and peeled the handkerchief from my arm. 'You have cut yourself. This needs cleaning,' he said, examining the wound. Still he held my arm, his fingers cool against the heat around the injury. I was fully aware of the potential seriousness of the situation. But surely he could not guess? It was too wildly improbable that he should imagine I had jousted against him.

Stanton took out a clean handkerchief of his own and

bound it around my arm. I sat still, feeling awkward to have him tending me like this, when I had deceived him so badly. I could feel my heart thumping painfully in my chest as I waited to hear what he might say next. At last he released me and sat back on his heels in the straw. His look was sombre.

'So I was right,' he said quietly. 'I can scarcely credit it, even with the evidence of my own eyes.'

'My lord?' I faltered, unsure of his meaning, but fearing the worst.

'You took your cousin's place in the joust. You knocked me from my horse,' he stated calmly, but there was a slight wonder in his voice. 'How did you dare? You might have been killed!'

'I don't know what you mean . . . ' I began, but Stanton waved my words away impatiently.

'Don't deny it. I know it for a fact, incredible though it may seem.'

'Maria told you?' I asked in a small voice.

'Maria? Good God, no. Was she part of this?' exclaimed Stanton in surprise.

'No, but she found out and shielded us, after . . . ' My voice trailed off. I didn't know what to say, and was afraid of saying too much. Stanton was still gazing at me.

'So why did you do it?' he asked again. 'Such a risk!'

'You thought you could force my hand with that hateful wager,' I replied angrily. 'I was not going to submit tamely to such a thing.'

Stanton looked taken aback. I swallowed and continued more quietly. 'In any case, I am not inexperienced in the joust, sir,' I told him stiffly.

'That much was obvious. I should rather suppose you were trained from the cradle,' Stanton retorted.

'Not quite. I was eleven when the castellan began to teach me alongside my brother.'

'And were you afraid today?' he asked, his voice suddenly softer. The question surprised me so much, I blinked at him.

'Afraid? Only a little. I was absolutely determined to get the better of you,' I replied honestly.

'Have I angered you so much, Eleanor?'

'I should think that must have been your intention, my lord. I can imagine no other reason for such ungentlemanly behaviour.'

Stanton did not defend himself, nor did he apologize. Instead, he gave a short bark of laughter. 'That was your reason for this outrageous masquerade? Very well, I believe you. No doubt it was your idea. I can hardly believe your cousin dreamed it up.'

'No, of course not. He was most unwilling . . . Sir, if Maria did not tell you, how did you know?'

'Several things. The way your cousin's mount was fretting for a start. You were clearly not the rider he was used to. That aroused my suspicions. Somebody had taken your cousin's place. But your style was unknown to me. I could not think who you might be.'

I bit my lip, and he smiled faintly. 'I'm really not quite as stupid as you seem to think me, Eleanor. I noticed you were missing from the stands during the final, and I was surprised. I knew, you see, that you had a vested interest in the outcome of that particular bout.'

He was teasing me again, and I glowered at him. The humorous gleam was back in his eyes.

'I was not going to let you win by withdrawal,' I said fiercely. 'If the rules did not forbid women, I could have ridden against you openly.'

'That would have been interesting.' He smiled briefly, and then grew serious once more. 'I cannot condone the deception you practised. I am most unhappy to have been apparently beaten by your pitiful cousin.'

'He is not pitiful,' I exclaimed indignantly.

'Pitiful,' repeated Stanton firmly. 'But I find myself in awe of both your considerable courage, and your skill with a lance.'

I did not know where to look. Stanton sounded, for once, quite sincere.

'Thank you, I suppose,' I said at last. Then I added: 'If it had not been for that hateful wager, I never should have done it.'

'That would almost have been a pity.' Stanton took my left hand in his, and kissed it. I shuffled uncomfortably.

'Can I escort you to Mistress Maria?' he asked, dispelling my embarrassment.

Stanton descended the ladder first and then insisted on my jumping down so he could catch me, despite my protests that I could manage perfectly well. In the end, I agreed. He caught me, his hands on my waist, and held me a moment before setting me on my feet. I grimaced a little, my side still sore from the first blow of the lance.

'You are hurt?' asked Stanton, looking concerned. He was still holding me. I hurriedly disengaged myself.

'Only a little bruised. I have often been hurt in training. This is nothing.'

'I reproach myself for injuring you,' Stanton told me.

It sounded most unlike him. I lifted my brows incredulously, but he met my eyes, his own sincere. Then he turned to the door.

Before we walked out into the yard, I paused, stopping him with a hand on his arm.

'You are not going to tell Sir Walter, are you?' I asked, looking anxiously up at him. 'That I took Gregory's place, I mean.'

The look he gave me in response was enigmatic. I was puzzled and then it struck me.

'Of course. You cannot tell, can you?' I crowed gleefully. 'For then everyone will know you were beaten by a mere girl, which would be even more humiliating than being beaten by my cousin! That's a double defeat for you, my lord!'

Stanton bowed stiffly. '*Touché*, Eleanor. Your round, I think.'

# CHAPTER TWENTY

'Good evening, Betsey,' I greeted the cook, as I entered the kitchen an hour later. 'Is this Mother's supper tray?'

'Indeed, Mistress Eleanor,' she replied. 'But where the chaplain is, I cannot say. How were the joust, Mistress? I heard your cousin did win!'

'He did indeed! I am very proud of him!' I agreed. 'Betsey, would you be a dear, and draw me a mug of ale?' I asked the harassed cook. 'I'm so very thirsty.'

I did not usually ask Betsey to wait on me, especially not when she was so busy, and she shot me a surprised look. But she took down a mug without a word, and went to the barrel to draw the ale. As soon as her back was turned, I emptied the contents of my twist of paper into the goblet of wine on Mother's tray. A fine grey dusting of powder spilled onto the tray beside the goblet. With a trembling hand, I wiped it away and quickly stirred the wine with a knife that was lying on the table. When I looked up, Betsey was regarding me in astonishment, my mug of ale in one hand.

'Whatever are you doing, Mistress Eleanor?' she demanded. I felt a stab of annoyance. Why did she have to turn round so quickly?

'I . . . it's to help Mother,' I whispered frantically. 'I have to get the chaplain out of the way.'

Betsey clutched my arm. 'It's not poison, Mistress Eleanor?' she gasped.

'No.' I shook my head, and took the mug of ale from her hand. 'Thank you, Betsey.'

I stood sipping the yeasty beverage, while Betsey looked fearfully at me. Her mouth opened, but then shut again with a snap. She was looking past me. I heard the heavy footfall and breathing of the chaplain behind me. He was no longer soft-footed as he used to be. He puffed and wheezed as he walked.

'Here again, Eleanor?' he asked, eyebrows raised. 'You neglect your guests.'

'They'll not miss me,' I said as nonchalantly as I could. I noticed I was shaking, and held myself rigidly, the fear of discovery or failure tormenting me. My hands were damp with perspiration.

To my relief, the chaplain picked up the tray, complete with the goblet of drugged wine, and left. As he reached the door, I made a movement to follow him, but then paused and glanced at Betsey.

'Take care, Mistress,' she whispered. I nodded and set down my mug. I had a sudden impulse to hug her. If my plan went well, I would not see her again. I hesitated, and found that I lacked the courage for such an unfamiliar gesture. And so I simply turned and followed the chaplain, staying out of sight. I cursed my fashionable dress which rustled as I walked. It used to be easier to remain unnoticed in servants' garb.

Doubts kept assailing me as I walked. Suppose the chaplain no longer drank Mother's wine? Suppose he gave it to her and for some reason she broke her self-imposed rule and drank it herself? I could be drugging my own mother instead of rescuing her. She would not be able to escape, and would suffer the ill effects of the drug.

Should I stop the chaplain as he went to the tower? Knock the tray from his hands? If only there was some way I could warn Mother. Then, just ahead of me, I heard the chaplain's door bang shut. If he had gone into his own chambers, all was presumably safe. I breathed deeply, telling myself he was sure to drink the wine. He always did.

I hid myself in an alcove and waited. New worries began to torment me. How long did the powder need before taking effect? Was it instant? If the chaplain did not re-emerge, I supposed I would have to knock on his door. I stood anxiously trying to come up with a reason to speak to him. A false message from my father? No, far too risky. A question about scripture? That would make him suspicious. I was not known for my piety.

I need not have worried. After what seemed an eternity, he emerged, tray in hands. As far as I could see from my hiding place, he had eaten the choicest titbits, but I could not see inside the goblet. I cursed quietly under my breath. How could I find out?

At that moment the dinner trumpet sounded. I shot out from my hiding place in pursuit of the chaplain and caught up with him on the stairs.

'Do you not come in to dinner, Father Rankin?' I asked him innocently. He sent me a repulsive look in return.

'Yes, yes, shortly,' he replied impatiently. Then he added: 'I'm touched by your concern. Should you not be making *your* way to dinner?' His voice was loaded with sarcasm, but I cared not. I had seen the wine goblet had been emptied and refilled with water. My greatest fear was dismissed. The chaplain had drunk the powder; there was no danger now that Mother would get it.

But I now had to keep the chaplain in sight. He could be overcome by the effects of the drug at any time. I followed him to the Lady Tower and hid at the bottom while he ascended. I hoped he might pass out up there, and waited with baited breath. But to my disappointment, I heard him coming back down the stairs some ten minutes later. Were his footsteps a little more sluggish, a little heavier than usual? I could not be sure.

By the time he reached the passageway leading to the great hall, his tread was definitely slower. His steps faltered and I saw him stop and lean his head on the wall briefly. I approached him. 'Are you well, Father?' I asked. Sweat was beaded on his forehead and his eyes were blurred and bloodshot. He had to struggle to focus on me at all. 'Should I help you to your room?' I asked him hopefully. 'You look ill.' I should have been rejoicing to see my enemy overcome, but instead I felt guilty and sick at the sight. What if the powder was poisonous after all? Father Rankin might die.

'No,' he gasped. 'I can't . . . I just need a little wine.' Then with a most uncharacteristic outburst, he snarled: 'What are you following me about for?' He pushed me away from him and staggered into the hall. I followed helplessly, wishing I'd found some way of diverting him from such a public place. How would I get the key unnoticed if he collapsed in front of the entire hall?

The hall was filling up, but not all the guests had

arrived, and the servants had not yet begun to serve the food. The chaplain crashed into the nearest table and clutched it. I looked around fearfully, but the noise of voices and laughter had drowned the sound. No one seemed to have noticed. Taking his arm, I heaved his dead weight onto a bench, wincing as the effort made my own injuries smart, and summoned a nearby servant. 'The chaplain is unwell,' I said. 'Bring him a glass of wine at once.' He hurried to do my bidding. My order had drawn one or two curious looks from the men at the other end of our table, but they were deep in a discussion of today's jousting outcome and when they saw the chaplain take a goblet of wine and drain it, they lost interest in him and returned to their conversation. I caught a few words— 'Never thought he had it in him . . . ' and 'Stanton will have a task to live this one down . . . ' but they washed over me as though they were from a different world. My attention was all on the sweating, swaying clergyman beside me. Pass out, I thought over and over again. Don't make a scene so that everyone's watching. The chaplain had his head in his hands, and I looked longingly at the bunch of keys at his waist. Somehow I had to get them before anyone else joined us.

Suddenly the chaplain grasped my sleeve. 'It's you,' he uttered thickly. 'You've done this to me. What are you after?' His eyes widened and as he stared at me, I saw some spittle run slowly down his chin. He seemed unaware of it, but I shuddered with disgust.

'You speak nonsense,' I told him. 'I don't understand.'

'You won't get her,' he rasped in a hoarse whisper. His fingers fumbled at his keys and he clutched them tight.

'She's mine, and you're never taking her away from me . . . ' Even as he spoke, a gasp was wrenched from him. I watched, horrified, as he slowly collapsed forward, his head striking the table with a dull thud. Saliva drooled from his mouth and sweat trickled down his face. I could not tell whether he was poisoned or asleep, but at least he was not blue or writhing in agony. It was bad enough without that. Had I killed him? Not that I cared about him, but it was a hanging matter.

Even as these thoughts passed through my mind, I was fumbling at his cord, trying to free the keys. They had slipped from his now nerveless fingers. People were starting to stare at him. I was forced to raise the alarm before I had secured the keys.

'Help!' I cried, feigning concern. 'Oh, please someone help. The chaplain is ill.' That gained all the attention I could have wished for. Those closest to me looked round, and one or two rushed forward. I heard someone mutter, 'Drunk, belike,' and someone else tried unsuccessfully to raise him. Another man was feeling for his heartbeat.

Unseen under the table, my fingers continued to tug with increasing desperation at the cord which bound the keys. I was going to fail. Any minute now, they would lift him away from the table and all would have been in vain. I could not bear it.

Suddenly the knot gave, and the keys slid from it into my hand. It was such a surprise; I fumbled and nearly dropped them. I took a new grip on them and concealed them in the folds of my gown. I have them, I thought numbly. I actually have the keys.

'Can you move away, Mistress Eleanor?' one of the

men asked, taking hold of the chaplain under his arms. I slid away along the bench to make room for them to help him. Once they moved him onto the floor and became engrossed in searching for signs of life, I got up and fled. As I left the hall, I cast a hurried glance at the top table. Sir Walter was listening attentively to the king and appeared not to have noticed the disturbance as yet. I could not see Maria and that gave me a moment's concern. There was nothing I could do about it, however, so I made straight for the Lady Tower, clutching the chaplain's keys. My feet felt as though they scarcely touched the floor as I ran through the castle. I had the keys again. I was going to see Mother.

This time I knew which key unlocked the first door. I climbed the spiral stairs as fast as my trembling legs would carry me and twisted the second key in the lock. As I flung the door triumphantly open, Mother started and looked around, the daylight showing me her wasted face as I had not seen it in the darkness last time I came. Then she realized it was me.

'Oh! Eleanor!' she cried, joy lighting up her countenance. 'You have truly come! Oh, how I have longed for this moment . . . '

I paused a moment. My eyes took in more of her appearance: 'Mother, how thin and pale you are!' She looked almost like a ghost and there were new lines of care and age about her eyes and her mouth.

'I have been very sick,' she admitted, and her voice sounded as thin and weak as she looked. 'I think I nearly died.'

We embraced awkwardly, unaccustomed to one

another's proximity. A stale sour smell of unwashed body and linen hung about her. I held her tight despite this.

We broke apart and gazed at each other.

'How you have grown up, my dearest daughter,' Mother whispered, tenderly smoothing my hair with a hand that shook. We both seemed frozen in the moment, unwilling to say anything to interrupt it. I was the first to pull myself together.

'There is no time to waste, dearest Mother,' I said at last and took her hand in mine. 'Come.'

This time, there was no hesitation. Though she looked fearful once more, Mother followed me willingly out of her tower prison and down the spiral staircase. When she paused, it was only to lean against the wall and catch her breath.

'I fear I am sadly lacking strength,' she murmured. I stared at her appalled. We needed to get right across the castle and then we would have a long, hard ride ahead of us.

'Mother, you must try,' I urged her and squeezed her hand. 'We'll rest as often as we can, but there's not much time. This is a bad time of day, and my theft of the keys might be discovered at any moment.'

'I can do it,' she assured me. 'I must.'

I led Mother swiftly along the main corridor. I judged it safer than the servants' passages at this time, when most guests should be at supper. Sure enough, we met no one. We avoided the great hall by going down one floor and through several storerooms, finally reaching the inner court by a side door. I paused and listened at the door, trying to ignore Mother's ragged breathing behind me. I could hear footsteps, and dragged Mother into a nearby room while we heard someone pass. I did not see who it was. Mother was shaking piteously at this shock, her breath now coming in stifled sobs, but I led her firmly out into the court.

'The chaplain will never let me go,' she whispered. She sounded terrified. 'He will pursue me.' She bent over, clutching a stitch in her side.

'Not tonight he won't,' I replied. 'I've drugged him. I left him unconscious in the great hall.' I heard Mother gasp, but I tugged at her hand and got her moving again. As we moved on, I thought she seemed a little stronger.

'What about Walter?' she asked suddenly. 'We can't leave little Walter.' I paused and regarded her in astonishment. It had not occurred to me in my wildest dreams that we would take my brother with us. Then, with a pang, I remembered him as he was when last Mother had seen him: a bonny, trusting lad of four summers, full of affection.

'Mother, he would not come,' I said as gently as I could. 'He is not as you remember him. He is his father's boy now. A champion jouster and sword fighter, he thinks of nothing else.'

'Surely not,' Mother protested faintly, but I took her hand and led her on, unwilling to spend any more time discussing Walter just now.

Crossing to the outer court, we ran straight into Maria. There was no avoiding her on the narrow bridge. I felt my stomach lurch with the shock.

'Eleanor!' she said, before I could gather my wits. 'I've been to the stables looking for you. Sir Walter is most perturbed by your absence.' She spoke in her usual honeyed tones, but when she looked at Mother, her jaw dropped in surprise. The light was fading in the sky now, but it was not yet so dark as to make our faces indistinct.

'Maria!' I uttered, turning hot and then cold in turns. 'This is . . . um . . . my Aunt Beatrice. She just arrived . . . and . . . er . . . wanted to be sure her horses had been well rubbed down before she came in to supper. Please don't tell Sir Walter she's here. She would like to surprise him.' My lie sounded quite plausible, I thought. I looked pleadingly at Maria, willing her to believe me, or at least to play along as she did after the joust.

'Your Aunt Beatrice?' repeated Maria blankly. 'That would be . . . your father's sister?' she asked. 'Or . . . ?' To my misery, I could see comprehension dawning.

'Aunt Beatrice?' I urged Mother. 'Tell Mistress Maria that it is so!'

'Yes . . . I . . . ' faltered Mother. But then to my chagrin, her face crumpled and she began to cry. I turned to Maria and grasped her sleeve. 'Please, Maria!' I begged. 'Just go into supper and tell Sir Walter I have had too much sun today and am laid upon my bed with a headache. You have been a good friend to me once, today, Maria. Please be so once more.'

'It is Lady Hungerford, is it not?' asked Maria, her eyes fixed on my mother, a strange expression on her face.

'Yes,' I answered for Mother. 'And I trust you to help us.'

'I'll make your excuses,' said Maria turning to me abruptly. 'But where do you plan to go?'

I sighed with relief. 'Thank you! We're heading for London. On horseback. We shall ride as far as we can tonight and then find somewhere safe to rest I'm hoping our flight won't be discovered until tomorrow.'

Maria smirked and bridled as was her wont, and then she kissed my cheek. 'Go,' she said. 'I'll do what I can.'

'Thank you,' I said warmly, before leading Mother swiftly to the stables. A couple of stable hands crossed the yard, but barely glanced at us. They were too young to remember Mother. 'Send Tom to me!' I ordered them, heading for the stalls. Tom arrived by my side in seconds.

'Mistress Eleanor,' he gasped. 'My lady.' He bowed to my mother, keeping his voice low. She had regained her self control, and nodded to him. Tom turned back to me. 'I've unsaddled the horses,' he groaned. 'I'd given you up for today.'

'Then let us saddle them again, quickly!' I ordered him. Tom passed me the bridles to put on, while Tom went running for the saddles. To my frustration, my injured hand hindered me. My fingers were numb and the wound painful. Tom saw when he returned, and took over.

'Must I indeed ride, Eleanor?' asked Mother tremulously. I paused a moment, remembering how much she disliked being on horseback.

'I'm afraid you must, Mother,' I told her. 'There is no alternative. I cannot order the carriage out, and we would be forced to stay on the roads if I could.'

'But, Eleanor,' Tom interrupted suddenly, in the middle of tightening Arianna's girth, 'how's you going to get out through the gatehouse at this time o' night? You can't pretend you're just going for a ride like you planned.'

'I've thought of that. Just get Mother on to Beau and

keep the horses hidden until I come back—no matter what you hear.'

So saying, I unhooked the lantern from the doorway and slipped out into the dusk. I ran across the yard to a lean-to where straw for the horses' bedding was stored. It stood hard against the curtain wall, and far enough from the stables not to be a danger to the horses. Neither would there be any danger to the main castle from here.

Putting down the lantern, I shook out a pile of loose straw from one of the sheaves, and placed the lantern on top of it. I fed straw into the flame, until a smoky, choking fire was well and truly burning. I stood back, coughing, and watched the flames spread, curling and blackening the stalks of straw. Soon I needed to retreat from the smoke and the heat. Leaving the door swinging open, I ran towards the gatehouse.

'Fire!' I cried. 'Help! The stables are on fire! Quickly!'

The guards were alert when I reached them but still at their posts. 'It's the stables!' I cried again. 'We need everyone to help!' As I spoke, a tongue of flame shot up into the sky beyond the stables. We could all clearly hear the flames crackling, and a coil of smoke rolled across the stable yard towards us.

'You go,' shouted one guard to the other. 'I can't move from here. The castellan'll have me flogged if I leave the gate.' But as he spoke he looked fearfully at the smoke and flames.

I stared at him in dismay. If he stayed there, how were we to get out? I had to get rid of him.

'Sir Walter will have you flogged if you let his guests' horses burn to death!' I shouted. I could see the indecision in the guard's face. There was a crash of falling timber in the distance and a dull red glow in the sky. I turned and ran back towards the stables and to my relief I could hear the guard's feet pounding behind me.

As the grooms ran to the well to help the stable hands draw water, I turned and slipped back into the stables. The horses were restless, pulling at their halters and whinnying with fright at the noise and the stench of smoke. I could smell them sweating with fear.

'Get them all out safely, Tom,' I pleaded. 'If the fire should spread.'

'I will,' he promised.

I spoke a soothing word to Arianna. Tom threw me into the saddle and squeezed my uninjured hand. 'Go, Eleanor,' he urged. I clung to his hand for a moment, looking down into his familiar face dimly lit by the remaining lantern. 'Go,' he repeated. I released his hand and gestured to Mother to follow me. We headed towards the gatehouse. Nobody noticed us go, their attention fully occupied by the fire.

Once we were over the drawbridge, I urged Arianna into a brisker walk and she stepped out obediently up the steep hill, Beau following close behind.

'Are you well enough, Mother?' I asked anxiously, turning in my saddle. I had had no thoughts to spare for her for the last many minutes.

'Yes,' she answered breathlessly, clutching her horse's mane. 'But I fear I cannot go far.'

'Then let us at least go swiftly,' I said. As the horses reached the brow of the hill, I urged Arianna into a canter. It was almost dark now, but I could hear Beau keeping pace beside us. Both horses were fresh and covered the ground swiftly.

The evening air was clear and cool after the warmth of the day. I felt exhilarated. I had done it. We were free. I wanted to smile at Mother and rejoice in our escape, but even as I turned towards her, my ears caught an ominous sound. A thunderous drumming, some distance behind. Hoof beats. We were being pursued.

# CHAPTER TWENTY-ONE

Mother had heard the horses too. We looked fearfully at one another.

'We must gallop!' I said, urging Arianna on.

'It's not safe, in the dark,' my mother moaned in fear.

'It's not safe to be caught either,' I replied. Our horses were willing to brave the dark, and stretched their legs into a gallop. The sound of pursuit faded behind us. How could Sir Walter have discovered our flight so quickly? He must have been in the stables within minutes of us leaving.

Several miles further on, I slowed Arianna to a trot, and then a walk, leading the way off the road and into a wood. We paused, while I listened to the sounds of pursuit. We waited, holding our breath, praying they would not notice we had left the road. The horses passed by us, continuing on the road towards Bath and London. Mother sobbed with mingled fear and relief. She was swaying in the saddle. 'Eleanor,' she whispered. 'I cannot . . .'

I thought quickly. Sir Walter would soon realize what had happened and turn back to look for us. We could not outride him all the way to London. Even alone, I doubted I could do it. Neither could we hide. Sir Walter knew the land around Farleigh as well as I did. And he might have dogs with him. That thought gave me a sharp spur of fright. There was only one option that I could think of.

'Mama, do you think you could ride as far as the priory?' I asked. 'Dr Horde will shelter us, I'm sure of it.'

'Yes, I could manage that. But he's a friend of Sir Walter's, Eleanor!'

'Yes, I know. And of Cromwell's. But he will not hand us over. He is good man, a man of God. Come!'

I led Mother through the woods, glad of my familiarity with the paths in this gloom. Even so, twigs snagged in our hair and snatched at our clothes as we pushed our way through the trees. I heard Mother cry out softly as a small branch that I had not been able to hold out of her way whipped her face. We crossed a field and emerged into a narrow lane that led through a small hamlet. Our passing set all the dogs barking.

'Who goes there?' cried a rough man's voice.

'A friend!' I replied, and heard him grunt in dissatisfaction at my words, but I wasn't about to give him my name. We drew away from the houses and could see the priory lights glimmering in the distance. 'Look, Mother!' I said, keeping my voice low. 'We're nearly there. Let us be swift.'

Arianna pricked up her ears and quickened her pace at the sound of my voice. It seemed she was enjoying this nocturnal outing. But then she paused, laying her ears back again. I listened intently. At first I could hear nothing. My ears were not as sharp as Arianna's. A few moments later, however, I heard the unmistakable sound of hounds baying.

'They've tracked us!' I cried. All caution was thrown to

the winds. We broke into a crazy gallop. What matter noise, when there are hounds following your scent? I was afraid for the horses, galloping like this in the dark, but I was even more afraid of the dogs and men behind us. A hedge loomed suddenly before us, and Arianna almost sat on her haunches to stop, crashing into the branches, snorting with fright. I hunted frantically along the hedge for the gate I knew must be here somewhere. Having wasted precious minutes finding it, I fumbled with the wooden latch, knowing it was useless asking Mother to jump a gate. As we passed through, I banged it shut behind us, hoping it might slow our pursuers. Then we were flying through the darkness towards the lights of the priory. But the dogs were very close now. One, ahead of the rest, was already snapping at Arianna's heels. I felt rather than saw Arianna kick out at the dog. There was a sudden yelp of pain, and then it was no longer there. I patted Arianna, surprised. She was trained to ride to hounds. But it seemed she knew as well as I did that we were the hunted, not the hunters, tonight.

At long last the iron gates of the priory appeared before us. But when I leaned down to open them, they were already locked for the night. Desperately, I tugged on the rope, and heard the bell pealing inside the building.

'Help!' I shouted. 'Help us, please!'

A brother appeared, and made his unhurried way towards us across the courtyard. His robes swept the ground as he walked and his face was hidden in his cowl. As he reached us, he put it back and peered at us.

'Who asks for admission so late?' he asked calmly.

'For the love of God, let us in,' I begged. 'Here are the

Lady Elizabeth Hungerford and her daughter Eleanor, and we are pursued with dogs, though we've done no wrong! We are in danger of our lives.'

I could hear the horses crashing through the undergrowth behind us. I could even hear a voice, raised in a curse, in the distance. The monk blinked at me in surprise, but made no move to unlock the gate.

'We are friends of Doctor Horde,' I said in desperation. 'I request sanctuary.' I had said the right thing. The monk produced a key, fitting it into the lock. I could now hear the panting of the hounds as they raced through the darkness behind us. As soon as the key clicked in the lock, I threw my weight against the gates, pushing them open and obliging the monk to step smartly out of the way. The leading dog appeared out of the darkness behind us. At the sight of us, he flung back his head and howled. There were answering barks behind him, and as we led our horses quickly through the gates, I heard the triumphant shouts of the men too. I flung myself out of the saddle and shut and locked the gates. One dog tried to dart through as I banged them shut, but lost his nerve at the last minute and fell back.

I turned the key and removed it, and began leading the horses to the stable. Mother was still mounted on Beau, clinging weakly to the pommel of the saddle.

'Can we stable our horses?' I addressed the monk.

'Madam, you still have the key to the gates,' he protested, bemused.

I pretended not to have heard him.

'Would you please send for Doctor Horde?' I asked. 'And tell him I desire urgent speech with him? And whatever you do, please don't open the gates to anyone else, especially not to Sir Walter.'

'Doctor Horde is at evening prayer,' said the monk indignantly. 'He is not to be disturbed. And he would be most annoyed if I were to deny entry to Sir Walter, who is a friend and benefactor of the priory.'

'In that case, it is certainly better that I retain this key until I have had speech with him,' I said, surprised at my own boldness. A shout at the gate diverted the brother's attention from me.

'Halloo there!' called my father's voice. 'Gate!' The monk hesitated. After standing indecisively before me for several minutes, he finally turned back to the gate. I led Arianna and Beau to the stables, praying the brother had not a second key.

When I helped Mother to dismount, she could barely stand upright. I put an arm around her waist. A groom appeared, tousle-haired and heavy-eyed.

'Asleep?' I asked him scornfully. 'At this hour?'

'No,' he retorted unconvincingly.

'See our horses rubbed down and watered,' I requested him. 'We are expecting to stay the night.'

'Wot, two ladies? 'ere?' he asked rudely. 'I don't fink so.'

I ignored him and supported Mother through a side door into the priory itself. There we found a bench, onto which she sank down gratefully, overcome with exhaustion. I thought how long she had stayed in one room, with no activity or exercise of any kind and realized how strenuous and frightening this evening must have been for her.

It took about ten minutes for the prior to arrive, by

which time I was fretting with anxiety and impatience, wondering every minute what my father was saying at the gates.

Dr Horde entered.

'What is this I hear, Eleanor?' he asked, and then he saw my mother. 'Gracious Heaven, Lady Elizabeth!'

He fell back in shock, looking as though he had seen a ghost.

'We desperately need your help,' I began. But at that moment the monk from the gate hurried into the room. He bowed hastily to the prior and spoke his name breathlessly.

'Brother William,' said Dr Horde. 'You interrupt.'

As he spoke the sound of raised voices from the front gate reached us. Dr Horde looked bewildered. 'What is going on? Do we admit some guests, and leave others to call at our gates in vain?' Brother William looked embarrassed.

'No, indeed, Doctor,' he replied. 'But you see . . . ' and he gestured helplessly towards me.

'I took the key,' I explained. 'After the brother let us in. Please let me explain. We are being pursued. Our lives are in danger.'

Dr Horde's bewilderment turned to astonishment. 'But, Mistress Eleanor, who is chasing you at this hour of the night?'

'Sir Walter,' I said.

The prior paled, and his expression became grave. I hurried to explain: 'Mother has been imprisoned for four years. She is not mad, as Sir Walter pretends. We need your help.'

Mother spoke in her soft voice: 'Doctor Horde, I know

my husband is your friend. But I swear to you, I was not ill when he imprisoned me in that tower. I have only been ill since as a result of the treatment I have received at his hands.'

'But that would be monstrous,' Dr Horde exclaimed, grasping the back of a chair. 'There must be some mistake . . . ' He stood there for a moment, apparently lost in thought, and then he seemed to come to a decision. 'The key, please, Eleanor,' he said firmly, holding out his hand. I looked beseechingly at him, but he did not relent. I thought he looked at me with kindness, not like a man who was about to betray me, so I gave him the key. Dr Horde turned to Brother William. I held my breath, waiting to see what he would do.

'Please ask Sir Walter to have patience a few moments,' he said. 'Apologize to him from me and assure him he will have my full attention as soon as possible.' I noticed that he kept the key, and I sighed with relief.

'Now, my lady,' said the prior, turning back to my mother. 'Tell me, if you please.'

My mother related her tale of imprisonment and poisoning. It was a fearful one. There were details even I had not known. She told how on some days, before I began to send her food, she had even had to drink her own urine to survive. Then there were references to the chaplain that I did not completely understand, but I understood he had caused Mother great suffering.

The prior's face grew graver and graver as he listened, and when she had done, a look of great sadness, even grief, came over him. There was a long silence, broken only by the crackle of the fire in the grate.

'Oh, Eleanor!' he sighed at length. 'Why did you not come to me four years ago? In those days, I was a man of standing and influence. Now, I fear . . . ' He paused, as though lost in thought.

'I tried,' I told him. 'I came here, but you were away. Sir Walter discovered I had been here and punished me. I did not dare try again.'

The prior looked sad.

'This is a difficult and dangerous situation,' he said at last. 'Far more so than you realize.' He sighed heavily, and I waited for him to continue. 'I pity you, Lady Elizabeth, from the bottom of my heart. I am certain God will reward your sufferings. I will help you. I promise you.'

'Surely you are not going to turn us away?' Mother asked fearfully. Dr Horde looked at her and his face softened, though the sadness remained.

'How changed you are, my lady,' he said, looking into her eyes. I could see he was deeply moved. 'It is not in me to turn you away at this time of need. But understand this. My position here is precarious. Houses of God like this one are being shut down all over England. Their wealth is robbed, and goes to fill the king's coffers, their brethren disbanded. At Henton, we continue to survive purely as a result of the friendship I enjoyed in happier days with Sir Walter and Lord Cromwell. Do you understand me? If I keep you here, if I anger them, I will lose that protection. It may be a few weeks, or even a month, but then this monastery will be torn apart, as countless others have been before us.' He looked sadly around the room. 'So many years' devotion and service, and we are come to this,' he sighed.

I squirmed, racked with guilt. How could we possibly

stay here and bring such trouble upon him? But the alternative was also dreadful to contemplate. How could we calmly give ourselves up to my father? I was distressed at the choice. Dr Horde must have seen some of this in my face, for he smiled faintly at me. 'Do not blame yourself unduly, my child. The end would have come sooner or later in any case. I am telling you so that you know that I cannot shelter you for long. You will not be safe here. You can, of course, resume your journey at any time, but meanwhile I will use my influence on your behalf—write letters and so on.'

I nodded my understanding. 'You are very kind. I am truly sorry to bring such trouble upon you,' I told him. 'We were heading for London, but they came after us so soon . . . I have managed so badly.'

The prior straightened his shoulders. 'I must speak to Sir Walter,' he said. 'Brother Thomas will see that you are given comfortable quarters for the night.' So saying, he bowed and left us.

We were shown to a small but comfortable guest apartment at the back of the building, in which a fire had recently been lit. A bowl of hot broth was brought for each of us, which we drank gratefully. A jug of water was then brought for washing, and the monks withdrew for the night. I bathed Mother's hands and face and combed her hair, and she sighed with pleasure.

'It is so good to see you again, Eleanor,' she said, her voice hoarse with weariness. 'But I am so unused to so much excitement and exertion.'

'Sleep,' I told her. 'I will wake you when it's time to leave.'

Mother was quietly asleep within minutes. I, on the other hand, could find no rest at all. All was quiet both inside and outside the priory, so I assumed that Dr Horde had persuaded Sir Walter to return home without us. I paced the room, angry with myself for failing to get us properly away. I waited for the dawn in a fever of impatience to resume our journey. It was folly to be lingering here, but I knew Mother had to rest.

Long before first light, I heard the peal of the bell once more and a shout outside the gates:

'Open the gates! Lord Cromwell demands admittance in the name of the king.'

# CHAPTER TWENTY-TWO

I flung open the door of our chamber. No one was in sight, but I could hear the brothers moving about and the sound of agitated voices. I ran along the passageway to a window that overlooked the front gate. There were a large number of mounted men beyond it, all of them armed with swords and spears. A few carried crossbows.

We had left it too late to make our escape. I cursed myself for not setting out when it was quiet last night.

As I watched, Dr Horde himself crossed the courtyard, flanked by two of his brethren. He held himself very upright and walked with measured, unhurried steps. But I remembered what he had told us the night before, and I felt afraid. Not only was he unable to keep us safe, he might be about to lose his priory. And it was my fault. I felt dreadful for him—for all the good monks here. What would become of them?

I suddenly thought there might be a back way out of the priory. That Mother and I might get safe away and all may yet be right. I ran back to our room and roused Mother. She was heavy with sleep and struggled to waken.

'Get up, Mother! Cromwell is here. Outside the gates. We need to try and escape.'

I pulled my cloak around me as I spoke. Mother looked

as though she could not take in what I was saying. She looked dreadfully ill in the early morning light, with deep shadows, like purple bruises, under her eyes. When she rose from her bed, she was stiff and sore from yesterday's short ride. She sank back down onto the bed, tears shining in her eyes.

'I cannot do it, Eleanor,' she said shakily. 'We will have to submit. And yet I would rather die than return to Farleigh.'

'No!' I cried. 'I need you. I am also afraid to be dragged back to Farleigh. Do you really think I will go unpunished for helping you escape?'

Mother struggled to her feet and wrapped her cloak around herself without another word and followed me downstairs. In the hallway, we met Dr Horde returning from the gate.

'Have you admitted Lord Cromwell?' I asked, peering fearfully over his shoulder.

'I have stalled them,' replied the prior. He passed a hand across his face, looking suddenly old and tired. 'I have to write Lord Cromwell a letter, formally resigning the priory to the crown. They wanted to come in and stand over me while I did it, but I have persuaded Cromwell to wait while I write it.'

'Oh, I am so very sorry,' I cried. My stomach churned with guilt for what I had done to the good brothers. 'I have made such a mess of everything,' I cried, wringing my hands. 'I have brought all this upon you, and have not even helped Mother. Did he mention Mother and me?'

'There was no need,' said the prior heavily. 'He knows you are here as well as I do.'

'Doctor Horde, is there a back way out of the priory?'

The prior looked at me sadly. 'Yes, there are two. Hungerford's men have stood guard over them all night. We have been watching them for you, hoping there might be an opportunity for you to escape. There was none.' He sighed, and then continued: 'It was a great misfortune for us that both the king and Cromwell were so close by, at Farleigh. Normally it would take weeks to get a warrant.'

I felt weak with despair. 'Then we are trapped,' I said hopelessly. I turned to my mother and she put her arms around me. I hugged her back, as tightly as I could. 'I have let you down,' I apologized into her shoulder. I was ashamed.

'You have not,' she said. 'You have been brave and strong, Eleanor. And you will continue to be so.'

The monks began hurriedly packing their few belongings while Dr Horde withdrew to write his letter to Cromwell. Mother and I sat by the fire, trying to make the most of our last few moments of freedom together. It was difficult. I kept jumping to my feet with new ideas of how to escape, each more wildly impracticable than the last. I suggested leaping down from the priory walls or cutting our hair and dressing as monks. Mother begged me to be calm, but it felt too dreadful to just sit here quietly waiting to be recaptured.

The prior emerged with the letter he had written and paused as he passed us.

'Lady Elizabeth, I am more sorry than I can say. You will have to return to Farleigh for the time being. Eleanor, do not despair. I will help you both. You have my word; I will do what I can to aid you.'

'Thank you, good brother,' said Mother, taking his hand and kissing it. 'We depend upon you.'

The letter of resignation was handed to Cromwell, the gates were opened and his soldiers marched in. I had heard tales of the sacking of the monasteries. Of violence and theft, of desecration and burning. Of unspeakable cruelties to the monks. But if these things took place here, it was not done in our presence. Everything seemed orderly, almost polite. Perhaps the soldiers did not dare commit any atrocities with Cromwell himself present.

Cromwell sat astride his horse in the priory courtyard, giving orders. The brethren filed past him, eyes downcast, clutching their bundles. They were allowed to leave in peace, some would even get pensions. They wished to do nothing to anger the representatives of the crown. The prior handed over the keys of the priory to Cromwell himself. I could hear him pleading for our safety. Cromwell did not reply.

At last Mother and I were led out into the yard, where Cromwell regarded us steadily.

'Sir Walter will be most relieved to see you safe, Lady Elizabeth,' he said. I knew it was not true. Sir Walter would have been glad to find Mother dead so he could marry Maria.

I thought Cromwell should dismount and bow to Mother properly. It was rudeness to sit there on his horse as though Mother were merely some peasant woman. But then Cromwell always had been a very ordinary little man, sadly lacking in manners. His recently bestowed titles had not changed that.

'And you, of course, Mistress Eleanor,' Cromwell added as an afterthought. As he spoke my name there was a harder edge to his voice. I longed to hit him. I opened my mouth to insult him, but Mother laid a warning hand on my shoulder. So I said nothing. I spat at him instead. I missed his face, but got him on the shoulder. He wiped it away with one leather-gloved hand.

'You will be sorry for that,' Cromwell said. 'Tie her hands!' To my utter humiliation, my hands were tied firmly together in front of me. Our horses were led up to us, already saddled. We were assisted to mount, our reins firmly held by a soldier apiece. Cromwell was taking no chances.

We were led back to the castle at a sedate pace. With every step Arianna took, my spirits sank lower. As the shadow of the curtain wall fell on us, I felt chilled and despairing. After all the effort and courage it had taken to escape, here we were, back again. All that we had gained was the promise of help from Dr Horde.

We crossed the drawbridge into the yard under the curious eyes of the castle guards. The sight of the charred and blackened remains of the bedding store frightened me. I had caused so much trouble. I knew I would be punished.

It was still early morning when we reached the castle. Only the servants were stirring. There were none to see us led through the silent corridors. I was locked into my chamber, and Mother was led away, presumably to be locked up in the Lady Tower once more.

The day passed in a haze of dread. I was exhausted and slept some hours, always awakening with a lurch of fear in my stomach. What were they doing to Mother? And what was going to happen to me: these were the constant themes that occupied my feverish mind. Would I be beaten? Would I still be made to marry Stanton? Or had I disgraced myself too badly even for that?

An hour before supper, I heard the key grate in the lock. I leapt to my feet and backed to the wall. My mouth felt dry suddenly as I wondered who was about to come in and why.

It was Maria. As she entered the room, I sighed with relief. But she was tight-lipped and severe, and did not greet me in her usual affectionate manner.

'I'm to help you dress for dinner,' she said.

'Dinner?' I asked, surprised. But when I thought about it, it made sense. My father would want to hush up the incident. No doubt he would be pretending I had gone for a late ride and got lost or some such thing. Maria pushed me into a seat and began combing my hair. It was tangled and neglected and I winced as the comb snagged.

'Where is Mother now?' I asked.

'She is back in the tower.' Her voice sounded very cold.

'Thank you for your help last night,' I said softly. 'Even though we did not succeed, I am grateful to you.'

It cost me something to thank Maria, but my sense of justice demanded it.

In reply I got a sharp tug of the comb that made my eyes water.

'You are hurting me,' I told her.

She did not reply, but continued dragging the comb through my tangles.

I caught her wrist in my hand and turned to look at her.

'Maria?' I asked. 'What is wrong?'

Maria glared at me and I recoiled as I saw the hate in her eyes. I began to understand.

'It was you who alerted Sir Walter of our escape last night,' I said, my voice small. When Maria did not answer, I shook her wrist. 'Was it you?' I asked.

Angrily, Maria pulled her wrist out of my grasp. She looked as though she was fighting to keep control over herself. Abruptly speech burst from her: 'Of course it was me, you stupid girl,' she hissed. 'I was never your friend! Did you really think I enjoyed your company for one second? You are a conceited, odious, wild little slut, with no care for anyone except yourself and your mad mother!' The words poured out of her like poison from a boil. I watched her with horror as her face contorted with rage. I began to shake. How could I ever have believed, even for a moment, Maria was my friend? I had trusted her and she had gone straight to my father.

'Sir Walter will marry you off to Lord Stanton in less than two weeks, and it's more than you deserve. I pity the man!' Maria flung at me. 'I hope he can tame his women as well as he tames his horses.'

I gasped in shock. Her cruel words lashed me.

'You are so angry. Why? What have I done to you?' I asked.

'You have caused me nothing but trouble. Sneaking about, hiding, being rude and disobedient. And Sir Walter was in such a rage last night when I took him the news. He blamed me for letting you leave the castle. But what could I have done? I ran to him as swiftly as I could.' She looked aggrieved. I felt no pity, only a kind of numb hurt.

'What do you have to gain in all this?' I asked her, shaken.

'I? I gain a husband, a title, a castle and become a woman of consequence at the king's court!'

'You cannot marry Sir Walter. He already has a wife,' I objected. I had never understood her interest in my father.

'Have you never heard of divorce?' asked Maria triumphantly. 'He will divorce your mother, and marry me. He has already asked me.'

'You are welcome to Sir Walter and Farleigh and all the rest,' I said. 'But *why*, why could you not have let us go?'

'Because Sir Walter wants you both here,' she said. Her voice was under control again now, cold and hard, but I was still shaking with anger.

'So why did you pretend to be my friend?' I demanded. 'Why did you help me after the joust?'

'Because Sir Walter asked me to befriend you, you little fool, and gain your trust. And concealing your disgraceful little secret did the trick, did it not? You trusted me enough to tell me exactly which direction you were going to take.' Her voice had a triumphant note in it. She was enjoying telling me how she had betrayed me.

It all made sense. Everyone was ranged against me. There was nothing I could do against so many.

I felt low and depressed as I submitted to dressing for dinner. I followed Maria miserably down to the great hall and hung my head in shame as we entered. It was hard to face everyone after such a defeat. Several people asked solicitously after my health, and I understood that they had been told I had been indisposed once more. They knew nothing of my escapade.

'So what was wrong with me this time?' I hissed at Maria after the third enquiry.

'A touch of the sun,' Maria replied under her breath 'The exposure during the tournament gave you a severe headache.'

'I'm glad to know it was nothing serious,' I replied sarcastically.

I found I could eat little at supper. I realized, with a sickening jolt, that as long as I was locked in my chamber, Mother would get no food at all. Unless Alice took her some bread that she could ill spare from her own family. How could I dine on venison and sweetmeats while she starved? I pushed my plate away in despair.

Was there no one within the castle on my side? Was there no kindness or mercy? It seemed not. I looked around at the faces in the hall. There were fewer than yesterday. Some had already left now that the tournament was over. Not that it made any difference to me. Gregory caught my eye and sent me a look so full of heartfelt sympathy that it brought hot tears to my eyes. I blinked them back. I could count on one friend in him.

Lord Stanton, too, was still present. I was certain he was an enemy. Stanton caught me looking at him and kissed his fingertips to me across the room. I looked quickly away, but to my dismay, I saw him get up from his place and come towards me.

Unwillingly, I gave him my hand, and he surprised me by kissing it.

'You have been ill?' he asked quietly. He sounded genuinely concerned. I felt confused and unsure what to say. Did I confirm the lie that had been told about me or deny it? While I hesitated, Stanton leaned closer and spoke in a voice intended for my ears only: 'I hope this was not a result of your . . . ah . . . exertions?' He indicated my injured arm as he spoke.

He clearly attributed my indisposition to my injury at the joust. No doubt Sir Walter had taken great care to let him know nothing of his future bride's wild conduct last night.

'No, I am quite well,' I assured him briefly.

'I am greatly relieved to hear it,' he murmured, bowing and returning to his seat. Strange, I mused, as I watched him make his unhurried way back across the hall and seat himself gracefully again. There was no mocking note in his voice at all. It was almost as if he meant what he said. I felt touched by his kindness and had to remind myself fiercely that he was no more my friend than Maria was.

There was no formal entertainment that evening. Directly after supper, Maria escorted me to my chamber and locked me in. I removed my headdress and cast it onto the floor then I flung myself upon my bed.

'Dear God, please help us!' I uttered into the bedding, my voice muffled in my sheets. I groaned. How could we escape now? Dr Horde was our only chance, for I could think of no plan at all. I had never felt such despair. I lay unmoving, numb with hopelessness. I neither undressed nor drew the covers over me, but simply lay there as the night deepened outside the castle. I did not sleep.

It seemed like hours later that I heard the key in the lock once more. The door opened and Maria stood there again. She entered with a servant, looking flustered.

'The king has sent for you,' she said.

# CHAPTER TWENTY-THREE

The maid laid out my clothes and gave orders for a small bathtub to be carried up to my chamber, lined with linen and filled with water. Servants filed in carrying cans of water, some casting me curious glances. The steam rose and curled about the room. Meanwhile Maria sat beside me and explained to me that when a king sends for a young maiden at night, it is both an honour and a danger.

'What are you talking about?' I cried at length, my head in a whirl. 'Speak plain, for I do not understand you.'

'The king loves young women, Eleanor,' Maria explained. 'But his love is fickle and ever-changing. Do you understand?'

'No,' I said. 'I do not. I do not want the king to be in love with me. I am betrothed, he knows that! He sanctioned the betrothal. And I can undress myself, thank you.'

I was not accustomed to bathing, normally contenting myself with a wash from a basin of water. I was embarrassed to be completely naked in front of an audience. Maria dismissed the maids, and I hurriedly pulled off my nightgown and climbed into the water. It was warm and scented, but I was too confused and anxious to take any pleasure in such a luxury.

'What are these bruises?' exclaimed Maria, pointing to

my injured side. The marks from the impact of the lance were black and purple. I had forgotten how much they showed.

'They are from the joust,' I explained. 'Where Stanton's lance struck me.'

'As if your arm was not bad enough. Why must you be such a hoyden? I hope this will not disgust the king. If he mentions your injuries, you must say you fell from your horse.'

'He will not see them!' I exclaimed, outraged. 'Why do I need to bathe anyway?'

Maria began washing my hair. I was so angry with her, I could not bear her touch.

'Be still and stop fussing, Eleanor,' she snapped. 'The king likes women to be clean. He cannot bear dirt or body odour of any kind.'

'That's pretty unreasonable considering how he stinks and farts himself,' I commented, drawing a gasp of shock from her.

'How can you speak so about His Majesty, Eleanor?' scolded Maria. 'I hope you can conduct yourself with propriety in his presence.' I scarcely heard her. An appalling thought had struck me, which made sense of all her previously incomprehensible words.

'He doesn't want me as his *mistress*, does he?' I asked, my voice low with horror.

'I doubt you'll be so favoured,' sneered Maria. 'I imagine you will serve to amuse him for one evening only. And not even that if you offend him, Eleanor.' She tugged my hair; it was a warning: 'Your father has gone to great trouble and expense to entertain the king and gain his favour. If you undo it all by being rude or coy, I cannot begin to imagine what he'll do to you. I hope you know the honour due to the king of England.'

I sat hugging myself in the bath, rigid with dread at the ordeal that lay before me.

'Cannot you say that I am unwell?' I begged at length.

'You cannot refuse the king,' was all Maria said. I got nothing more from her.

In less time than I would have liked, I was walking towards the king's chamber. I had been washed in places I hadn't known I had, and was cleaner than ever before in my life. A new gown, the only one I had not yet worn, rustled about me. My hair had been rubbed dry and then combed out and left loose. It fell to below my waist in an auburn cascade.

We passed few people in the corridors. It was late now, and most had retired. Maria ushered me into the king's presence and, as I sank into a deep curtsey, I heard the door close behind me. I was alone with the king. My heart hammered as though it would escape from my chest. My mouth felt dry and my hands were trembling.

As I rose shakily from my curtsey, I remained where I was, staring at the floor just in front of my feet.

'Welcome,' I heard the king's voice say. 'Come and sit down.'

I looked up and saw the king seated on a small settle before a roaring fire, despite the warmth of the evening. He was smiling benignly at me, and patting the small space that was left on the settle beside him. I felt my stomach lurch. I approached hesitantly, casting my eyes around for another chair I could sit on instead. 'By me,' repeated the king, once again patting the settle. I sat gingerly down. I could not help brushing against him, there was not enough space for two. With one pudgy hand, he reached out and began to stroke my shoulder. My skin crawled under his touch. I was overawed by the king's presence and the importance of not doing or saying anything that might offend him. The heat of the fire scorched my skin. I felt dizzy.

'I confess, I am curious about your *indisposition*, Mistress Eleanor,' said the king. I glanced up at him briefly, then hurriedly lowered my eyes. He was too close and watching me like a hunter about to pounce on its prey.

'My . . . indisposition, Your Majesty?' I faltered.

'It must have been a strange affliction, my dear,' he murmured. His hand was now caressing my neck. 'It began with a lack of appearance at the dancing, where I, you know, had been looking forward to dancing with you. Then it continued with a fire in the stables, I have been told. Most odd. And then it necessitated Lord Hungerford riding out from the castle for much of the night, and even entailed a warrant for the sudden dissolution of Henton Priory.'

His hand crept up into my hair, which he began winding around his fingers. I concentrated on breathing steadily, trying to keep from fainting.

'I . . . don't understand, Your Majesty,' I attempted to say. It came out as a croak. The king released my hair and sat back with an impatient sigh.

'I am many things, Mistress Eleanor, but I am not a fool. I am also an early riser, and observed your dawn return to the castle, bound at the wrists. I dislike being lied to. So do not dissemble, I pray.'

I shook my head, trying to clear it. I realized the king could be the one person who could perhaps help me. This spurred me into action. I threw myself upon my knees before him, heedless of my dress and the closeness of the fire.

'I am sorry you have been lied to, Your Majesty,' I pleaded. 'It was not me who wished it so.'

'Spare me your protestations, and tell me the truth,' interrupted King Henry. 'Where were you going and why?'

'Sir Walter has my mother, his wife, locked up in the south-west tower, Your Majesty,' I began. 'She has been there four long years.'

The king waved his hand impatiently.

'I know this. The poor woman is mad. Sir Walter told me so himself.'

'Please, Your Highness, she is not mad, she is as sane as . . . ' I had been about to say 'as you are', but realized at the last minute that this might be deeply disrespectful. I bit my lip and continued after an awkward pause: 'As sane as anyone in the castle. I believe Sir Walter thinks of a new marriage to increase his wealth and power.'

The king observed me steadily. His small black eyes gave little away. He looked as though he were weighing my words, trying to sum me up. I sought desperately for something more to say. Something that might convince him.

'You could help us, Your Majesty,' I pleaded. 'You could see to it that she was set free.'

He made an impatient gesture, a slight shrug. He was not interested. Instead, he took my hand in his and drew me back onto the settle. He put an arm around me and held me close, placing a whiskery kiss on my cheek. His stinking breath fanned over my face, making my eyes water.

'And is that all this little adventure was about?' he asked coaxingly. Now his free hand was stealing round my waist. I felt sick. 'There was nothing more to it than that? It seems unlikely that Sir Walter would lie to me for so slight a reason.' He was pulling me round to face him now. I knew he was going to kiss me any minute and I had to prevent him.

'Sir Walter is a traitor, Sire,' I heard myself say. Then I gasped at my own words. I was terrified of what I had said. Of what the king might do.

'Go on.'

I swallowed hard and forced myself to go on: 'I overheard him plotting against you.'

King Henry released me so suddenly, I almost toppled into the fire. The look on his face was thunderous. I was suddenly terrified; no longer for myself. 'Tell me!' he ordered, his voice like iron. I wished that I could have taken back what I said. But I could not.

'I . . . he . . . ' was all I could utter at first.

'Who was he speaking to at the time?' demanded the king.

'Lord Cromwell,' I admitted in a very small voice. I felt dreadful. Like a thief or a murderer.

'And what was said? The exact words if you please.'

'Um . . . something about a boy king being easier to control,' I told him reluctantly. I dared not repeat the part about the king himself being unstable and dangerous.

I was afraid I might be cast into prison just for repeating the words.

'I see. My son Edward, no doubt. I knew it!' He stood up with some difficulty and began to pace up and down the chamber, striking one fist into the other hand. The relief of having him at a physical distance once more was great, but I could not relax, given what I had done to achieve it. 'And were they plotting to kill me?' he demanded abruptly, his voice enraged. There was a dark and twisted expression on his face that I had never seen there before.

'Not that I heard, Your Majesty. They were interrupted.'

'And did anyone else overhear this conversation?'

I thought of my cousin hiding beside me in the dark, his hand in mine. I remembered his fear afterwards, and I quickly shook my head. 'No, Your Majesty.'

Slowly all the sordid details were dragged from me. I had no honour left in me. I had descended into being an eavesdropper and a sneak. I had not even secured a promise of help from him. When I told him of Father Bird and the horoscope, he flew into a fearful rage, snatching up a jug from the table and smashing it on the floor.

'By God, they will pay for this,' he swore. 'Leave me!'

I dared not try again to interest him in Mother's plight, but fled the room at once. Maria was awaiting me outside the chamber, on the edge of a chair. She leapt to her feet when she saw me.

'So soon?' she exclaimed. 'What was that crash?'

'A jug,' I replied shortly. I felt ashamed and exhausted. I did not want a conversation with Maria.

'You clearly did not give the king much pleasure!' she remarked.

'I believe I did not,' I replied, knowing she meant something quite different. She asked me questions all the way back to my chamber, clearly consumed with curiosity. I told her nothing of what had passed. She lingered in my room, but I lay down upon my bed, turning my back on her until she gave up and withdrew, locking the chamber door behind her.

I lay there in silence. I was unable to cry, I certainly could not sleep. The conversation with the king went over and over in my mind until dawn. With first light came sleep at last which released me from my troubles for a few short hours.

I awoke with a headache. I was living in a nightmare and there was no prospect of it ending.

The king wasted no time. At breakfast the next morning, he announced his departure for later that very day. I was seated at the top table under Maria's and Sir Walter's eye, and so had a clear view of their reactions.

'So suddenly, my liege?' asked Sir Walter. It was clear the king had not announced his intentions to his host before he told the company at large. His face betrayed an almost ludicrous disappointment.

'I hope you know, Sire, that you are welcome to return here whenever you like,' Sir Walter assured his king.

'I know how to value such loyalty as yours, Lord Hungerford,' said the king with a wolfish smile. My heart jumped in my chest and I watched my father closely to see how he took this dubious compliment. Apart from a small furrow on his brow, however, he appeared to take the remark in good part. I could not see that the king treated Cromwell or Sir Walter any differently to before. They still spoke together and laughed and toasted each other. It was only that sour, down-turned pout to King Henry's mouth, I thought, that gave him away. And perhaps I only saw it because I knew.

As the king took his leave, and everyone gathered in the outer court to see him off, it was freely whispered that Catherine Howard had sent him word to join her, and it was to her side that he hastened. People were only surprised that he had lingered at Farleigh so long. I hoped that they were right, but in my heart I knew there was another reason.

I felt no satisfaction in my betrayal. A younger Eleanor might have rejoiced at paying back her father for all the cruelties he had inflicted. But I was wiser now. I knew there was neither virtue nor satisfaction in such revenge. The consequences were too grave.

Locked once more in my chamber, I spent some anxious hours imagining Mother alone in the Lady Tower with only the chaplain for company, if he was well enough to attend her. She would also be suffering from hunger and thirst. I imagined her faced with the choice of slow and painful starvation or of taking nourishment that might be poisoned.

Sir Walter drank heavily at supper that night. His temper, soured by my attempted escape, had been strained to breaking point by the sudden departure of the king. The servants were nervous and careful around him, expecting him to explode at the slightest fault.

Our company was much reduced. Many of the tables had been removed and the great hall felt echoing and spacious once more. My father sat at the top table, scarcely touching his meat, but downing goblet after goblet of wine. He was silent and brooding, often casting repulsive looks in my direction. I knew he was deeply disturbed by the king's sudden departure, but he was also furiously angry with me. I could be punished, while the king could not. I grew fearful, and longed for the meal to end.

Suddenly my father stood up and hammered on the table for silence.

'My lords, ladies, and gentlemen,' he called, his voice only a little slurred from all the wine he had taken. I noticed he was gripping the edge of the table to hold himself steady on his feet. 'I find I must reduce my stable!' he announced. 'I have a horse I would like to auction.' There was a hush then a sudden buzz of interest around us. Sir Walter was looking directly at me. I felt my stomach tighten with sudden fear. Surely he would not?

'What's wrong, Walter?' called out one of my father's cronies from another table. 'Got an unsound beast you want to be rid of?' There was a burst of good-humoured laughter. Sir Walter waved the suggestion away, his hand not quite steady.

'Not unsound, William!' he cried. 'Don't have unsound horses in my stable! She is no longer needed, that's all. And I must retrench, you know. You have been eating me out of house and home, my good friends.' There was more merriment at this, and Sir Walter was toasted uproariously.

'You've been a good host, Sir Walter!' called another of his friends. 'None better! We'll buy all your horses from you!'

'Just one that needs to go: an eight-year-old grey palfrey. A fine horse, Arab blood in her. Currently known by the ridiculous name of Arianna.'

Sir Walter was looking at me. I pressed my lips tightly together and remained silent. There was nothing to be gained by betraying my emotions to Sir Walter. Inside, I was in turmoil. My beloved Arianna was to be sold. I could not bear it.

'She's used to carrying a lady,' Sir Walter continued, 'but will bear a gentleman just as well. Who will bid for her?'

I held my hands tightly clasped in my lap, gripping my fingers together to stop them from shaking and to stop myself from crying out. There was a lump in my throat. Surely he could not do this to me. I would rather he beat me.

'Are we not going to see her first?' demanded Sir William. 'Or do we take our chances on a mystery horse?'

'Do you expect me to have her brought in here to dine with us?' demanded Sir Walter belligerently. 'You take your chances. Who will open the bidding?'

I caught Maria casting sideways glances at me. She looked highly amused, as were many of the guests. They were bidding goblets of wine and boots in exchange for Arianna and the hall was echoing with laughter. But to me this was deadly serious. Arianna, my dear friend and companion of the last years, was being taken from me. I sat as still as a statue and prayed that Sir Walter would declare this a bad joke, and stop the auction. But he did not. Small sums of money were now being offered and he was grinning stupidly as he took the bids.

I saw Stanton raise his hand, and I felt a stab of betrayal.

'I'll give you two sovereigns for her!' he called out lazily.

'Two sovereigns?' roared my father. 'Gad, you insult me, sir!'

Someone else bid three and then four. Those who were not bidding cheered on those who were, calling out advice, sensible or otherwise. Everyone seemed delighted with this new form of entertainment. Through it all, I sat sick and silent. I wanted to get up and leave, but I knew I would not be permitted to do so. I also had a grim need to know Arianna's fate.

The price rose. My cousin Gregory caught my eye. He looked sympathetic. He was not bidding, but there was nothing he could do to help me.

Arianna was almost sold to a Sir John, a heavy-looking, bad-tempered man, for twelve sovereigns. But at the last minute, Lord Stanton raised his hand again. 'I'll give you twenty sovereigns,' he offered. There was an audible gasp from the assembled guests. It was a fantastic sum for an unseen horse. Sir John shook his head, and Sir Walter banged his fist on the table. 'Sold!' he shouted. He gave a bark of satisfied laughter and sat back down again. I glared at my plate, choked with misery and anger. I found I could hate more than I had ever imagined. I hated Sir Walter for selling my beloved Arianna. But I hated Stanton just as much for buying her. Just as I thought we had reached a slightly better understanding, he turned on me.

# CHAPTER TWENTY-FOUR

Sir Walter left Farleigh the next day. He said he had business to attend to in London, and would return in time for the wedding. If I thought his departure would bring about any increase in my freedom, I was gravely mistaken.

The other guests all departed too, including my cousin Gregory, and even Lord Stanton. The latter had departed with my horse, as Maria took great pleasure in informing me. He did not take his leave of me.

With no guests in the house but Maria and a couple of her friends, I was kept locked in my room around the clock, allowed out only for breakfast and dinner, and not always then. In between, I paced my small chamber in a fever of boredom and anxiety. How slowly the hours passed. How had my mother endured four years of this? I forgave her every sign of weakness during our brief escape, and longed only to hear that she was well. I had no news of her, and no way of knowing whether she was safe.

I was measured for my bride clothes one morning. I was to wear a long kirtle of white satin under a gown of white brocade edged with lace, stitched with tiny pearls. A white veil was to cover my face and reach almost to the ground behind me. Maria's friends sighed over the fabrics and the length of the veil, and told me they envied me. I, however, thought of the man I was to marry, the man who had ridden off with my horse with no word of apology.

A few days before the wedding, they began to decorate the castle. The chapel was hung with lengths of white fabric draped from the ceiling in long elegant folds. Flowers were brought in by the armful and arranged in both the chapel and the great hall. Every time I saw them, I was reminded of what lay ahead. I wondered if Dr Horde was trying to do anything to help us. If he did not come soon, it would be too late for me, though he might be able to free Mother.

After a week of dark thoughts and loneliness, and only two days to go before the wedding, there was a soft knock at my door. It was midday, and I was expecting no one till supper time. I was lying on my bed, and raised myself up on one elbow.

'Who is it?' I asked, wondering who, now, had the courtesy to knock.

'Johnson, the castellan,' came the response. 'There's a letter come for you, Mistress Eleanor.'

I rose from my bed and hurried to the door.

'For me?' I asked, surprised. Then I thought the letter might be from Dr Horde, and felt renewed hope.

'Yes, Mistress Eleanor. All letters are supposed to go to the steward. But I . . . intercepted this one. Are you well?' His voice sounded kind and concerned.

'I am well enough,' I said. 'Can you not let me out?'

'I'm sorry, Mistress. I do not have the key.'

I was disappointed. But there was still the letter. It might contain good news.

'Who is the letter from?'

'Mistress Eleanor, I cannot read, but I understand it's from your aunt.'

As he spoke, there was a rustling sound, and the corner of a piece of parchment appeared under the door. I bent down to tug it through, but it stuck. We both tried to wiggle it under the gap, but to no avail.

'Please would you break the seal?' I begged him quietly. 'If it were opened, it might fit underneath.'

'Aye, if you are happy for me to do that, Mistress,' he answered. I could hear the sound of the wax seal being broken away from the parchment, and then the crackle as he unfolded the page. The letter came through this time, only slightly torn.

'I have it!' I said. 'Thank you!'

'You are most welcome,' he said and then I heard the sound of his footsteps fading away. Eagerly, I took the letter to the window and spread it out to read:

*London June 1540*

*Dear Eleanor,*

*You will scarcely remember me, my dear niece, but I am your Aunt Jane. It has been many years since we met.*

*I am deeply concerned about the welfare of both yourself and my sister, Lady Elizabeth. If I tell you the good prior, Dr Horde, came to call on me several days ago, you will comprehend the rest. With this in mind, and in the knowledge that Sir Walter is currently in London, I journeyed immediately to Bath. From here I shall undertake the drive to Farleigh in my carriage in hopes of seeing*

*you. I intend to be in Farleigh tomorrow, June the 22nd. If you*
*cannot contrive to meet me on the road, I shall call at the castle.*

*Your loving aunt,*
*Lady Jane Cranbourne.*

My aunt! I could not remember her, but I recalled Mother speaking of her. I experienced such a mixture of emotions on reading this letter that it took me some time to untangle them.

So Dr Horde had been true to his word, even after all the trouble I had brought upon him: that was kindness indeed. I felt joy and hope that others cared about us still. I also felt anxious that my aunt would be fobbed off. Perhaps she would be told that my mother was not here when she came. I had no problem imagining Maria telling her some such convincing lie. And here I was under lock and key, as helpless as Mother while my aunt was arriving tomorrow.

I needed to get out. I shook the door handle in frustration. Though I knew it was locked, I tugged at it and kicked at it in my frustration. 'Damnation!' I shouted.

I raged helplessly for some time before the first inkling of an idea came to me. It would take some courage, but it might just work.

I poured some water from my jug into my washbowl and washed my face, in an effort to calm myself. Then I lay down upon my bed and attempted to compose myself and rest. But, alas, I had never learned patience, and soon found myself pacing the chamber again.

The weather was wet the following morning, with the kind of rain that soaks into everything and turns the fields to bogs. It was cool for June, so it drew no remark from Maria that I took a shawl down to breakfast. I noted the chaplain was at his usual place in the hall, looking no worse for the effects of the sleeping drug I had given him.

During the course of the meal, when Maria was engaged in conversation, I seized a sharp knife from the table and concealed it quickly under my shawl. I felt my quickened heartbeat and breathlessness as I looked around to see if anyone had noticed. My hands shook a little as they clutched the knife.

As Maria escorted me back to my room after breakfast, I gripped the knife tightly, steeling myself to threaten Maria with it, or even use it. But in the event it was not necessary. As she stood before me, unlocking my door, she said over her shoulder:

'Your wedding gown is ready. The seamstress is bringing it for you to try on this afternoon.'

'I can hardly wait,' I replied. As Maria half turned, looking puzzled, I gave her a great shove. Caught off balance, she tumbled full length into the chamber with a cry of pain and shock. Quick as a flash, I slammed the door shut between us and turned the key. Maria's howl of rage when she picked herself up and discovered she was locked in made me glad that this room was so far from the main castle apartments.

As I turned to go, I had a shock myself. The castellan was a few paces away, looking at me with a worried expression on his face.

'Mistress Eleanor! I saw you take the knife at breakfast. I was afraid . . . ' He looked from me to the locked door in some trepidation.

'I did not use it,' I hurriedly assured him, as Maria screamed and banged on the door behind me. He looked relieved. 'Are you willing to help me?' I asked the castellan. 'You have done so much for me over the years, will you do me one last service?' He hesitated a moment, and then nodded.

'I'll help you, Mistress Eleanor,' he assured me. 'And I'm not the only one.'

'What do you mean?' I asked him, moving away from my door and Maria's furious shrieks, down the corridor.

'You and Lady Elizabeth have more friends here than you realize,' he replied. I was surprised and pleased, but had no leisure to ponder his words. I had to succeed in escaping today.

'What I need is some of Maria's clothes,' I explained. The castellan looked at me blankly. I explained: 'So that Mother can wear them, and pretend to be her. Oh, and her horrid little black veil as well. Can you get those for me, please?'

'I can. That's a better plan than setting the stables alight,' he said with a grin. 'But what are you going to do? I cannot be party to you sticking that knife into anyone. Not even Father Rankin.'

'I do not intend to *actually* stab him,' I replied earnestly. 'But I may need to threaten him.'

'I should come with you,' said the castellan at once. 'You cannot deal with him alone.'

'I can and I want to,' I assured him. 'No one must know that you helped me. I can't let anyone else suffer for us. But . . . ' I hesitated, thinking of a better plan than searching for the chaplain myself, 'you could ensure that he goes to the tower. Could you perhaps find him and ask him if I have permission to be visiting Mother, as you saw me going up the stairs?'

The castellan thought about this for a moment, then he smiled his slight, thin-lipped smile.

'Certainly,' he told me. 'And, Mistress Eleanor, can I once more advocate caution in the use of that knife?'

'I promise,' I said seriously.

He hurried away to find the chaplain, and I ran to the Lady Tower, heedless of who saw me. I had barely concealed myself behind a door near the foot of the tower when I heard the chaplain's wheezing breathing as he approached. He was not hurrying, and he was carrying Mother's tray. I watched Father Rankin, wondering whether the castellan had had time to find him, or whether he had come unprompted. As he jangled the keys, and then thrust the right one into the lock, I crept softly up to him and pressed the knife to his neck. He gasped and froze.

'Keep unlocking that door,' I ordered him. 'And do not turn around. If you do, this knife might slip. Right into your throat,' I said with relish. I did not feel sorry for him. My mother had suffered for four long years at his hands. The chaplain gave a strangled whimper and slowly turned the key in the lock. The door swung open.

'Good. Now hold that tray with both hands and walk very slowly all the way up to the next door.'

I followed him, keeping the knife at his throat as he mounted the stairs before me.

It was dark on the stairs. They were lit only by arrow slits in the walls, and it was as gloomy as a winter's day out there. I could hear the rain falling as we passed each opening, and feel the cold damp air on my skin. It seemed to take forever to shuffle up the stairs, but we reached Mother's door at length. 'Now open it,' I ordered the sweating chaplain.

There had not been a sound from Mother, and I almost feared to look upon her as the door swung open. I was sure she would be thinner and weaker than ever. She stood quietly on the far side of the room. Her eyes were wide with surprise as we entered, but she looked no worse than before.

'Mother,' I ordered her, 'go to the foot of the stairs and wait for me there.'

'That man,' said my mother, her voice quivering slightly. 'Eleanor, I'm not leaving you alone with him. You do not know what he is capable of.'

As she spoke the chaplain twisted round, smashing the tray into my elbow. I cried out in agony as the tender elbow bone was struck. The pain almost blinded me, and I felt the knife fly from my hand. Plate, goblet, jug, and food all went flying through the air, striking me and smashing onto the floor. The noise was incredible. Gasping, eyes watering, I looked frantically for the knife. It lay at some distance from me on the floor. I dived towards it, heedless of the pain in my arm, but the chaplain was faster. Stretching full length, he snatched it up.

I gave a yell of mingled pain and fury, but even as I cried out, I saw Mother's foot come down on the chaplain's hand, crushing his fingers. There was a sickening crunch, and he released the knife. 'Take it!' shouted Mother over the chaplain's screams. I did so, and pushed myself up to kneel beside the chaplain, the knife tip now pressing against his ribs.

'I would dearly love to stick this into you,' I told the man as menacingly as I could. He stilled his cries, lying still but for his panting. 'In fact,' I continued, 'I'd like to slice you right open and spill your guts like a pig on butchering day. If you give me any more trouble, I shall do just that. Do you understand?' The chaplain gave the faintest of nods, seemingly frozen with fear, but I did not trust him. 'Shall we tie him up?' I asked Mother. As I looked up at her, I saw her looking down at the chaplain, her face a mask of disgust.

'If I broke your fingers,' she told him, 'I'm not sorry. It can be a reminder to you of all the unnecessary suffering you've caused me these four years.'

She turned and pulled the sheet off her bed, tore it into strips, and bound the chaplain with them. She pulled the knots tight, and then went to the door, waiting for me there. I stood up, and felt dizzy for a few seconds with the pain that was still throbbing in my elbow. Then I threw the knife onto the floor and left, locking the chaplain in. Mother and I did not speak. We simply hurried, hand in hand, down the steep spiral steps. As I locked the second door behind us, the castellan appeared, clutching a bundle of clothing. He bowed respectfully to Mother and held the bundle out to her.

'Put them on,' I urged her, ushering her into the privacy of a nearby room. 'You are to be Mistress Maria. We are riding to Bath to meet your sister.'

'My sister Jane?' asked Mother. I could see the curiosity in her face.

'She sent a letter, I'll explain later.'

I left her to change and went back to thank the castellan.

'There's precious little to thank me for,' he said dismissively. 'The chaplain was already on his way here. Are you hurt?' He indicated my dishevelled garments. There was a wet stain down the side of my dress where the water from the tray had spilled, and my gown had been torn slightly in the scuffle.

'I'm well enough,' I told him shakily.

'Are you going to give me the keys?' asked the castellan gravely.

'No.' I shook my head. 'No indeed, I have quite other plans for them.'

He frowned but did not press me.

'And so I am to lose my pupil,' said the castellan quietly. 'And Walter will lose his jousting partner.'

'Whether I run away, or stay here to be married, it makes no difference.' I shrugged. 'But I shall be sad to give up the training. Tell me. Were you satisfied with your pupil's performance at the tournament?'

'I was very pleased with Walter, of course.'

'And how pleased were you with your other pupil?'

The castellan looked puzzled.

'The final against Stanton?' I prompted him, enjoying the way his eyes widened as he tried to take in what I was telling him.

'Mistress Eleanor, that was not you,' he said uncertainly.

'Johnson, it was,' I assured him. 'My cousin was too injured to ride the last heat. I took his place.'

I pulled up my sleeve to reveal the cut on my arm, healing nicely now.

He gasped.

'I never dreamed . . . Mistress Eleanor, you were magnificent.'

I felt myself glow with his rare praise.

At that moment, Mother emerged, dressed in Maria's gown, hood, and veil. I thought she looked like Maria. Thinner, of course, but I trusted the guards at the gate would not notice.

The castellan led us swiftly to the stables where two horses awaited us already saddled and bridled. Our cloaks were also awaiting us there. They would be very necessary in such weather.

There were grooms working in the stables but none spared us much more than a cursory glance. If they wondered at us at all, it was why we were riding out in the pouring rain. They did not appear to question our identity.

One of the waiting horses was Beau, the other one of my father's hunters, an ugly, large-boned animal, strong but steady. Tom was tightening the girths as we entered the stable, and grinned at me.

'Your father owes you a horse, I reckon,' he said quietly. He bowed awkwardly to my mother and offered her a leg up onto Beau. I looked at my mount, taking in his raw, inelegant appearance, and felt a rush of sadness for Arianna as well as a stab of resentment towards Stanton who had taken her from me. The castellan offered to throw me up in the saddle. I hesitated.

'Tom,' I asked, 'why is this unspeakable animal wearing a side-saddle?'

The castellan replied for Tom: 'On my orders,' he said. 'I considered it sensible to make a good impression on your aunt.'

'How did you know my aunt was coming? You told me you cannot read.'

'True.' The castellan gave me a quick smile. 'But I had a long talk with your aunt's groom when he brought the letter.'

Once I was seated awkwardly in the strange saddle and arranging my skirts, the castellan patted the saddle bags behind me. 'Betsey's packed you enough food for half of Bath,' he said in a low voice.

I found that all this kindness brought tears to my eyes as my suffering here had never done. I leaned down and grasped Johnson's hand. 'Thank you,' I said tremulously. 'Thank you to everyone who has helped us.'

'Something tells me you have courage enough for this,' he replied with a tight smile. 'Travel safely.' The castellan turned to Mother.

'God bless you, my lady,' he said. 'That's a brave daughter you have.'

'Thank you, Johnson,' she replied faintly.

As we prepared to ride out the castellan forestalled us: 'Just let me go and chat to my lads on the gate. If I greet your ladyship as Mistress Maria, they will not question you leaving.'

We watched as he strolled over to the gatehouse and began to exchange idle conversation with the guards. As I turned my horse towards the gate, I reached down and gripped Tom's shoulder. I said nothing, but we exchanged a long look. I hoped he knew how sorry I was to leave him, though I found I could not say it.

Passing through the gatehouse and crossing the drawbridge should have been the moment of greatest risk. But the castellan's presence robbed it of danger. The guards would not question us if he did not.

He bowed to us as we passed and called, 'Ride safely, Mistress Maria, Mistress Eleanor! You will get very wet, I fear!'

The guards stood to attention and let us pass without question. Our horses' hooves clumped over the wooden drawbridge for the last time. As we crossed, I leaned out and dropped the chaplain's keys into the moat. They fell into the water with a satisfying splash. And then we were free, riding along towards the Bath Road in the pouring rain.

# CHAPTER TWENTY-FIVE

We rode in silence at first, with many anxious backward glances. I could scarcely believe that no one was following us. At last, after a mile or so, my mother spoke:

'Have we succeeded, Eleanor?' she asked cautiously. 'It seems scarcely possible that it could be so easy.'

'Easy?' I thought of the fight with the chaplain and how I had locked Maria in my room. 'Did you say *easy*?' I threw back my head and laughed, overwhelming relief mixed with my joy. The rain poured down into my face, the heavy drops splashing onto me and running into my mouth.

'We're free!' I shouted, startling my horse. 'We've done it. But, Mother—I would not have called that easy.'

She regarded me with some surprise, which made me laugh all the more.

'We had many kind helpers,' I said, once my mirth subsided. 'I did not realize how many of the staff were loyal to you rather than to Sir Walter.'

'Nor I, indeed,' sighed Mother. 'And the good villagers too. They all heard about our escape to the priory, you know. I was sent so much food that I could not eat it all.'

'How kind,' I said touched. 'I was so afraid that you would starve once I was locked up too.'

'So was I. I was certain you would be imprisoned, after that night, and I have feared greatly for you.'

'But as you can see, I am quite well.'

We smiled happily at one another, and Mother leaned over and took my hand, giving it an affectionate squeeze.

I related to Mother how Dr Horde had sought out my aunt and told her our plight. Mother exclaimed, and shed tears of gratitude.

'Does Jane know we ride to meet her?' she asked at length.

'There was no time to write. And indeed, she did not give me her direction in Bath. But she said she was coming to Farleigh today and asked us to try and meet her upon the road.'

'But, Eleanor, what if we should miss her? Or if she does not set out in such weather?' I saw there was a worried crease in her brow, and I hastened to reassure her.

'We cannot miss her. She will be coming along this road,' I said confidently.

'Eleanor,' began Mother hesitantly, 'do you . . . have any money?'

I shook my head. 'No, none. But I have a few things we could sell. This gold necklace for one.' I showed the gift Maria had given me. 'Do not fear, Mother. I shall take care of you.'

Mother gave a small laugh. 'Indeed, 'tis I who should be taking care of you,' she murmured sadly.

We rode towards Bath for another half an hour or so. The horses slipped and slithered down the long descent into Limpley Stoke, struggling to hold their footing. Often they sank into the mud and freed themselves with difficulty. I began to fear one of them might cast a shoe, and began looking out ever more anxiously for my aunt. There was no one on the road today, however. Anyone who had any choice had not set out in such weather. Although I said nothing to Mother, I began to feel uneasy. Despite my assurances, I had no idea how we would go about searching for my aunt in an unknown city.

The rain had penetrated our cloaks now, and I could feel ice-cold trickles running down the back of my neck. My hair was plastered to my head. I could see Mother's clothes were drenched through. I felt a stab of anxiety for her. I knew her health was not strong. She had thrown back Maria's veil, and the rain was streaming down her face.

'What is it like?' I asked, breaking a long silence. 'To feel the rain and the wind again after so many years indoors?'

'If you had asked me an hour ago,' Mother replied, 'I would have said it was like a taste of heaven. But now, I must confess to being soaked through. I shall look forward to a warm fire at our journey's end.'

We reached the ford at the bottom of the hill, and I rode my horse cautiously out into it.

'The water is higher than usual, Mother,' I called over the rush of the river. 'But it is safe to cross.'

Mother urged the reluctant Beau out into the water. The horses surged up the bank on the far side and we began the ascent.

'This is the last real hill before Bath,' I said encouragingly to Mother. At the top there were wonderful views of the valley spread out below us, with neatly cultivated fields and wooded hillsides, vividly green in all their summer finery. I could see Mother drinking in the beauty of the view.

While we lingered, two horses appeared around the bend of the road. I had not heard them, and there was no time to hide in case it was someone we knew.

'Mother, pull down your veil,' I said. She did so at once.

I looked at the riders and my heart leapt into my mouth. One was a servant, but the other I recognized instantly.

'Well met, my dear Eleanor. Whither away? And in such weather too!'

'Lord Stanton.' I bowed stiffly. I could feel myself going hot and cold with shock. Lord Stanton was bowing to Mother, and he was looking slightly puzzled.

'Good morrow . . . ah . . . Mistress Maria?' he said. Mother bowed and remained silent. This was sensible, but so unlike Maria that I imagined Lord Stanton would be suspicious at once. But it was me he was looking at, his brows raised. I resolved to brazen it out.

'Mistress Maria has had word her sister is come to Bath,' I informed him boldly. 'She is desirous of meeting with her at once. So I offered to accompany her.'

'Most generous of you, Eleanor. And in such weather too. But is the castle now so thin of company that no one remained to escort two ladies on such a long ride?'

I bit my lip, vexed. I decided to play upon the recklessness he had once accused me of.

'Indeed we needed nothing so stuffy as a groom trailing after us,' I scoffed, tossing my head. 'We will not detain you, sir.' I bowed slightly by way of farewell and urged my horse forward. It was unfortunate that he chose that moment to miss his footing and stumble into a deep rut. He slipped and floundered before recovering himself. I kept my seat, but it was enough, apparently, for Lord Stanton.

'Wait!' he called. I halted again, fuming with vexation. I was desperate to get away from him. 'I cannot possibly leave you to ride alone,' Stanton said, wheeling his horse about and coming abreast of me. 'You would be at the mercy of every scoundrel and thief on the road, and with no one by to help if either of you have an accident. I will be pleased to be your escort.'

There was a note of sincerity in his voice which made me think he was trying to be kind rather than teasing me. But indeed, his kindness could not have been more ill judged. 'Are you thinking of horse thieves, my lord?' I asked sharply. 'Indeed, I believe we may already have met one.' He did not look as though he understood my allusion, so I continued, saying firmly: 'Your escort will not be necessary.' But he was no longer listening. He had turned and was giving orders to his servant to ride on to Farleigh. Mother and I told our horses to walk on, exchanging anxious looks.

'Who is he?' Mother mouthed from under her veil.

'Stanton,' I breathed back. She looked blank.

Lord Stanton caught us up again and all chance of private conversation was at an end. As he brought his horse alongside mine and smiled, I scowled.

'What are you doing at Farleigh again so soon?' I asked.

'Why, I have come for our wedding tomorrow, Mistress Eleanor. Or had that unimportant event slipped your mind entirely?' he asked. I heard the sharp intake of Mother's breath. Stanton heard it too, and turned politely to address her, leaving me no opportunity to retort to his jibe.

'And which of your sisters will you have the pleasure of seeing in Bath, ma'am?' he asked. Mother remained silent. I could sense her desperation and hurried into speech.

'Maria has had a sore throat and has lost her voice,' I said. 'I think it was . . . er . . . your sister Harriet, was it not, Maria?'

'Mistress Maria, it was most unwise of you to ride out in the rain with a sore throat,' said Stanton, earnestly. 'How could you be so careless of your health?' I cast him a suspicious look, which he met limpidly, but I could see small creases of amusement about his eyes, and realized that he had guessed at least a part of what we were trying to hide.

'Do you not fear to become seriously ill?' Stanton continued, turning back to my mother. 'You risk an inflammation of the lung at the very least. And there is the danger that you could pass it to your sister, you know. Have you not considered this?'

I realized too late what a stupid lie I had told. I was also sure now that Stanton was amusing himself at my expense once more. Mother remained stubbornly silent.

'Though of course,' Stanton continued, 'you no doubt consider your "sister" quite safe from illness as Mistress Maria has no sisters—only a brother.'

I was stunned into silence. Stanton waited patiently for a response as our horses battled forward through the mud, their hooves squelching and the sodden harness squeaking. I was frantic. I did not trust him. Not for one second. But I had no way of warning Mother.

At length Mother lifted her veil and looked directly at Stanton.

'I am not Maria,' she said calmly. 'I am Lady Elizabeth Hungerford.'

I could not see Stanton's face as he heard this. Surely he must be surprised. Whoever he expected to be under the veil, it could not have been my mother.

'Lady Elizabeth.' He bowed courteously. 'A most unexpected pleasure.'

Mother was pale, but looked quite serene. I admired her courage.

'I am fleeing Farleigh for reasons of my own,' she explained. 'No blame attaches to my daughter.' Stanton glanced at me, a fleeting look of surprise on his face.

'Is that so?' asked Stanton. I could clearly hear the laughter in his voice now. 'In my experience, ma'am, Eleanor is usually in the thick of any mischief.'

My mother paused before replying, and when she did her voice was very low.

'Sir, this is no jesting matter. I have been kept a prisoner without grounds for several years, and treated most cruelly. Indeed my life was constantly in peril. Without Eleanor's help, I would have died.'

Stanton frowned. 'How so, my lady? I understood you were gravely ill, and being nursed.'

You understood no such thing, I thought. Stanton must be a good liar to sound so innocent and surprised at my mother's words.

'Not at all,' replied Mother. She explained the truth with a quiet earnestness that defied disbelief. Her pale face, her child-like innocence, and her trembling voice all lent her story utter conviction. When she had finished, we rode in silence for some time.

'I see,' said Stanton. 'Your tale explains much that puzzled me before.'

'Are you going to ride off and tell Sir Walter where we are?' I asked bitterly. It was the first time I had spoken since Mother lifted her veil. Stanton looked taken aback.

'What makes you think that I would do that?' he asked.

'Eleanor,' Mother reproved me, 'that was not polite.'

I stayed silent, but I remembered what Sir Walter had told me weeks ago. Stanton was in the plot to be rid of my mother. He was just pretending to be on our side. He would find out where we were going and betray us, I was certain of it. But it was pointless accusing him of this. He would simply deny it, in that sincere way he had that made one certain at once that he was to be trusted. Well, I would not trust him. I pressed my lips firmly together and said nothing. The next time Mother looked at me, I sent her a warning look.

It did no good. Mother seemed to have fallen completely under Stanton's spell. He was treating her in a respectful, deferential way, and she was smiling up at him, telling him everything. Furious with both of them, I kicked my horse on, and pulled ahead. How could she trust this man Sir Walter had foisted on me? He had tormented me at every turn.

My clothes were now so wet, they were chafing my

skin. My cloak hung heavy and cold from my shoulders, and I longed for the ride to end. I could see it was impossible to shake Stanton off now. We could neither outride him nor overpower him. We had no choice but to pretend to accept his help until such a time as he left us.

As we approached the walls of the city of Bath, I sneezed several times. Stanton rode forward until he was beside me.

'You have caught cold, Mistress Eleanor?' he said.

'I never catch cold.'

'I am concerned for you. It has been a long wet ride.'

'Your concern is entirely wasted. I am quite well. In fact, now that we are safely in Bath, we can dispense with your escort. Will you not leave us and ride back to Farleigh?'

'I wish to see you safely bestowed. Your mother is not strong, and has already agreed to allow me to install you at an inn while I make enquiries for your aunt.'

I made an angry sound in my throat. Mother was so gullible. Now Stanton would be able to tell Sir Walter exactly where we were staying.

'You still do not trust me, Eleanor?' Stanton asked softly. 'I wish you would.'

I shook my head.

'Eleanor, I must ask you something,' said Stanton. When I did not respond, he continued anyway:

'Do you intend to return to Farleigh once your mother is safe with your aunt?'

I looked at him in astonishment. 'Return? Of course not!'

'I see. You will not have forgotten that we are to be

married tomorrow. Is it only your father you are fleeing from, or is it our wedding also?'

'Both,' I said, my voice sounding tight and hard. 'I never wanted to marry you.' I stole a quick glance at his profile. There was a slight frown upon his face, but otherwise I could read little there. 'And I know you did not wish to marry me either,' I added.

'That was long ago. I supposed that you and I had reached a better understanding. Was I mistaken?' He sounded disappointed.

'I can only suppose you wished to marry me for the pleasure of continuing to torment me,' I said.

'You are quite wrong. I desire your happiness as well as mine. Is there nothing I can say or do to change your mind?' Stanton's voice was humble. He was making this more difficult than I could have imagined possible. I clutched my reins tightly.

'I just want you to leave me alone,' I said.

There was a pause, then Stanton said sadly: 'I do not know if I can do that.'

I said nothing. Was he refusing to release me? After waiting in vain for a look or a word, Stanton turned his horse about and rode back to Mother. I felt strangely bereft when I should have felt satisfied. Triumphant even. I had looked forward to this moment after all. But I did not. I felt confused and upset.

Stanton took us to a comfortable inn where our wet and weary horses were stabled. Mother and I were shown into a private room where a warm fire burned.

'You would scarce think it was June, would you, ladies?' said the landlord, ushering us in, and bowing so low, he almost touched his knees. 'You warm yourselves by the fire. What can I be getting you in the nature of refreshments?'

'Hot wine for the ladies, please,' Stanton replied for us. 'And some bread and meat, if you have it.'

'Oh, yes, sir,' the landlord assured him, bowing again. 'That we do, sir. My missus has just roasted a nice side of beef, and I said to her, I did, you mark my words . . . '

'Thank you, roast beef would be most welcome,' Stanton interrupted him, holding the door open for him. 'As soon as you can manage please. The ladies are quite famished.'

'Yes, sir, at once,' replied the landlord and hurried out. Instead of admiring the masterly way Stanton dealt with his garrulousness, I flung myself into a chair, yawned and remarked: 'I really should have preferred ale. And chicken.'

Stanton's lips twitched.

'You will find the hot wine and beef most sustaining however, Mistress Eleanor.' I hunched an impatient shoulder.

'Oh, yes, indeed. What luxury. You are so kind,' murmured Mother faintly.

'Can I take your wet cloak, ma'am?' Stanton responded, all attentive kindness at once. He helped her remove it and spread it over a chair before the fire where it began to steam. 'And yours, Eleanor?' he asked.

'I can manage myself,' I replied ungraciously. Stanton bowed stiffly and turned back to Mother, taking her hand in his.

'I hope you will be comfortable here, my lady. I will go

at once and make enquiries for Lady Cranbourne. I shall return as soon as I have news.' He kissed her hand and left. I sighed with relief as the door closed behind him.

Mother sighed also, with relief of a different sort, as she sank into a chair by the fire. She looked almost grey with exhaustion after the long ride. 'I do not know how I stayed in the saddle all that distance,' she said faintly. 'I was truly thankful for Lord Stanton's help. But I was sorry indeed to see a daughter of mine so deficient in manners, Eleanor. Truly, you have been without a mother's guidance for too long. What were you thinking of?'

'We cannot trust him, Mother,' I said at once. Her words had stung me and I could feel my temper rising. 'How do you know he is not even now sending a messenger post-haste to apprise Sir Walter of our whereabouts? This could be a trap!'

Mother waved a weary hand at me.

'Not now, Eleanor,' she said. 'I am too tired, and thankful for the help he has given us. Without him we would be riding around Bath in the rain asking at every inn, only to find that my sister is staying with friends. Because we have met with unkindness, Eleanor, you mistrust everyone. This is a mistake. There are good people in the world too.'

'I know,' I cried. 'But Lord Stanton is not one of them. He was in on the plot to murder you. I'm sure of it.'

My mother looked visibly shaken. 'Eleanor, surely not?' she gasped turning pale.

'He was. Sir Walter told me so himself! When you advised me, that night I came to the Lady Tower, to speak to my future husband about your situation, Sir Walter

237

overheard. And he told me afterwards it would do no good, for Stanton was on his side!'

'He said Stanton was aware I was to be poisoned?'

'No, not exactly. But he said he knew everything.'

'I think you must have been mistaken,' my mother said anxiously. 'Lord Stanton seems a truly good man. I am very happy to find you so eligibly betrothed.'

I gaped at her in disbelief. 'But I am n-not going to *marry* him!' I stammered, appalled. 'I'm running away with you!'

'Yes, of course,' Mother replied with a smile. 'But he tells me he is most desirous of marrying you, despite that.'

'Mother, how could you?' I cried. 'Is that what you two were talking about behind my back?' I could hardly believe what I was hearing. 'He is an odious man, and I loathe him. I thought you of all people would understand.'

At that moment there was a knock at the door and the landlord entered once more, carrying the hot wine. He was followed by his wife, who begged to take our cloaks and gowns for drying, and by a maid carrying plates of meat.

There was no more opportunity to speak privately. Without Lord Stanton to rid us of him, the landlord stayed in the room. He insisted on serving us himself and on entertaining us with endless stories of lords and ladies who had honoured his inn in the past.

I sipped the hot wine and tasted the food, but without relish. My interrupted conversation with Mother had taken my appetite from me, and there was an uncomfortable constraint between us.

When the meal was over and the landlord had at last

absented himself, Mother came over to me and embraced me.

'My dearest Eleanor, let us not argue. I am so happy to be here with you. Let us leave everything else for the future.' I hugged her back, and we sat in silence for some time side-by-side, my head resting on her shoulder. Together we watched the fire in the hearth die down to a gentle glow. It would have been peaceful but for the barely concealed anxiety we both felt at every sound of a carriage or footsteps on the street outside.

'I am so afraid that Sir Walter will burst in on us at any moment,' I admitted to Mother at one point.

'I too,' she confessed nervously. 'It has been several hours now. I do hope your suspicions were not justified.'

When the door at length opened, we both leapt to our feet in alarm. But a lady stood upon the threshold. I could see at a glance that she must be my aunt. She was as stout and robust as my mother was thin and frail, but she had a great look of her nonetheless.

'My dear Eliza!' she cried and enveloped Mother in a hearty embrace. Mother promptly dissolved into tears in her sister's arms.

'Oh, Jane . . . my dear Jane! To think . . . I should see you once more!' she uttered brokenly. I offered them our seats by the fire and withdrew to a table by the window. I watched them happily for a few minutes, delighting in tracing the similarities between them as they hugged one another and spoke a jumble of words, neither attending greatly to the other in the first burst of their joy.

To my annoyance, Stanton entered the room and came to join me by the window. I ignored him.

'Well, Eleanor, are you not going to thank me for bringing your aunt to you?' he asked me provocatively.

'Thank you,' I said stiffly. He smiled faintly.

'I do believe you would rather hit me. Or at least knock me off my horse once more.'

I glanced at him, surprised he should refer to that event. But there was no resentment in his face.

'Shall we agree that you *could* have managed by yourself?' he asked. '*You* did not need my help. But believe me; it was much better for your mother to rest quietly by the fire than to go from inn to inn in the rain.'

I regarded him with smouldering resentment, which grew as he looked blandly back at me.

'Come, Eleanor,' he said at last. 'We have sparred with one another long enough. Can we not at least be friends?' He offered me his hand, and I looked at it without taking it.

'I still do not know if I can trust you,' I said bitterly. 'So how can we be friends?'

Stanton looked grave again in an instant and withdrew the proffered hand. 'I see,' he said. 'Well, there is nothing I can say to convince you. I can only trust that time will reveal the truth to you.'

I felt embarrassed and ungracious at once. It occurred to me for the first time that my father could have lied to me. He might have told me Stanton was on his side simply to prevent me confiding in him. I no longer knew whom to believe.

Stanton got up, and took a polite leave of my mother and my aunt, waving aside their thanks. 'I shall do myself the honour of calling upon you tomorrow or the next day, if I may?' he asked Mother. 'To assure myself that you have recovered from the journey.'

'Please do!' said Mother at once. 'We would be happy to see you.'

I am very sure I scowled as she said this. But when Stanton came over to me and offered me his hand once more, I did not withhold mine. There was something very perverse in my nature it seemed; for I found I was disappointed when he had gone.

# CHAPTER TWENTY-SIX

When the door had closed behind Stanton, the three of us looked at one another.

'What a charming young man,' my aunt remarked. 'And so *handsome*! How very fortunate that you should have chanced upon him on the road. I was just telling your mother, my dear Eleanor, that I was forced to delay my visit to Farleigh as a result of the atrocious weather. Now, shall we not remove to my lodgings at once? We can be more comfortable there.'

'Indeed, it was not fortunate!' I cried, springing to my feet. I ran to the door and opened it a crack, to see that Stanton had really gone. 'Stanton knows now where you are staying. He is not to be trusted. I have tried to warn Mother. I believe he will go straight to Sir Walter with the news of our whereabouts.'

'Surely not?' asked my aunt, shocked.

'I have already told Eleanor I do not believe it,' said Mother.

'We can trust no one from Farleigh,' I insisted. 'They pretend to be my friends, and as soon as I trust them they betray me. Maria already has. Stanton's father is a close friend of Sir Walter: they arranged our betrothal between them. Can you really believe he is on our side?'

'But, Eleanor, he is such a gentleman!' implored my mother. 'He has honesty written all over him.'

'I admit, I, too, was most favourably impressed,' agreed my aunt.

'Having a handsome face and polished manners does not make him honest!' I cried in frustration. 'And even if he is and wishes us well, he may still feel it is his duty to tell Sir Walter where we are.'

It seemed I had struck a chord at last. As Sir Walter's wife and daughter, we had no status, no rights of our own. He practically owned us, and society would condemn our running away.

'But in that case, what are we to do?' cried Lady Jane. 'Where will you go if you cannot come to me?'

'Can we not remove to London at once?' I asked. 'It would be easier to hide there.'

'It is far, and we would be easily traced along the way,' said my aunt doubtfully. 'Are you really so certain that Sir Walter will come looking for you?'

'We are sure,' I said. Mother and I related the story of our previous escape.

'Dr Horde told me some of this,' nodded Lady Jane. 'It seems in truth that the utmost secrecy and discretion are required. Eleanor, do you have any ideas on what course we should take now?'

'We should remove to somewhere which has no connection to either us or you, Aunt, and stay there awhile under false names.'

Mother nodded her agreement. 'Indeed, I think Eleanor is right,' she said. 'We cannot be too careful.' I smiled at her gratefully, glad of her support.

'Well, there are any number of modest lodging houses in Bath,' said my aunt at last. 'But it is not what I wished for. I wanted to have you to myself and spoil you, after all you've been through, my dear sister.' She took Mother's hand and pressed it affectionately as she spoke.

'After my quarters in the tower, almost anywhere with a fire and my daughter's company will be luxury,' Mother assured her with a wan smile.

My aunt heaved herself to her feet. 'If it will make you feel safer, I will go and find somewhere for you now. Landlord!' she called, opening the door.

The man came hurrying in so quickly, I suspected him of hovering outside the room. 'Yes, ma'am?' he asked, with a low bow.

'My friends need their gowns and cloaks, if you please. And I would like their bill.'

'Oh, madam, that's very kind of you, I'm sure, but the gentleman what was here earlier—a real gentleman, by his fine manner and generous ways—settled the bill already. But is there nothing else you'd like before you go? My missus has a nice leg of lamb roasting as we speak, and it's always a pleasure to be serving such honoured guests . . . ' The landlord bowed low again.

My aunt looked surprised for a moment, then said: 'Just the cloaks, please,' and nodded dismissal to the man. 'Well, that was generous of Stanton, at any rate,' she remarked to us once the landlord was out of earshot. 'He's not all bad then, Eleanor, you see.'

I put my chin up defiantly, and refused to be drawn.

I had to prevent Aunt Jane from asking the landlord the names of some decent lodging houses, pointing out how easy it would be to trace us that way. We enquired instead of a respectable passer-by in the street, and an hour later Mother and I were installed in the top floor of a small house in Cheap Street under the names of the Mistresses Wilson, two sisters travelling from Oxford. It was the best I could think of, tired as I was.

The lodging house was modest, but we were content. We had a small fire lit to ward off the damps of the evening, and we felt safe and comfortable at last. I requested a small bathtub be carried up to our room, so that Mother could bathe as I had done at Farleigh.

When Mother climbed into the bath, she sighed with pleasure. 'It is so many years since I had a bath,' she said softly. 'This is luxury indeed.' She reached out one of her wet hands for mine, and pulled me down to sit beside the bath.

'Thank you, dear daughter,' she said. 'I owe you so much. This feels like a dream, but if we are left in peace, God willing, I may come to believe it by and by.' I felt proud at her acknowledgement, and smiled. After a few moments silence, Mother asked: 'Have you had any thoughts on what we might do next? Once it is safe to leave here?'

'I had dreamed we might find a little cottage somewhere, where we could live together, you and I,' I said. It had been the picture I had had of our future for several years, but as I said it out loud, I realized how silly it sounded.

'A cottage?' asked Mother with a laugh. 'How romantic. Should we have roses growing over the front door and keep a cow at the back?' I laughed with her at this image, but felt rather hurt to have my idea treated as a joke. 'And what should we do for company?' Mother asked me.

'We would have each other, of course,' I said, but Mother shook her head.

'It might do for me, Eleanor. But you are young and need friends of your own age as well. You will wish to marry. And you are the daughter of a nobleman. You cannot spend your life in some obscure cottage.'

'I would be happier than I was at Farleigh,' I assured her fiercely. 'I shall never marry. I made up my mind about that long ago.'

'My marriage turned out badly, Eleanor,' said Mother sadly. 'But not all marriages do.'

I shook my head sceptically. 'I will not risk it,' I declared.

'Few of us have the good fortune to decide over our own destiny,' said Mother seriously. 'Women least of all. You will be fortunate indeed if you have any sort of choice. And you are forgetting something. How shall we manage for money? We have nothing.'

'I had not forgotten that,' I said, my voice low. In every dream I had ever had of our future, in every plan I ever formulated, I had come up against this one insurmountable problem.

'The best future I could wish for you is marriage to a good husband who would care for you,' said Mother.

I gasped with shock.

'Like Sir Walter cared for you?' I demanded. 'I'd rather marry a dung beetle and live in the midden.'

I bit my lip once the words were out, remembering

how Mother disliked it when I was unladylike in my speech. But to my surprise, Mother threw back her head and laughed. It was the laugh I remembered from my childhood: like a peal of merry bells. I could not help but join in. I was so pleased to hear her laugh again.

'I doubt you would find that a comfortable way of life, my dearest,' she chuckled. 'Now, pass me that soap please, before the water grows quite cold. I am going to wash my hair.'

I slept deeply that night, and woke, much refreshed, to the sound of a quill scratching. I sat up and saw Mother, wrapped in a blanket, sitting up writing.

'What are you doing, Mother?' I asked her curiously, rubbing my eyes and yawning.

'Writing to Thomas Cromwell,' replied Mother.

'What?' I asked, astonished. 'Why?'

'He should know,' said Mother. 'Sir Walter should not go unpunished for what he did to me.'

'He *does* know!' I exclaimed. 'Have you forgotten he was present when you were arrested four years ago? That it was he who took us from the monastery? He's been in the plot all along.'

Mother continued writing, the quill scratching rhythmically. 'I cannot believe he knows the full story,' she replied. 'He would not let me explain that day at Henton. But he will have to read a letter.'

'Please yourself,' I said, snuggling back down between the sheets. 'But he's Lord Cromwell now, Earl of Essex. And he's plotting treason against the king.'

Mother cried out in shock. 'Eleanor, do not say such dreadful things! What do you understand of treason at your age? Now I have made a blot, and shall have to begin again.' She took a fresh sheet of parchment. I lay in bed feeling once more the sick sense of guilt that I felt every time I thought of my conversation with the king. I tried to tell myself nothing would come of it. That it had been my duty. But these excuses brought me no comfort.

The day was long and tedious. Once Mother had finished her letter, we waited for Lady Jane to come. She had promised us some books and embroidery to pass the time, but she did not appear. By mid-afternoon, we were both fretting with impatience and anxiety.

'Perhaps she has been taken ill?' suggested Mother.

'She would have sent us a message. Perhaps she has been kidnapped by Sir Walter.'

'Now you are being ridiculous, Eleanor,' said Mother nervously. 'Perhaps she has had an idea for our future, and wishes to surprise us.'

Our speculation was fruitless. By the time evening arrived, I was feeling confined and bad-tempered as well as anxious. I began to admit to myself that perhaps a small cottage might not suit me after all. At last, under cover of dusk, a knock came upon the door. Lady Jane entered, shrouded in a cloak. She looked flustered and had spots of red on her cheeks. She sat down plump in a chair and began to fan herself energetically.

'What a day,' was all the response we got to our exclamations and questions. 'Oh dear me, what a day. I need to catch my breath before I can tell you.' She sat breathing heavily while I bit back my impatience to know what had happened.

'I have been entertaining Sir Walter . . . all day,' she said dramatically after a suitable pause. Our reaction was all she could have wished. 'Oh yes, 'tis too true! He brought the constable with him and had the confounded impudence to search my rooms for you!'

'No,' said Mother faintly. 'And is he coming here?'

'Not if I have anything to say to it,' declared my aunt. 'I took great care not to be followed, I can promise you! Would you believe he had some doctor with him— nothing but a mountebank if you want my opinion—who he claimed had certified you insane, Elizabeth!'

'What?' cried Mother, quite overcome.

'It is the story he has put about concerning you,' I told her sombrely. 'To explain your confinement to the world. He has told everyone you are sick in mind.'

'A dangerous lunatic was the term they used, no less!' exclaimed Lady Jane indignantly.

Mother sat down limply on a chair, her face grey. Her sister leaned forward and patted her hand reassuringly. 'Never fear, sister. I shall take care of you. He won't come anywhere near you if I can prevent it. And my husband will aid you, too, never fear. No, Sir Walter got nothing from me this day. I expressed shock and astonishment. I admitted I had come to Bath in hopes of seeing you, but denied that I had done so. I wept for my poor sister till Sir Walter became quite embarrassed. I considered having hysterics, but that would have been too fatiguing. I contented myself instead with clinging to him in the most irritating way, and begging him to protect me from you!'

I could not help a small chuckle escaping me at the picture my aunt's words conjured, but a glance at Mother showed me she was far from amused. She was leaning back in her chair, clutching her side, her lips tinged with blue. I rushed to get her a glass of wine, while my aunt chafed her hands, and comforted her with soothing words.

When Mother seemed to be recovering, I asked my aunt in a low voice whether Sir Walter was searching the town.

'That he is,' she replied in the same low tones. 'His men have orders to enquire for you at every hostelry in the city. So you were quite right, my dear, to come here and give a false identity. But it wasn't his lordship who betrayed you. I had the story from Sir Walter himself. He arrived at Farleigh some two or three hours after you left it, to find all in an uproar, the chaplain locked in the south-west tower, and the key nowhere to be found.'

I nodded, thinking of Stanton. I had been unwilling to trust him the day before, but I was pleased to know I had been mistaken in this at least.

'But Eleanor said Sir Walter was in London,' said Mother faintly. She appeared to be recovering from the shock.

'He was returning for my wedding,' I replied in a low voice. 'It was supposed to be today.' It was a strange thought that I should have been married by now.

'And why does my own husband want me dead or certified?' asked Mother.

'He wants to marry again,' I replied hesitantly 'Mistress Maria, whom you met, is certainly expecting him to marry her.'

'Maria Sheldon?' asked my aunt knowledgeably. 'Yes, she'd be a very wealthy bride: and her father and uncle are close to the king. It is power and influence he seeks. Much good may it do him. Mistress Maria! Ha! I could tell some stories about her!'

I was curious, but Mother was weeping now, tears trickling down her cheeks. 'We cannot stay here!' she sobbed. 'Where can we go?'

# CHAPTER TWENTY-SEVEN

We agreed to stay overnight in the lodging house, mainly because we could think of nowhere safer to go. The following morning, when we went downstairs to breakfast, Mother paused in the hallway to exchange a few words with our landlady. She was a business-like matron past middle age. The house door opened and a man walked in. Mother jumped and made to withdraw at once, but he had recognized her.

'Lady Elizabeth!' he lisped, stepping forward, his hand held out.

I stared at the man. He was a stranger to me. He was tall, thin, and dark haired, with a very dainty, fussy air about him. And he looked completely oblivious to there being anyone else present.

'Why, Sir Thomas!' Mother responded, putting her hand in his without hesitation. And then she blushed. Mother actually blushed.

'*Lady* Elizabeth?' asked the landlady. 'Do you know something I don't, Sir Thomas?'

Her voice seemed to bring the man back to a sense of his surroundings. I was biting my lip, looking for some sign from Mother, because it seemed to me we were undone. The landlady had heard her real name.

The man called Sir Thomas turned to the landlady and said: 'Yes, indeed, Mistress Myers, this is . . . was Elizabeth Hussey. I was page to her father for a number of years, and we have met infrequently since. Elizabeth, Mistress Myers is my old nurse. She runs the boarding house now, and I visit her from time to time.' He bestowed an affectionate smile upon the landlady, who beamed back at him. 'But in the name of all that is wonderful, Elizabeth, what are you doing here? You married Lord Hungerford and were living at Farleigh—I heard you were ill.'

'It's a long story,' said Mother, with a glance at me.

'Well then, don't stand in the hallway telling it!' exclaimed Mistress Myers good-naturedly. 'Come into my parlour and sit down comfortably. I'll bring your breakfast in there.'

I tried to send Mother a warning glance as we were ushered into the parlour, but she was not attending. And after all, I thought, it was a little late for caution now.

'Eleanor, dear,' said Mother a little breathlessly once we were in the room with the door closed behind us. 'Can I introduce to you my good friend, Sir Thomas Throckmorton? Thomas, this is my daughter, Eleanor.' Sir Thomas shook my hand warmly.

'Delighted to meet you,' he said, but it was clear that he had eyes for no one but my mother. I stood by and listened while she poured her whole tale into his ears. I was vexed. I could see no reason to trust him, but Mother seemed to have no hesitation in doing so. Under his adoring gaze, she blossomed. A delicate colour rose to her cheeks and her weary eyes glowed with pleasure.

I felt left out. After a while, I slipped away, fetched a veil from our room and made my way across the city to the stables where we had quartered our horses. I unlatched Beau's loosebox and slipped into the gloom, stroking his nose and breathing in his comforting horse scent. He was not a beautiful horse like Arianna, but he was familiar and I felt soothed as I leaned my face into his neck.

'What is to become of us?' I asked him softly. 'Mother trusts anyone who smiles at her and Sir Walter is hunting us all over Bath. If he thinks to search for our horses we shall be in trouble.' Beau let out his breath in a snort and shifted his weight. 'Is that all you can say?' I remarked. 'I expected more sense.'

Mistress Myers knocked and entered our room in an anxious flutter early the next morning.

'Two guest houses in the next street have been searched this morning!' she gasped. 'What shall I do if they come here? They may have a warrant to search the building!'

Mother and I exchanged frightened glances. We did not know what to say.

'Mother,' I said, 'we must leave Bath. We cannot stay here another day.'

Mother nodded, looking pale and drawn. 'Perhaps Sir Thomas may be able to help us,' she said hesitantly.

'Who is this Sir Thomas?' I flared up immediately. 'Why do you trust him so unreservedly, Mother?'

'He . . . I . . . we loved one another, Eleanor,' said

Mother. Her eyes took on a faraway look. 'He asked to marry me. I wanted to say yes, but in those days he was not wealthy. His family live quietly and have no influence at court. My father hesitated to agree to the match. And while he was hesitating, Sir Walter offered for me: Lord Hungerford, the Earl of Heytesbury. There was no comparison. I was ordered to forget Sir Thomas.'

'I did not know,' I said softly. I looked at my mother in a new light. She had been married against her will, and then treated so badly. 'I thought you loved Sir Walter,' I said. 'You always seemed to, before . . . '

'I did grow to love him,' Mother admitted. 'He was my husband, and for many years he was a good husband. But I never forgot Sir Thomas.'

I did not ask any more. It seemed almost indecent to pry into my mother's private feelings. But I felt a new tenderness, a new solicitude towards her.

Neither of us could eat any breakfast. We kept to our room all morning, where we were soon joined by Sir Thomas. I tried to like him, for Mother's sake. He was perfectly friendly to me, but he had fussy, almost womanish, manners that I found irritating. He flattered her and fussed constantly about her comfort, placing a rug over her knees to protect her from draughts, and ordering refreshments in case she should be hungry. To all of this she patiently submitted, smiling tenderly up at him. After an hour or so of this, I felt like a fifth leg on a horse. I put on my cloak and went to check on the horses once more.

As I approached the stables, I almost ran into one of Sir Walter's men. He was standing on a street corner watching the passers by. I barely had time to dive down an alleyway before he turned. I stood concealed in a doorway and watched as he was joined by one of Sir Walter's grooms. To my dismay, I saw them disappearing into the stables. If they had not already found Beau and my father's hunter, they soon would.

When they emerged ten minutes later, Sir Walter was with them, and they were leading both the horses. I pressed myself back into the doorway, not even daring to watch them go. I felt despair at the loss of the horses, but I had one thing at least to be thankful for. The stables had no idea where Mother and I were lodging, I had been careful of that at least.

I fled back to the lodging house, frequently turning to check I was not being followed.

I burst into our room, panting and hot. 'Mother!' I cried. 'They have our horses! I was nearly caught by one of Hungerford's men! We are not safe here!'

Both Sir Thomas and Lady Jane were with Mother. They all looked up at my words.

'Ah! Eleanor!' exclaimed Lady Jane. 'We were just talking about you. Heavens, child! Whatever is the matter? You look as if you've seen a ghost!'

I related what had happened in a breathless disjointed way, and the adults exchanged serious looks.

'Are you sure you were not followed?' asked Mother fearfully.

'Quite certain,' I told her.

'Well, my dear, that confirms what we've just been saying,' my aunt told me. 'Although Mistress Myers is completely to be trusted and will protect you as much as she can, if they are searching the city, and they have a warrant, there will be nothing she can do. You need to leave Bath.'

'Yes, indeed,' I agreed warmly. 'But how? Will they not be watching the city gates?'

'Yes,' said Lady Jane briskly. 'But they are looking for a mother and a daughter. So you will have more chance of getting away undiscovered if you leave separately.'

This made sense to me, but I could see my aunt and Mother exchanging uneasy glances.

'What is it?' I asked. 'Tell me.'

'Eleanor, my dearest child, we think it safest if we are parted for a spell,' said Mother gently.

I jumped to my feet. 'No!' I cried.

Sir Thomas got up also and made me a fidgety little bow.

'Mistress Eleanor, forgive us, but this is for your own safety. My mother, who is an invalid living a few miles outside Bath, has need of a companion. Your mother has very kindly agreed to fill that post. Under an assumed name, of course. We believe she will be quite safe from your father there.'

I looked at Mother desperately. She rose and embraced me. 'It's for a short while only, I hope, my darling,' she said.

'Your mother,' I said to Sir Thomas. 'Does she live quite alone then?'

'Ahem, well, no, not quite. I am there much of the time to attend to the farm and other business. My house in Bath is not my main residence, you know.'

I regarded him with gathering hostility. 'It sounds as if

she already has a companion. So why does she need another?'

'Hem, well, female companionship, you know, is quite a different thing. I do not always have the leisure . . . '

'So, in fact, you are asking Mother to come and live with you,' I stated rudely. I could hear my mother and aunt murmuring protests in the background, but I ignored them.

'It will be quite proper, you know,' Sir Thomas assured me. 'It is a large house, and they will have their own apartments, quite separate from mine.'

'And what about me?' I asked. 'Where do I fit into all this?' I felt hurt and abandoned that Mother was prepared to consider any plan that separated the two of us.

'You are invited to stay with me and my husband in London for a spell,' my aunt said quickly. 'Posing as my young cousin, Mary. My friend Mistress Aubrey has promised to take you out of the city in her carriage this very afternoon. We will meet at the inn in the village of Box, some miles from Bath. It should be safe for you to travel with me from there. And I promise you, Eleanor: I shall look after you as if you were my own daughter.'

I looked at Mother again. 'This afternoon? And when do you leave?'

'I am going in an hour or so, Eleanor. Sir Thomas thinks it safest.' She took my face in her hands and looked at me lovingly. 'Please, Eleanor. It's only for a while. Just until the hue and cry has died down.' She looked as though she meant it. But then, as she let me go, I saw her exchange a glance with Sir Thomas, and

I realized they were in love. I felt a fierce stab of jealousy and resentment. I had gone through so much to be with Mother, and now she was going to be with this man instead. I knew, in some part of my mind, that I was being selfish. I knew Mother deserved happiness after suffering so much. But the truth was that I wanted her all to myself and I was hurt, angry, and humiliated.

'Very well, Mother,' I said tightly. I curtseyed stiffly to my aunt and said, 'Thank you, Aunt Jane, for your kind offer. I accept. But now, if you excuse me, I shall take a walk.'

No one stopped me. No one pointed out that I had had one lucky escape already that day. They understood that I needed some time alone to accustom myself. I walked the streets of Bath for an hour, not caring where I was going. I just needed to keep moving to hold my misery at bay.

When I returned, Mother was alone in our rooms, her few possessions packed. She held out her arms as I came in, and I went to her. As she held me close, I breathed in her sweet scent, soaking it up to remember her by.

'I know,' she said simply, and stroked my hair as I leaned my head against her shoulder. We stood thus until there was a soft knock upon the door. Sir Thomas had arrived to collect Mother.

# CHAPTER TWENTY-EIGHT

The journey to London took several days and was very tedious. I begged to be allowed to ride, but my aunt was afraid I would be recognized.

I had visited the city before, so its sights and smells were not completely unfamiliar to me. I quickly found myself longing for the hills and valleys around Farleigh. I missed the green of the fields and woods and the sweetness of the summer air, which here was turned to foul corruption. The narrow, dirty streets were filled with noise and bustle. They were crowded with carriages, street sellers, dogs, horses, and people in a hurry to get somewhere. I had been jolted for endless hours over bad roads and longed for peace.

We crossed into the city by way of London Bridge. It was evening, but being high summer, it was still light enough to see the grisly sight of heads impaled on the spikes. I looked at the rotting shapes and shuddered. My aunt followed my gaze.

'They parboil them, you know,' she said conversationally. 'To preserve them.'

'I am not sure I wished to know that,' I replied. Then I gasped with terror and a small scream escaped me.

'What is it, my child?'

I pointed to one of the heads, rigid with fear.

'Cromwell,' I whispered. 'I would know him anywhere.'

The sightless eyes of my father's friend stared at me, livid in death.

My uncle Sir Edward Cranbourne, a blustering, hearty man some ten years older than his wife, met us in the hallway of my aunt's London home.

'Welcome home, my dear Jane!' he said, greeting her fondly. 'I've missed you greatly whilst you've been jaunting around England! And this is Cousin *Mary*,' he said for the servant's ears, turning to me. 'Well, you are very welcome too. Come in, come in!' So saying he shook my hand and gave me a conspiratorial wink. He ushered us into a fine apartment, furnished with bright tapestries, and containing a large fireplace, unlit today in the warm summer weather.

'Have you heard the news?' he asked gravely as soon as the door was shut behind us.

'News, my dear?' asked his wife. 'We have heard nothing.'

'A week ago Cromwell was accused of treason and thrown into the Tower. He was executed this morning.'

'Oh my, then it was indeed his head you saw on London Bridge, my dear!' exclaimed my aunt. 'I scarcely credited it at the time.'

I nodded, but could not speak. I felt numb. If Cromwell was dead, what of my father?

'Oh, Edward!' said my aunt. 'Do tell us everything you know. When did the arrest take place?' She was agog with curiosity about this latest scandal. I sat silent, feeling sick, wondering if this arrest had anything to do with me. Another piece of news from my uncle startled me from my uneasy reverie.

'The king has had his marriage to Anne of Cleves annulled,' he announced solemnly. 'We heard a few days ago. He is to marry Catherine Howard instead.'

'Mercy!' cried my aunt, pleasantly shocked. 'Well, I declare, I've only been gone a couple of weeks, and the country has been turned upside down. What a lot we shall have to talk about, Edward. And we have not gone short of adventures either, I can tell you.' She leaned forward to pat her husband's hand and he twinkled merrily back at her. 'You shall have to tell me all about it at supper, for that is the bell ringing now,' he replied.

I was touched to see these two people so happy in each other's company.

Supper was served in a large, cheerful apartment, which overlooked the pretty garden, just now bursting with summer growth and flowers of every colour. I reflected how much more comfortable such a house might be to live in than a rambling, draughty castle.

As soon as the servants had withdrawn, my aunt recounted our adventures to my uncle, calling on me to corroborate many details. I was pressed to tell of the escape from Farleigh. Finally I summoned up the courage to ask the question which was troubling me.

'Sir, Cromwell has been executed. Have you heard anything about Sir Walter Hungerford?'

'No, though rumour has it he was not with Cromwell when he was taken. I heard he had set out for Farleigh some time before. General opinion is that he is in grave danger. He and Cromwell stand together, you know. They were too close not to be implicated in one another's actions.'

I nodded dumbly, my hands clenched together in my lap. It mattered not that I loathed my father: I still did not wish to be guilty in his downfall. More than ever, I wished my words to the king unspoken.

'At least if the scoundrel is arrested, you and your poor mother will have some peace,' my uncle said gently.

I got little rest that first night in London. The noise was far worse than anything Mother and I had endured in Bath. The town crier and the night watchman startled me awake several times, and the morning bustle of the city began very early. I arose heavy with tiredness to face an anxious day.

A week passed with no news. My aunt and I were sitting over our stitchery in the shade of the garden. It was stiflingly hot, and despite the abundant verdure surrounding us, the scents of honeysuckle and roses could not entirely mask the stench of the city beyond the garden.

I was bored to tears both with waiting and with sewing. I longed to throw it in the bushes and go for a ride over the hills or through the woods, anywhere where there would be some air. But I had neither Arianna nor access to pleasant countryside here.

Suddenly my aunt yawned and tossed her own embroidery aside. 'Well, that's as much as I can stand in this weather!' she announced, and rang for a servant to bring some drinks out to us. I laid aside my own sewing. My aunt was watching me, eyes twinkling. 'Do I detect some relief there, Eleanor?'

'To be honest, Aunt, my needle has never been my favourite occupation,' I confessed.

'Nor mine, indeed!' said my aunt merrily. 'I would rather sit idle and gossip at any time. But your mother— now there is a fine needlewoman! She is younger than me, you know, but I could never equal her neatness or her industry. Such beautiful work she did. Our mother was always holding her up to me as an example, shaming me with my own sloppy work! I thought your mother must have brought you up to sew like her, so I have been trying to set you a good example.'

I laughed. 'I wish you had told me before,' I said. 'Mother tried, but failed to instil any skill or love of sewing in me.'

'Well, now we know, Eleanor. We need only pick up our sewing when there is someone by to impress.'

I looked ruefully at my piece. 'Sadly, I fear this would impress no one,' I said. I told her the story of my sampler that Mother had thrown in the fire the very day she had been arrested. We laughed merrily together over this story, and then my aunt wiped her eyes. 'Your poor mother,' she sighed. 'I wish I had not believed Sir Walter's smooth tales of her illness. I had letters sent to her, you know. And begged to be allowed to see her. But he assured me that any visitors disturbed her deeply and that she needed absolute rest. If our parents had been alive, he would not have got away with it so easily.'

'You came as soon as you knew, Aunt Jane,' I told her soothingly, for she looked quite tearful. 'And I think Mother is happy now.'

'Yes, indeed,' smiled my aunt. 'Sir Thomas is a lovely man. I've known him for most of my life. Your mother will meet nothing but kindness at his hands.'

I must have looked sceptical, because my aunt spoke earnestly.

'I know it is hard for you, Eleanor, to let someone else in, when you have longed to be with your mother yourself. But nothing could be better for Elizabeth than this. She will be taken care of, respected and valued—'

We were interrupted. A servant entered the garden with a visitor following her. I did not recognize him at first. Then I gasped.

'Why, Doctor Horde!' I cried. Impulsively, I rushed to shake his hand. He embraced me and then held me at arm's length to look at me.

'You are looking very well, Mistress Eleanor,' he told me.

'You look so different out of your habit!' I exclaimed, before realizing how tactless such a remark was. A shade of sadness crossed Dr Horde's face.

'And how do you do?' I asked him hurriedly. 'Or should I ask *what* do you do now? I feel so dreadful that I brought all that trouble upon you. I am glad of the chance to say so. And I want to thank you from my heart for sending my aunt to us.'

Dr Horde and Lady Jane exchanged a smile.

'I told you at the time, my child, it was only ever a matter of time before the priory was closed. And as to

265

how I do, why I have been singularly fortunate. I have truly seen that God is good—and some men too.'

I clapped my hands delightedly. 'Tell me!'

'I have been so fortunate as to be befriended by a gentleman who has several livings in his gift. He was deeply sympathetic to my situation, and has most generously offered me one of them: I am to be a vicar, Eleanor. I exchange my priory for a comfortable parsonage and a village church. Hence my change in clothing.' He indicated his priest's robes with a sweep of his hands. 'It will be a great change, to be sure, but not an unpleasant one.'

'I am so happy,' I told him sincerely. It was a great relief to me to know that this friend at least had not been so very harmed by my actions after all.

'And so, who is this kind gentleman?' asked my aunt curiously. 'I know him, surely.'

'I imagine you do, my lady,' responded Dr Horde. 'Eleanor most certainly does, for I first met him at Farleigh, in the spring.'

I was intrigued at once. 'Who can it be?' I wondered.

'Can you think of no one, Mistress Eleanor, who is so charitable?' asked the Doctor. I sensed he was teasing me, and that there was a smile lurking behind his serious manner. I shook my head.

'Truly, sir, I took little notice of most of the guests, and became acquainted with few of them.'

'I think, though, that you had some acquaintance with Lord Stanton?'

I was dumbstruck. But Dr Horde clearly expected some response from me.

'I am certainly happy to hear he has been so kind to *you*, sir,' I said with a slight curtsey.

'What's this?' he asked, with a glance at my aunt. 'Are you not betrothed?'

'Yes, they are,' replied my aunt.

'No,' I said at the same time.

Dr Horde looked from one to the other of us, puzzled.

'Eleanor?' asked my aunt.

'I broke it off,' I told them, my voice sounding oddly tight. 'At Bath.'

'But, Eleanor!' exclaimed my aunt. 'It was not in your power to do so! That would be breach of promise. You could be sued. Did he accept your decision?'

'Not exactly. I am not sure. If he wants to sue me, he'll have to find me first,' I said. I was angry with them both. What did they mean by standing there looking at me disapprovingly? 'The betrothal was not of my making,' I added.

'No, it was the king himself who blessed the proposed union,' said Dr Horde seriously. 'Such a contract cannot lightly be put aside.'

'Well, I believe Lord Stanton accepted my refusal,' I said defiantly, but their words had made me anxious. Could he really insist on my marrying him?

To my relief, my uncle walked out to join us, causing a welcome interruption. I smiled at him, but his face was grim. He came up to me and took my hands in his.

'Eleanor, I have grave news.' I could feel my heart beating quick in my chest and could sense the hushed expectancy in the others too.

'Is it Sir Walter?' I asked. 'Or Mother?' He paused a moment before speaking.

'It is indeed Hungerford,' nodded my uncle. 'He's been arrested and brought to London under armed guard.'

'And?' demanded my aunt. 'What more?'

'He has been accused of treason and attainted.' The other two gasped. I heard the word treason and felt faint with terror.

'Uncle, what . . . ' I faltered. 'What does attainted mean?' I had never heard the term before.

'A bill of Attainder means that all Sir Walter's lands, possessions, and titles are forfeit to the crown,' my uncle explained gently. 'Farleigh Castle has already been seized. It also means that Hungerford can be sentenced without trial. The king must be angry indeed. He is likely to show him little mercy.'

I swallowed. There was a lump in my throat.

'May God have mercy on his soul,' said Dr Horde. 'He was a good friend to me for many years, and I would not have him meet such an end. No matter what his crimes,' he added.

I tried to speak, but I found I could not, so I only nodded my agreement.

'His crimes were heavy indeed,' said my aunt. 'But he is likely to pay with his life. The consolation, my dear Eleanor, is that you and your mother will be safe. In a few weeks or months, Lady Elizabeth will be a widow, and she can marry that nice Sir Thomas.'

'My dear,' chided her husband, with a warning look in my direction.

'Marry him?' I cried aghast. 'Surely not?'

'Oh, it was plain Sir Thomas was besotted with Elizabeth,' said my aunt comfortably. 'He won't care about the scandal living quietly in Bath, away from the king's court. He'll make your mother as happy as anything, you wait and see.'

'My dear.' Sir Edward tried again to stem his wife's outspokenness. 'Perhaps it would be more tasteful to discuss such matters at a later date.'

'But what will become of me?' I asked miserably. I did not wish to go and live with Sir Thomas and watch him and Mother making sheep's eyes at one another. Neither could I bear the thought of staying here in London. My uncle and aunt could not be kinder, but I did not enjoy city life. I missed my riding, and the sights and smells of the country.

'That brings us back to the subject of Stanton,' commented my aunt, and she proceeded to relate to my uncle what I had said of my refusal to marry Stanton and the possibility of breach of promise.

'I will look into it, as discreetly as possible,' my uncle promised.

I rose abruptly and took a turn about the garden. As if I could think of marriage in the midst of such dreadful events. I would know no peace now.

'Oh!' I cried out suddenly. 'What of Walter? Little Walter, my brother. What has become of him?'

My uncle hurried to reassure me: 'I have already thought of that, Eleanor. I despatched a messenger to your mother before I came out to speak to you. I have recommended that Sir Thomas take some men to Farleigh with him and take charge of the boy, if he is still there.'

'If?' I cried, distracted. My brother and I had grown so far apart over the years, but he was still my brother whom I had played with when he was a baby.

'Your mother is the properest person to take charge of him now,' said my uncle soothingly. And with that, for the time being, I had to be content.

I had thought we should have to wait a week at the very least to hear from Mother. I was astonished the next day when a message arrived from Bath and was brought to me as I sat at breakfast with my aunt.

I turned the letter over with shaking hands. 'Perhaps Mother has heard of Sir Walter's arrest?' I said.

'Open it, Eleanor, and we shall know,' said my aunt sensibly. I broke the seal, and spread the parchment on the table. I read aloud:

*My Dearest Eleanor,*
*Please convey my warmest regards to your uncle and aunt.*
*Sir Walter was arrested yesterday at Farleigh and taken to London. Lord Stanton and Gregory Hungerford brought me the news, and they also brought me my dear Walter.*

'Oh, Aunt Jane! Did you hear that? My cousin took Walter to Mother!'

'And Lord Stanton, you see. He is a good man, Eleanor.'

'How did he know where to find Mother?' I asked wonderingly.

Aunt Jane looked momentarily uncomfortable.

'I told him,' she confessed after a pause. 'He called on me before we left Bath.'

'Aunt Jane!' I exclaimed reproachfully. 'I told you we could not trust him. Does he know where I am too?'

My aunt did not reply, but instead drew my attention back to the letter. 'What else does Elizabeth say?'

*Imagine my joy, Eleanor! To be reunited with my son.*

'There are several paragraphs about that,' I said skimming over them. 'She says Walter is very unhappy and wishes to go back to his father and Farleigh.'

'I daresay he'll soon settle in,' said my aunt.

'Yes, if Sir Thomas turns his home into a jousting ground and a sword-fighting arena,' I remarked. 'And if he buys him horses.'

'You should not be so censorious of your brother, Eleanor. Your mother is happy, I'm sure.'

'Yes, and I am truly glad for her, and for Walter too,' I replied more generously. 'Perhaps I am just a little jealous . . . ' It cost me something to admit it, but I had been thinking over my aunt's words just before Dr Horde's visit and I had come to believe she was right. There was nothing really amiss with Sir Thomas. My own hurt and envy had made me dislike him.

My aunt nodded kindly. 'Is there anything else in the letter?' she urged.

'Oh, just some nonsense about Lord Stanton being our friend,' I said carelessly. 'You can read it if you wish.' I passed her the letter and began to pace the room.

'Dearest, you know very well that I cannot read,' objected my aunt. I stopped short and stared at her.

'But you wrote me a letter!' I exclaimed.

My aunt shook her head. 'Of course I did not, Eleanor. Your uncle wrote it. Generally, women do not read, my dear. You and your mother are an odd—I mean you are unusual,' she corrected herself.

I could picture Lord Stanton clearly, his handsome dark face and his laughing eyes. Something stirred in me that was neither anger nor dislike. Had we been wrong about him after all? His recent actions seemed all unselfish kindness. I wondered if he had been at Farleigh when Sir Walter was arrested. It only surprised me that he had not left at once, knowing that his bride had fled.

Hearing of his generous behaviour made me see my own conduct in a different light. I remembered how I had planned to humiliate him by leaving him standing at the wedding without a bride, and I felt ashamed. I had not treated him well, either, in Bath. How childish he must have thought me. That was an uncomfortable notion. I hoped my aunt would not say too much about him. I did not think I could bear it.

'Eleanor, come and read the rest of your letter,' my aunt chided me. I picked it up and looked through it.

'Oh, my mother asks me to bring my visit to an end soon, and join her in Bath,' I said, dismayed. I dreaded joining Sir Thomas's household. 'Could I . . . could I not stay a little longer? At least until we hear more news?'

'Of your father?' asked my aunt. 'Do not depend on that matter being resolved in a hurry. Prisoners often languish in the Tower for months before the king takes a decision about them. But your uncle and I would be happy to have you.'

'Thank you, Aunt Jane!' I said, embracing her affectionately.

'And you see, Eleanor, I think we must not be too hasty in our judgement of Lord Stanton. He has acted honourably here it seems, at no small trouble to himself.'

I hung my head a little at her words. 'Yes, Aunt,' I said meekly. 'But indeed, I cannot make him out.'

'If you assume Sir Walter was lying to you about his involvement in his plots, his character makes perfect sense,' Aunt Jane pointed out.

It was possible. I had to admit it.

# CHAPTER TWENTY-NINE

It was the last week of July when my uncle came in with a grave face once more. Lady Jane and I had just sat down to supper, but I jumped to my feet at once, flinging aside my napkin and overturning my soup bowl.

My aunt cried out at my heedlessness and called a servant to clear up the mess. But I paid no attention, running instead to my uncle. He took both my hands and held them in a firm clasp.

'Prepare yourself, Eleanor,' he said sombrely. 'Sir Walter Hungerford is to be executed at Tower Hill tomorrow morning at dawn. The vicar of Bradford dies with him.'

'The charges?' I said weakly.

My uncle looked uncomfortable for a minute.

'There are many,' he said evasively.

'Please tell me,' I begged.

'Well, among other things, he is accused of having ordered a horoscope to be cast to predict the date of the king's death. That is reason enough on its own. Further he is accused of having imprisoned his wife.'

My heart jumped into my mouth. The king *had* listened to me that night. Seeing my face, my uncle added comfortingly: 'There are worse ways to die, Eleanor.'

'I can think of few,' I said bitterly. The good memories of my father rose unbidden in my mind: Sir Walter playing with my baby brother, and making Mother laugh. Sir Walter smiling at my joy the day he brought home Arianna for me. His shouts of laughter echoing round the hall in the happy days. Now he was to die, and it was my fault. If it had not been for that, I could have borne it better.

'We must pray to God for a swift and painless blow,' said my aunt. I nodded blindly.

'I could have wished for a long imprisonment for my father,' I said at last. 'That he might know how Mother suffered.'

'No, Eleanor,' said my aunt at once. 'It is better for you and your family that this is settled at once.'


I could not sleep that night. I tossed and turned on my bed as though it were a pile of rocks. Was my father dreading the dawn? I could find it in me to pity him.

I could not stop thinking about my part in all this. My mind was drawn irresistibly to Tower Hill. And inevitably, as though I had known all along what I intended to do, I climbed out of bed, pulled my clothes on as noiselessly as I could and crept out of my room.

The boards of the hallway and the stairs creaked unpredictably. I eased myself cautiously forward, making almost no sound. I groped my way down the stairs and along the hall. The bolts on the front door were well oiled and slid back noiselessly.

The night was hot and humid as though the very air

was breathing out damp, noxious fumes. I hurried along the deserted, dark streets, lifting my skirts to keep them clean and side-stepping the piles of refuse that lay strewn everywhere. From time to time, a tavern door opened, spilling light out onto the dark, narrow street. I could hear drunken voices and smell the fug of stale air mixed with ale. I shrank into doorways each time someone came along the street, terrified that they might notice me. It was not safe on the streets of the city of London at night. That much I knew.

I had no idea of the time, and looked fearfully at the sky expecting at any moment to see the grey of first light appearing. I also was not sure of the way. Used to the hills and valleys of Wiltshire, I quickly became confused by the tangled maze of streets and alleys that made up London. Eventually, as a few people began appearing on the streets, I was forced to stop and ask an old woman the way. Her eyes lit up when she heard my question.

'The Tower, is it?' she said in a harsh, grating voice. 'And what does a pretty young mistress want there? Goin' to see the executions, are we?' She grinned at me, exposing toothless gums.

I recoiled from her in disgust. 'Just tell me the way,' I begged her.

'For a coin, I'll lead yer there,' she offered.

'Very well,' I nodded, 'but as quick as you can, please.'

'Two coins, if you wants me to 'urry,' she added, shooting a sharp look at me. I felt in my purse for the few remaining coins of the allowance that my uncle and aunt had so generously bestowed on me, and agreed. Muttering about her old bones, the crone started to hobble along the street. 'You'll not get a good view this late,' she paused suddenly to tell me. I lifted my handkerchief to my nose to keep out the stench of rottenness that hung about her. 'What you goin' to do about that?'

'I hadn't thought,' I responded faintly. 'Surely one can get close enough to see something?'

''adn't thought, 'adn't thought,' she echoed, resuming her lurching gait. She led me through narrow, unfrequented ways until I became disorientated and afraid. I asked once or twice where we were going, but she only muttered in response. Eventually we came to wider streets and grander buildings. Finally the shadow of the Tower itself fell upon us. The old woman pointed up the hill. I could make out the outline of a scaffold silhouetted against the sky. The hillside was teeming with people. The scaffold was on the summit and surrounded by a ring of soldiers, every one of them armed with pikes and swords to keep the crowd back. My heart thumped at the sight and I felt a cold sweat break out on my skin.

I offered the woman my coins, which she took eagerly. And then I climbed the hill towards the crowd. The confused noise of voices grew louder as I approached, and the stench of unwashed bodies, of sweat, and of urine grew stronger. Most people were on foot, others on horseback, or seated in carts. More and more were arriving every minute.

I stood awkwardly on the edge of the crowd, feeling vulnerable and alone. Why had I come? I was not sure I knew the answer. I had been drawn here by a kind of horrified fascination and a sense of fate. I began to push through the crowd, working my way steadily forwards. I could see little. I was not even sure I would be able to make out my father from here. As I moved further forward, the crowd became more tightly packed, and people were less and less willing to let me through.

There was a sudden cheer from the crowd. I looked up and could see the prisoners being led to the scaffold. It was time. There was no drum roll, no parade of soldiers, no speeches. Just two figures bound and led to their deaths by armed guards. I had to stand on tiptoe and crane my neck to see the men. The first man was being dragged onto the platform already. Even by the pale morning light, I knew my father.

They blindfolded him as he stood there before the crowd. But as they tried to lead him to the block, there was a sudden commotion. My father was fighting the guards who held him, screaming obscenities at them and refusing to move. The crowd roared with excitement around me. My view was obscured suddenly as the unruly onlookers surged forward. I was pushed backwards and came up against the bulk of a horse. Its rider leaned down and put a hand on my shoulder.

'Eleanor!'

I looked up, and saw Lord Stanton leaning down towards me. I was so preoccupied that I was not, at that moment, surprised to see him.

'My father . . . ' I said distractedly, standing on tiptoes to try and get a glimpse of the scaffold. I could see nothing.

Stanton held his hand down to me. 'If you are sure you want to see, climb up before me,' he said.

I did not hesitate. The last moments of my father's life were slipping away. If I was to see him once more, this was my only chance. I put my foot on Stanton's, took his hand and he pulled me up onto the pommel of his saddle, seating me sideways across it.

The scaffold was a scene of commotion. Sir Walter was still twisting and yelling like a madman. He had torn off his blindfold. Four guards were attempting to restrain him. I watched, transfixed with horror, as Sir Walter was pulled forward inch by inch towards the block itself, where the executioner waited, axe resting on the platform and a black hood covering his face. Sir Walter fought every step of the way. When he reached the block he refused to kneel down. Clearly impatient at this delay, one of the guards kicked him behind the knees, causing his legs to buckle under him. Now he was kneeling down, but still he would not lay his head upon the block.

'A thousand curses rain down upon you,' I could hear him screaming at his gaolers. I felt sick. It was a terrible thing to see a man, once brave and strong, brought to face such a terrible death.

'Oh, why will he not submit?' I moaned quietly.

'He is beside himself,' Lord Stanton said. His voice so close to me made me jump. I had forgotten whom I was with. 'I would say he is frenzied—quite mad.'

'It is not usual, then . . . to resist execution?'

'No,' said Stanton quietly. 'Are you sure you want to watch this, Eleanor?'

I made no reply, my eyes fixed upon my desperate father.

The guards had forced his head down now, but the

executioner could not swing his axe without risk of injury to them.

'They are binding him,' said Lord Stanton. He was right, I could see the ropes now, being pulled taut around my father's resisting body. The guards stepped back. The executioner raised his axe. There was a moment's sudden hush, and the blade fell. I heard the thud, and saw the great spout of bright blood that sprayed the scaffold.

A wave of nausea rose in me. I turned my face away, and pressed it into Stanton's shoulder. I felt his arms around me and was a little comforted. At this moment he was not my enemy, but a friend in a time of need.

I became aware of the crowd around me cheering, and looked back to the scaffold. I should not have done. The axeman was holding my father's head up by the hair, displaying it to the bloodthirsty spectators. I felt sick and dizzy once more, and closed both my eyes and mouth tightly.

When next I opened my eyes, they were half leading, half carrying Father Bird to the scaffold. He appeared to be shaking uncontrollably, almost unable to walk. But unlike my father, he did not attempt to resist his fate. They made him kneel at a block already slick with my father's blood.

I did not want to watch as this miserable man's life was snuffed out. I turned my face into Stanton's shoulder once more and breathed in the scents of rosemary and lavender that hung about his clothes, shutting out the rank, unwashed stench of the mob around us.

I heard the axe come down; there was no blocking out the sound of it. I heard the collective gasp of the crowd, but this time I did not make the mistake of looking up. Then it was over. The crowd slowly began to disperse around us. I made a move to disengage myself from Stanton and he released me at once. I sat as straight as I could on the front of the saddle.

'You are unwell, Eleanor,' Stanton said, his voice concerned. 'Do your uncle and aunt know you are here?'

I shook my head, not meeting his eyes. I felt as though I might be sick if I tried to speak. I wondered for a moment how he knew where I was staying. Then I remembered he had spoken to both my mother and my aunt.

'I will escort you home,' he said, and turned Caesar away from the scaffold and back towards the Tower that loomed nearby. I sat, weak and shaking, allowing him to support me with an arm about my waist. I could think of nothing but my father. He was dead. What that might mean to me was not yet able to penetrate my frozen mind.

# CHAPTER THIRTY

We passed the Tower and continued towards the city. My mind was filled with the sights and sounds of Tower Hill. I became aware of my surroundings when Stanton pulled Caesar up outside an inn. He dismounted and held his arms up to help me down. I slid down obediently and was set on my feet. To my great shame, my legs refused to carry my weight. I stumbled and would have fallen, had it not been for Stanton catching hold of me.

'I thought as much,' he said. 'You are hungry and exhausted. Can you walk a few steps if I help you?'

'I do not need help,' I insisted, pushing his arm away. I managed to walk into the inn unaided, though my legs shook under me. Stanton engaged a private parlour and in no time at all, I was handed into a chair by a table and had a goblet of wine pressed into my hand.

'Drink it,' Stanton was urging. His voice sounded distant and for a moment I wondered whether I might be about to faint. I took a sip of the wine, shuddered and choked a little. I took another sip and the world seemed to come back into sharper focus.

'Is that better now?' my companion asked.

I nodded. My mind was a whirlpool of guilt and shock. The guilt was the worst. I had to tell someone. I could not keep the secret any longer. At that moment I forgot that Stanton was my enemy. He seemed a safe person to tell.

'It's my fault,' I said in a low voice.

'What is your fault?' Stanton asked.

'The executions,' I told him. 'It was I who betrayed them.'

'That is not possible,' stated Stanton calmly. 'These were state matters. In what way could you have been involved?' He spoke soothingly, but it only inflamed me.

'You know nothing of the matter!' I said fiercely.

'Then tell me,' was the calm rejoinder.

'I overheard them plotting against the king,' I said, my words coming out in a rush. 'Cromwell and my father. At the banquet, the night Walter won the joust.' I paused and swallowed. My mouth felt dry with fear as the memories came back to me. I sipped my wine again and then put the goblet down.

'I would have done nothing about it. Only the king summoned me to his chamber some nights later,' I explained. I heard Stanton catch his breath.

'The king summoned you? I knew nothing of this.' He grasped my wrist as he spoke, but I pulled it away.

'I told him of the conversation I had overheard, that was all.'

There was a moment's silence before Stanton spoke:

'And what had you overheard?'

'It was to do with the divorce of Queen Anne. Cromwell was afraid it spelled ruin for him and for my father. They spoke of putting a boy king on the throne. And of the horoscope Father Bird had cast.'

'I see.'

'What do you see? That I am guilty? It was dreadful to have betrayed them. I did it because I was so afraid. But I did not mean it.' I hung my head and waited for Stanton to say something. I did not know what to expect. Would he despise me for being an informer or would he tell me it had been my duty?

Stanton sat silent. I looked anxiously at his profile. There was a frown on his brow, but he did not look angry. At last he turned to me. Drawing his chair closer to mine, he took my hand and held it firmly. I did not pull away this time.

'You are mistaken, Eleanor,' Stanton said at last. 'You are not responsible for these deaths. You must not think that you are.' He paused again, as if unsure how to continue. When he spoke again, his voice was gentler:

'Cromwell was right. The king has been looking for an excuse to be rid of him. Many of the old nobility have been fiercely jealous of his influence. Until recently, their slanderous talk fell upon stony soil. Cromwell was too efficient, too clever, too favoured. But the marriage he arranged with Anne of Cleves was disastrous. From that moment, it was only a matter of time.'

'But it was still I who gave him the excuse,' I said. 'I still bear that guilt.'

Stanton shook his head. 'No. The king has—forgive me, Eleanor—better sources of information than a fifteen-year-old girl. You told him nothing he did not know already. He has spies everywhere. When people are investigated for treason, there is no hiding anything. Not even crimes they did not commit.'

I did not know whether Stanton was telling me the

truth or not, but I wanted to believe him. Perhaps I had not caused my father's gruesome death. I could feel the knot of dread and guilt, which had been in my stomach since the night in the king's chamber, begin to loosen.

'Thank you,' I said simply. There was a short silence.

'How came you to be at Tower Hill this morning?' I asked. I was surprised I had not thought to ask this sooner.

'I had been visiting my own father, who is also being held in the Tower,' replied Stanton. 'I did not intend to watch the executions.'

'So . . . why did you?'

'I saw your cousin Hungerford. He and his father were making arrangements to collect Lord Hungerford's body after the . . . Well, in any case, after I had spoken to him, I saw you. I was concerned to see you alone and followed.'

'I see. So my father's body will be buried? They . . . they boil the heads, don't they? My aunt told me.' I could not prevent my voice from shaking.

'Try not to think about it.' Stanton lifted my hand to his lips and kissed it tenderly. I withdrew it in some embarrassment.

'And your father: will he be executed too?'

'He fell under suspicion because of his association with Hungerford,' Stanton replied. 'But I am hopeful we may yet persuade the king that he is innocent of any crime.'

'And is he?' I knew I should not ask such a question, but I could not stop myself. 'And what about you?' I asked before he could reply. 'Were you involved?'

'Eleanor, no!' exclaimed Stanton. He looked shocked. 'Can you really suspect me of such a thing? I have no interest in politics or intrigue!'

'You knew of Sir Walter's plot to kill my mother. You were involved in that,' I accused him recklessly.

There was a moment's silence. I bit my lip; half wishing I could unsay my words, half curious to know what he would say in his own defence.

'You are misinformed,' cried Stanton passionately. 'I have never plotted against anyone. Not against the king, and certainly not against you or your mother. I had rarely ever seen Sir Walter before I came to Farleigh. The proposed marriage had been sprung on me just days before the visit, as it doubtless had been on you.'

'I had known of it for weeks,' I replied bitterly. 'Though I had not been told your name or anything else about you.'

'What made you think I knew about the plot?' Stanton asked.

'Sir Walter told me himself.'

'It is not true,' Stanton breathed. He looked as though I had slapped him.

I sat still, waiting for him to say more. I hoped he would convince me that it was not true. I wanted him to reassure me.

From the beginning, I had been determined to dislike Stanton and to suspect him of everything bad, and he had proven me wrong at every turn. The realization struck me with some force. I did not think of Stanton as an enemy any longer. On the contrary, he had been good to me and my family, despite his teasing ways. But the possibility that he had plotted against my mother remained a barrier between us.

'You say nothing,' I pointed out when Stanton remained silent.

'What can I say?' he asked in a low voice. 'If I could produce proof that I am innocent I would do so. But as it is, I can only swear to you that it is not true.'

I didn't reply, but I wanted to believe him. I wanted to believe my father had lied to me and that Stanton was telling the truth. But I felt confused.

'If that is what you think of me, no wonder you have hated me,' said Lord Stanton sadly. 'You still do, don't you?'

Stanton took my chin in his hand and made me look up at him. I tried to hate him still, and found I could not. I forced myself to meet his eyes. It wasn't easy. He looked both hurt and vulnerable. I had never seen such a look in his eyes before.

'I don't dislike you . . . any longer,' I admitted. It cost me an effort to tell him so.

Stanton scanned my face for some moments, before releasing me.

'I'm glad of it,' he said, but he sighed. When he spoke again, his voice was strained.

'Eleanor . . . I must ask you something else,' he said hesitantly. 'Although I hardly know how to voice it.'

'Yes?' I asked, surprised.

'One of the king's charges against Lord Hungerford. The one concerning yourself. Was that your accusation?'

'Concerning me?' I asked blankly. 'I know nothing of this.'

What had my uncle omitted to tell me?

'Did you tell the king . . . that during your mother's imprisonment, that . . . that *monster*, I mean your father, had committed unnatural crimes against . . . you?' Stanton's voice shook as he spoke.

'Unnatural crimes?' I asked, at a loss. 'I don't understand.'

Stanton looked at me eagerly. 'Then it is not true?' he asked. 'Your father did not . . . did not force you against your will.'

It suddenly dawned on me what he was saying. I recoiled in disgust.

'*No!*' I cried. 'He was not accused of such a thing, surely? For the whole of England to hear?' I felt my face flame red with shame and covered it with my hands.

'So it is not true?' asked Stanton.

I shook my head, too embarrassed to face him.

'No. Never, not ever. Not that,' I mumbled.

I felt Stanton's hand on my shoulder. 'I'm so relieved, for your sake, that it was a lie,' he said softly.

I nodded, my face still in my hands.

Stanton knelt down before me and gently pulled my hands away from my face.

'You have nothing to be ashamed of,' he told me. 'Even had the charge been true, it would not have been your fault, Eleanor. You see now how the king invents charges where none exist?'

I met his eyes briefly, and saw kindness there. But then the shame of it all overwhelmed me again. I had some inkling of the scandal that would be attached to me.

'I should go,' I said abruptly.

'You have already agreed to let me escort you home,' Stanton reminded me.

'I have? I do not remember that. I am quite able to go alone.'

'I am aware one should never contradict a lady, but I am afraid I must insist. You have had a great shock.'

I was almost glad of an excuse to quarrel once more, to put the shocking news of my father's supposed crimes further from me.

'You have no right to make any decision concerning me,' I told him.

Stanton bowed his head at once. 'I have not forgotten that you withdrew that right, Mistress Eleanor,' he said meekly. 'But though you do not wish to marry me, and cannot trust me, can you not at least accept my escort? I am concerned for your safety.'

Truth to tell, I was weary and footsore, and glad not to have to face the long walk home.

'Very well,' I said, giving in. 'I will go with you.'

I followed Stanton out into the yard. Caesar stood ready and Stanton swung himself into the saddle. He reached down a hand for me as he had done at Tower Hill. I grasped it and placed one foot upon his boot where it rested in the stirrup. Stanton pulled me up and settled me sideways across the pommel before him, one arm about my waist to support me.

'Are you comfortable like this?' he asked.

I nodded. It was not true. The pommel was awkward beneath me and my back was twisted. Moreover, I had not noticed Stanton's closeness to me at Tower Hill. I had been preoccupied by the scene on the scaffold. I found that I was acutely aware of his close proximity now. I was forced to lean against his chest, and I could feel the warmth of his hand where it rested on my side. The painful discussion we had just had made my embarrassment worse.

Stanton appeared not to notice it however. He turned Caesar, holding the reins in one hand, and headed him out of the inn yard. We threaded our way along narrow streets, circling out of the centre of the city.

'You seem to know London well,' I commented at length, feeling the need to make conversation.

'I have been obliged to spend more time here than I would have chosen,' was Stanton's response. 'My father is much involved with the king's court, and has insisted on having me with him ever since he deemed me old enough to be trusted.'

'Old enough?' I asked, surprised. 'But you are quite old!'

'I am but three and twenty, Eleanor. But no doubt that seems ancient to you.'

'Now you are teasing me again,' I said, uncertainly.

'Not at all,' he assured me, and looked down at me with a smile that made me feel strangely breathless. It's because he is so close, I told myself. I have never been so near to a gentleman before.

Caesar was walking at a leisurely pace, and the streets, though busy, were not thronged with crowds as they had been further back. The pommel of the saddle was beginning to cause me pain, but I was not sure how to say so.

'May I not walk again?' I asked at last. Stanton's arm tightened a little around me.

'It is a long way,' he objected 'Are you not comfortable?'

'Not very. Can you not at least stop one moment?' I asked him. As Stanton pulled Caesar up, I leant back against him and swung one leg over the pommel, so I was sitting astride. It was a great relief to sit straight, but I could not help sliding back against my companion. He did not seem perturbed, and threaded his arms under mine.

'Will you not allow me to take the reins?' I asked.

'I am the one who knows the way,' he said, giving Caesar the office to move on again.

'Or perhaps you prefer to direct your own horse?' I hazarded. 'Rather than trusting me to do so?'

'Not at all,' Stanton said at once. He handed the reins to me and placed his hands on my waist instead. I suspected I had been somehow outwitted again. I felt Caesar's mouth with the reins and he blew gently through his nose in response. He was a fine horse, far better mannered than my cousin's mount.

'Do your skirts not incommode you, Mistress Eleanor?' Stanton asked.

'Oh—I had them made full so that riding would be no problem.'

I felt rather than heard Stanton chuckle.

'You choose to laugh at me?' I demanded.

'Not at all. I admire your forethought. A side-saddle must be most restrictive, though I confess I had never thought on the matter before.'

'Of course not. You are a man!' I pointed out. 'My cousin thinks it is immodest for me to ride astride,' I added. 'No doubt you agree.'

'On the contrary, I find it intrepid.'

'Now you are laughing at me again,' I accused him.

'I am sometimes serious, Eleanor,' Stanton responded.

I was surprisingly at ease now, enjoying the rhythm of Caesar's gait. I had not been on horseback since I had arrived in Bath, and I had missed it. We rode down street after street, and through a park, with Stanton giving me directions from time to time. I relaxed, leaning against him, guiltily enjoying his warmth against my back. There was a comfortable silence between us.

At last we turned into a street that was familiar to me, and I realized we were nearly at my uncle's house. I sat up a little straighter and began to wonder what my aunt had made of my long absence. Stanton spoke once more.

'Eleanor, before we reach your uncle's house, there is something I need to say to you.'

'Yes?' I asked, nervously, for his tone was grave.

'You told me in Bath that you did not wish to marry me. You expressed yourself strongly on the subject. I know why now.'

I felt my cheeks grow hot and found I had not enough control over my voice to reply, so I merely nodded slightly.

'Our fathers arranged the marriage. Yours is now dead, and mine imprisoned. I want you to know that if you still wish it, I release you from the betrothal, freely and unconditionally. I will not hold you to the promise you made. It was made under duress.'

There was a pause. I was not sure what reply to make. I felt confused and hurt. Was he releasing me for my sake or for his own? I could imagine it would be intolerable to be connected with the scandal attaching to my father's death and particularly given the charges of incest against him. No one would wish to take a bride who was thought to have lain with her own father. My throat was tight, and stupidly, I felt inclined to cry. But I never cry, I told myself angrily, fighting to regain control over myself.

'Do you understand, Eleanor?' asked Stanton at length.

'I understand, my lord,' I said. 'And I still wish to be released.' It almost choked me to utter the words, but I managed it. My pride required me to say them. I could not force such a scandal on any man.

'There will be no breach of promise,' Stanton assured me.

I cleared my throat and said: 'I understand, my lord. You are very generous.' My voice wobbled a little, but I hoped he would not notice.

Stanton reined in outside the front door and dismounted. As he reached up to help me down from the saddle, his face looked unusually grim. I slid down into his arms, and attempted to smile at him, and to find a lighter note for our parting:

'I am persuaded your lordship never cared for an unwilling bride,' I said brightly. There was no answering smile in his face as he looked down at me.

'No, Eleanor,' he said gently. 'I do not wish for an unwilling bride.'

I could feel the blood rushing to my face again. Stanton was so close to me that I could see every fleck of colour in his dark eyes and the outline of a small scar on one cheek. The thought came to me that he was near enough for me to reach up and kiss him. I wondered at myself.

What had put such a thought in my head? He no longer wanted a kiss from me.

Stanton stepped back from me, took my hand and touched it to his lips.

'Farewell, Eleanor,' he said and turned and pulled on the bell rope beside the door. I heard the familiar peal within and heard footsteps and voices approaching.

The front door was flung open, and my aunt issued from it, crying: 'Eleanor! Thank the Lord! Where have you been?'

'I found her at Tower Hill, Ma'am,' Stanton replied for me.

'We guessed as much. Oh, Eleanor, do you not know how worried we have been? Your uncle is out searching for you, we were so afraid . . . How could you? Lord Stanton, I cannot tell you how grateful I am that you have brought her safely back to us! Truly, you are our good angel.'

I remained silent, whilst my aunt hugged me and fussed over me, clicking her tongue over the state of my gown. 'Come inside, Eleanor. You must be worn out. Lord Stanton, you will come in also? My husband will want to thank you, I know. Come and take a glass of ale or wine.'

'Thank you, Madam, I have much business to attend to today,' Stanton excused himself, bowing courteously to Lady Jane. 'I will not intrude.' So saying he swung himself back into the saddle and took his leave. I watched him ride away up the street. He did not look back. As he turned the corner and disappeared from view it struck me that I would never see him again.

# CHAPTER THIRTY-ONE

I slept uneasily for several hours and awoke feeling miserable. I told myself it was my father's death that lay heavy upon me, but it was more than that.

My aunt was in the garden, seated in the shade, fanning herself. It was a hot day and the stench of the city was everywhere: in the garden, but also stealing into the house. It was a smell of things rotting; of death and decay.

I was heavy and listless, and could not concentrate on anything. Not on my stitching, not on my aunt's conversation. Aunt Jane wanted to know everything: how I had got to Tower Hill, how the two men had died, and how Lord Stanton had found me. When she asked what had passed between Lord Stanton and myself, I fell silent. I was still pondering all that he had said to me; turning his words over in my mind. I was not ready to share them. My aunt must know, I thought, of what my father was accused. She must wonder about the truth of it. But she does not ask.

I understood that my uncle and aunt were trying to protect me by keeping silent. It would have been a relief to talk about it. But when I thought of broaching the subject, I squirmed with shame and embarrassment.

'Eleanor, you look so very sad,' my aunt's voice broke in.

'I'm sorry?' I asked her, focusing my eyes on her with some difficulty.

'My dear girl, you have been miles away! I've been watching you staring into the distance. You haven't yet set a stitch. Are you unwell?'

'Just tired, Aunt,' I assured her.

'Or still shocked by what you witnessed this morning. It is hardly surprising.' She reached forward and clasped my hand warmly. 'I think you need to give your thoughts a new direction. How about an outing?'

'Oh, Aunt Jane, please, no. I could not . . . ' I uttered distractedly.

'Nonsense, my dear! A little shopping always does one good when one is feeling dismal. I shall order the carriage at once.'

I made a slight move to beg her not to, but she shook her head at me. 'It is vital that we both go into mourning as soon as possible. There will be scandal enough surrounding your father's death. We must take care not to add to it. So we shall go to my dressmaker and select some fabrics for her to make up. Will you not like to have a new dress? To be sure, it will have to be black, which is not what one would choose at this season, but still, it will look very handsome with your hair colour.'

'You are very good to me, Aunt Jane. I am sorry to be bringing such disgrace and so much expense upon you,' I told her.

My aunt looked sharply at me, but waved my apology away.

'Nonsense, Eleanor. You are the daughter I never had. It is a pleasure to have you here.'

I doubted her truthfulness, but I could not doubt her kindness. I made no more objections to the outing, which took the rest of the day. I made an effort to appear interested and engaged, but it was hard work. I was drained when we returned home.

A few days dragged by. My uncle and aunt were very kind to me. They talked about Sir Walter, about the loss of Thomas Cromwell and what that would mean to the kingdom, and about my mother and her probable marriage to Sir Thomas now that she was widowed. In fact they talked about everything and anything they thought might interest me. But none of it did. My thoughts were bleak.

Often, I found myself dwelling on the emptiness of my future. I saw myself an unwanted member of Sir Thomas's household, with nothing to look forward to but an endless spinsterhood. Not even the thought of being with Mother could comfort me when I contemplated it. I also wondered what she had thought when she heard the accusations against her husband. Perhaps she even believed them.

One morning a visitor was announced. My aunt had gone out to call on an elderly friend, so I went to greet the caller alone. He turned as I entered the room.

'Cousin,' I cried in delighted surprise.

'Eleanor,' Gregory said, stepping forward and grasping my outstretched hand. 'I can only stay a moment. I am on my way out of London. How are you?'

'I am well enough,' I told him. 'And you?'

'It has been a difficult time,' my cousin said sombrely. 'You have lost a father, and I an uncle.'

'Thank you for taking care of . . . the burial and all such matters,' I said awkwardly.

'Not at all. Eleanor, there is something I must tell you. The night before the execution, I stayed with your father in the Tower. He was no longer sane. He raved and shouted. But he also had lucid spells, where he could speak rationally. I asked him about Lord Stanton. I have never believed he was involved in the plot against your mother. Sir Walter admitted that he was not. He only told you that to prevent you confiding in him. Do you see? If you believed him to be involved, you would not seek his help. It was a lie.'

'That possibility had occurred to me. Do you think Sir Walter was telling the truth, Gregory?' I asked timidly.

Gregory took my hand again. 'Yes, I do. He did not say this with any tone of regret. In fact I felt he was still congratulating himself on the cunning of his plan. But I believe he was telling the truth.'

'I think he was too,' I said quietly.

Gregory stayed only a few moments more. He had urgent business on his father's estates, he told me. I was disappointed. I would like to have spoken to him at greater length. We stood looking at each other awkwardly, and then impulsively I embraced him. Gregory hugged me back.

'God bless you, Eleanor,' he said, and took his leave.


My aunt found me in my uncle's library, staring at a book

without reading it, and laid a gentle hand upon my shoulder.

'What is the matter, niece?' she asked gently. 'We are worried about you, Edward and I. We cannot account for your lowness. You are so pale and wan. My dear, I do not think I have ever seen you cry before.'

'I never cry,' I gasped, even as the tears ran down my cheeks. My aunt drew me gently into her arms and held me. This was my undoing and I began to sob in earnest. 'Oh, Aunt Jane, I am so unhappy!'

'I can see that, my love. We cannot understand that you grieve so deeply for your father.'

'It is not that,' I said, covering my face with my hands for shame. The tears trickled through my fingers, and I sniffed hopelessly.

'Can you not tell me? Here, take this.' My aunt released me, and held out her clean handkerchief, which I accepted gratefully, dabbing at my eyes.

'What then?' she urged, as I wiped my face. 'What else can distress you so? Was it Lord Stanton? Does he hold you to your betrothal? I confess, I had not thought he would do so.'

'No indeed,' I faltered. My throat felt constricted with sobs and my breath was short. 'He . . . released me from our betrothal. And Aunt Jane . . . I fear he no longer *wanted* to marry me.' My voice broke, and I hid my face in the damp handkerchief once more.

'Well, my dear, and where's the tragedy in that? You did not wish for the match. You made that plain enough.'

'I know,' I said. 'And I am not surprised he no longer

wishes to marry a girl everyone believes to be spoiled goods.'

I had brought up the dreadful subject at last.

'Dear God, who told you that? Not Stanton, surely?'

I nodded miserably. 'No one will ever wish to marry me now, will they?'

'My poor child. We tried to keep it from you . . . your uncle and I. I'm so sorry, we meant it for the best. It was very indelicate of Lord Stanton to discuss it with you. I never thought he . . . Surely he did not tell you that was his reason for breaking with you?'

'No, he did not. He only asked me if it was true. He . . . he was very kind.'

'And you said . . . ?' my aunt asked tentatively.

'That it was a vile invention, of course. And it *is*.'

My aunt let out a sigh of relief and stroked my hair comfortingly.

'It is a weight off my mind to hear you say so. I cannot tell you what we have suffered for your sake since we heard the accusation. People are saying Hungerford was quite insane, towards the end. We feared he might have been capable of any crime.'

I shook my head.

'Not that one,' I assured her. 'But what difference does it make? Everyone will believe it to be true.'

'It makes a great deal of difference to you, Eleanor. And so it is this news which has brought you so low. I can understand it, my dear, but have courage. You know it to be false, and the scandal will pass in time. As for Stanton, you did not care for him anyway, so he is no great loss.'

Her words brought tears of despair to my eyes.

'When I saw him last, I accused him of plotting to murder my mother,' I confessed, the tears running hot down my face again. 'You know that Sir Walter told me it was so, and I believed him. But my cousin has just been here. He told me it was all a lie.'

'Your cousin?' asked my aunt, surprised.

I waved this detail aside.

'I think, perhaps . . . ' I began, hesitatingly. The awareness that had been growing in me for days became certainty as I spoke.

'You think . . . ?' prompted my aunt, when I paused.

'I think perhaps I do care for Stanton . . . a little.' I spoke in a rush, embarrassed to be contradicting everything I had said about him.

'You do? Enough to marry him?'

'I don't know. Perhaps. But it is no use. He thinks I believe dreadful things of him. And he will not want such a scandal. I will never see him again.' I leaned my aching head against my aunt's shoulder.

I had not fully realized the truth till this moment. Only a part of my great sadness had been due to my public disgrace. By far the larger part was the loss of Lord Stanton just as I realized how much I cared for him.

'He can be so very kind, Aunt,' I confessed. 'Even when I accused him of . . . well, of wanting to murder Mother, he did not fly into a rage. When I think that I will never see him again, I feel so sad. I miss him already. I would not even mind him teasing me now.'

'My dear Eleanor. You are in love!' exclaimed my aunt.

I nodded miserably. It was true. I did not know when my heart had changed, but it had.

Aunt Jane hugged me tight.

'Do not despair. All may yet turn out better than you expect.'

'How can it?' I asked despairingly.

'I do not know. But it may.'

'I wish only that I might see him one last time. So that I might have the chance to explain how wrong I was to dislike him so. But it is not likely.'


The following morning brought me two things. Firstly our mourning clothes, which my aunt insisted we donned at once. Both kirtle and gown were sober black, with not a single thread of colour to lighten them. A new hood had also been made for me, which my aunt begged me to wear. Usually I went bare-headed in the house.

'There will be callers, Eleanor. Some will come to give their condolences, but most to gather gossip, so you must be correctly attired.'

Obediently I clad myself in the sombre garments and descended to the hall where my aunt already sat. 'There's a letter for you, Eleanor!' she told me as I joined her. 'Sir Thomas sent it by messenger.'

I tore open the letter, praying that all was well with Mother in Bath.

'Oh, Mother is to be married! Next month.' It surprised me to find I was happy for my mother. But I looked down at my black gown and then at my aunt. 'Aunt Jane, should not Mother be in mourning? It cannot be proper of her to be getting married so soon?'

'It is most irregular,' agreed my aunt, with raised eyebrows. 'But I daresay your mother feels she owes your father no proper observance after the way she was treated. I imagine it will be a private ceremony?'

I scanned the letter. 'Yes. And I am to be bridemaid. Oh dear, I am to go to her at once. The messenger will accompany me on the journey. He is going to hire a carriage.'

I did not want to leave London and any prospect of seeing Lord Stanton once more.

'It's natural that your mother wants you with her,' said my aunt, smiling at my crestfallen face. 'And I'm sure you will learn to like Sir Thomas.'

'Well, if Mother loves him, of course she must marry him,' I sighed. My aunt chuckled.

'Well, there's someone who has changed her tune! Now, I think we need to start packing, don't you?'

As I folded my kirtles and gowns and laid them in my trunk, I imagined walking down the aisle as a bridemaid. I could not help thinking that had I remained at Farleigh, I would have gone to church as a bride by now. Would I have fallen in love with Stanton if I had been forced to marry him? I could not tell, but I thought I would have done sooner or later. I became quite absorbed in imagining various possible scenes, and was scolded by my aunt for packing my shoes into my hat box.

When I descended for refreshments, my uncle and aunt were both waiting for me, with cheerful looks upon their faces.

'We have a little something for you, Eleanor,' said my uncle. 'Please accept this as a parting gift, and as a souvenir of your time with us.' He presented me with one of his beautiful books.

'Oh, Uncle!' I gasped. 'How can I accept this? It's far too precious!'

'Nonsense, my dear,' he said, accepting my embrace. 'I would like to think that you have it, and are reading it.'

'And I have a smaller gift for you, Eleanor,' said my aunt, holding out a second package. It was a prettily presented box of parchment, with several quills. 'So that we can keep in touch,' she explained, hugging me tight. 'Your uncle will read me your letters. And I hope you will come and stay with us again sometime.'

The manservant entered the room at that moment and made his stately way over to my aunt.

'Pardon me for interrupting, my lady, but there is a servant at the front door with a message for Mistress Hungerford.'

My aunt looked at him in surprise. 'Well, tell him to leave his message, Cooper.'

'Pardon me, but I have already done so. He insists on giving the message in person.' The servant coughed discreetly and added, 'Not a genteel personage, my lady, though he is dressed in livery.'

'Who is it, Cooper?' I asked, my curiosity aroused.

'He won't say, Mistress,' replied the servant.

'Well, this is most irregular!' exclaimed my aunt.

'Please do not trouble yourself, Aunt Jane,' I begged her. 'I'll go to him.'

'You'll do no such thing! Sit down and behave like a young lady. Cooper, you may show him in, but make sure his shoes are clean and do not let him out of your sight.'

'Very good, my lady,' he replied.

A moment later a tall young man in vaguely familiar livery appeared in the doorway, and stood there awkwardly, hesitating. My gaze travelled upwards from his shoes, past his smart blue tunic to his face topped with unruly curls and a cap. I did not recognize him at first, and as I looked at him, he reddened under my gaze.

'Mistress Eleanor,' he said apologetically, stepping forward, and I knew his voice at once.

'Tom!' I cried, leaping to my feet. 'Where the devil did you spring from?'

I heard my aunt clucking a faint protest at my language, but I saw a smile in Tom's eyes. I grasped his hand. 'I've never seen you look so clean!' I exclaimed. 'Explain!'

'I have a new place now, Mistress Eleanor,' said Tom, blushing again, but also smiling. 'And I've brought something for you.'

'Something from Farleigh?' I asked, surprised.

'Not exactly, Mistress. It's outside the front door.'

'Outside?' I echoed in astonishment. 'Why did you leave it out there?'

Tom bowed clumsily. 'If you follow me, Mistress Eleanor, you'll see.' He spoke stiffly, and it was obvious to me that he was trying to be on his best behaviour before my uncle and aunt. I tucked my hand in his arm.

'Lead on, Tom,' I told him, and then added in a lower voice, 'But for God's sake stop calling me Mistress Eleanor.'

'I can't call you Eleanor, not now.'

'Why not? You just did. Are you feeling very grand in those clothes, Tom?'

Tom grinned sheepishly, and I forbore to tease him further.

The servant threw open the front door when we reached it, and Tom stood back to allow me to pass through it first. Curious, I stepped out into the sunshine. I had no idea what to expect, and indeed the heat and the bright sunshine dazzled me at first so that I could see nothing. I stood blinking while my eyes adjusted. Two dark blurs resolved into horses. One was unfamiliar and unremarkable. The second horse I knew at once.

'Arianna!' I cried, hardly able to believe my eyes. I ran to her and flung my arms about her neck, making her throw up her head nervously.

'That's no way to treat a high-bred horse, Mistress,' Tom chided me. I ignored him. I was hugging as much of Arianna as I could reach. I pressed my face into her glossy hide, breathing in her familiar horse scent. She bore it patiently after her initial fright, and when I let her go, she lipped my hands, looking for carrots.

'I've nothing for you, dear Arianna,' I laughed, stroking her soft velvety nose. I was overjoyed to see her again. I had thought her lost to me for ever. To my disgust, I found I was having to fight back tears once more. Whatever was happening to me? My feelings seemed so much more intense these days. I was ashamed of my weakness. It would not do for Tom to see me blubbing like a girl.

I turned to Tom. He was standing at a respectful distance looking pleased with himself. I beckoned him closer.

'Tom,' I asked. 'How is this possible? Did not Lord Stanton have Arianna?'

'Yes, that's right,' Tom agreed. 'He's my new master.'

My eyes widened in surprise. Tom sounded both proud and happy.

'So he has sent Arianna?' My heart gave a jump but then sank again. 'But why did he not bring her himself?'

'On account of not knowing whether he was welcome, Mistress Eleanor,' explained Tom, far too cheerfully. 'He thought you might prefer to see me.'

'I am very happy to see you, Tom,' I told him, trying but failing to match his cheerful tone. I hesitated, and continued more quietly: 'But Lord Stanton is mistaken. I do not dislike him. I believe you have found a good master.'

I turned to Arianna again, and stroked her beautiful grey neck, trying to hide my disappointment. Lord Stanton would not even come himself. He had truly lost his regard for me. And no wonder.

'Is not Arianna beautiful today, Mistress?' asked Tom. 'I brushed her for hours this morning and oiled her hooves, look.'

'I've never seen her look so fine,' I agreed. 'Thank you, Tom.' I hesitated. 'And does Arianna return with you? Or am I allowed to keep her?'

'Oh, she's a gift, Mistress Eleanor. Did I forget to say? A gift from his lordship *with* his compliments,' said Tom. 'Dunno what it means, but that's what he said to tell you.'

'I am very grateful to Lord Stanton,' I murmured.

'You should be,' said Tom seriously. 'We've rode for

four days, him and me, to fetch her from that place where he lives. Can't remember its name. He comes in early one morning, dunno where he'd been, and says, "Saddle up, Tom. We're away to fetch Arianna for Mistress Eleanor."'

I felt moved at his words. All this time I had been thinking he had neglected to call on me, he had been riding to fetch Arianna. The thought kindled hope in me, but I also felt hurt. After so much trouble, could he not have brought her to me himself?

I saw Tom was mounting the other horse. Was he going to ride away without saying farewell?

'Tom!' I cried. I laid a hand on his knee. 'I shall miss you,' I told him. 'Very much.' His face was tight as he looked at me, but he said nothing. 'And please tell his lordship that I'm exceedingly grateful to him.'

'Well I could try, Mistress Eleanor. But them's not words as I can say, I reckon. So why don't you come and thank him yourself?' He grinned at me. 'He's riding Caesar in the park if you'd like to see him.'

I felt a flame of hope burst into life within me. He was nearby. I could speak to him once more. This was what I had wished for.

'Wait!' I ordered Tom, and dashed back into the house to tell my aunt where I was going. She smiled complacently when she heard my errand, and gave me permission to go, provided one of the manservants accompanied me.

'Tom will look after me,' I cried, running back out of the house before she could protest.

The joy of riding Arianna again put all else temporarily

out of my mind. She danced and sidled while I adjusted my stirrups, but when I told her to walk, she stepped out briskly, her ears pricked right forward.

'Oh, Tom! I cannot tell you what a pleasure this is! To be riding Arianna again. And she still knows me.'

'Of course she does. I have a fair idea how you feel about that horse, Mistress Eleanor.'

When we reached the park, I felt a flutter of nerves. Did Lord Stanton actually want to see me, or would he have preferred to avoid it? Was my reputation so tainted that it would harm him to even be in my company?

I told myself I hoped for nothing from this meeting. I could not expect any decent gentleman to have anything further to do with me after my good name had been so ruined. I was just here to see Stanton one more time, and if I could find the courage, to tell him that I no longer suspected him of plotting against my mother. My nervousness communicated itself to Arianna and she broke into a canter. I reined her in as I scanned the park for Stanton.

'Over there,' said Tom, pointing out a tall, elegant figure on a large black horse some distance away. 'I'll be waiting at the gates,' he added, turning away.

'Oh, won't you come with me?' I cried impulsively.

'You don't need me,' said Tom gruffly.

I bit my lip and rode boldly out across the park. It was too hot to go any faster than a trot, and so it took me several minutes to come abreast of Caesar and fall into step beside him.

Stanton's face broke into a smile when he saw me.

'I only came, my lord, to say thank you for sending me Arianna,' I said hurriedly, imagining he might wonder at my coming.

'You are welcome, Eleanor. I bought her for you in the first place, so it is only right that you should have her.'

'You did?' I asked, astonished.

'Well of course,' replied Stanton. 'What did you think? That I'd buy your favourite horse and take her away from you?' He paused and scanned my face. I felt it burning with shame, and could not meet his eyes.

'Good God. That *is* what you thought,' said Stanton grimly.

'I'm sorry.' I barely spoke above a whisper. 'But you seemed to love to provoke me; I thought it was another instance of . . . '

'Eleanor, we were about to be married. My possessions would have been yours. Your father was being unpardonably cruel, so I bought Arianna as a bride gift for you.'

'I was not thinking straight,' I cried. 'For I always intended to run away before we could be married, so I never thought ahead to . . . '

'To our married life together,' Stanton completed my sentence drily. 'I noticed.'

'But why could you not have said so?' I demanded. 'You never mentioned Arianna again.'

'I took her to my home in Hampshire, so she could be waiting there for you as a surprise. I had business there in any case.'

'I can see I have caused you a great deal of trouble.'

'Not at all,' Stanton replied politely. His words and

manner were a rebuff. Why did he not tease me? Tell me
that I was a thorn in his side and he was glad to be rid of
me? Then we would at least be on familiar territory once
more.

'I barely recognize your lordship, so polite you have
become,' I remarked. Stanton merely bowed slightly.

'It's clearly a great relief to be free of me,' I said with an
edge of bitterness to my voice. 'It has quite restored your
good manners.'

'I am sure you are right.'

'Oh, I never met anyone as provoking as you!' I
exclaimed.

'How so?' asked Stanton, apparently surprised. 'When
I am doing my best not to annoy you?'

'You understand nothing!' I flung at him.

'Then explain it to me. What do I not understand?'

That silenced me. I had imagined this meeting so many
times. In my visions we had spoken sadly, tenderly even,
before parting for ever. I had never dreamt that Stanton
would be infuriating, or that I might be in danger of
losing my temper.

We had come to the end of the park. Stanton turned
Caesar, and I followed.

'Do you wish to ride some more or shall I escort you
home?' Stanton asked.

I could see he did not wish for my company, and I felt
desolate. But I so needed to speak to him that I did not
immediately accept his hint.

'It's too hot,' I replied pettishly. I dragged off my hood,
and shook my hair free. That felt better at once. 'I should
like to walk a little,' I told him. 'In the shade.'

I thought perhaps if we were walking, I might feel braver, more able to speak freely.

'Of course,' replied Stanton, leading the way to some large trees. He jumped to the ground and hitched both of the horses. I tried to smile at him as he helped me down from Arianna but he did not seem to notice. At that point, I despaired. This was hopeless. I may as well go home without speaking. He did not want me, and I could not blame him.

'I fear Tom will miss you,' Stanton said, breaking in on my thoughts. 'Was I wrong to take him into my service? He was turned off from Farleigh when the castle was seized by the king. He is uncommonly good with horses.'

'He appears very satisfied with his new master,' I replied, not knowing what else to say.

'Unfortunately it seems Tom cannot serve us both,' murmured Stanton.

'Unfortunately?' I asked at once.

'For him,' he said smoothly. 'I was speaking of Tom.'

'Of course.' I took a deep breath and tried to steady my nervousness. If I was going to speak to him, it had to be now.

'My Lord Stanton,' I began.

'Please, Eleanor, do not be so formal with me!' Stanton exclaimed, completely throwing me out of my stride. 'If we are never to see one another again, can you not use my name rather than my title, just this once? I am Philip. Let me hear you call me that.'

I was completely taken aback.

'Very well, as you wish,' I faltered. 'Philip.'

It felt so strange to use his Christian name that I paused,

confused. 'Now I have forgotten what I wanted to say. At least not so much *what* as *how*.'

'There is no hurry,' replied Stanton. 'You do not need to speak at all. We can just walk a while under the trees here, and enjoy the cool air together.'

'But there is something I must say to you,' I said nervously. I steeled myself, hoping that my treacherous complexion would not betray my embarrassment. 'I wanted to tell you that when you came to Farleigh, I disliked you very much. No, damn it, that's not what I wanted to say.' I flung my hood onto the grass and ran my hands through my hair. 'I was angry and desperate. I had been ordered to marry you against my will. I was surrounded by spies . . . I thought you were one. I know now, that I was wrong. Not only that . . . I know now that you are a good person. A kind person.'

'You surprise me, Eleanor.'

'I know. I've been so rude to you, so hateful. You believed me when I said my father was falsely accused concerning me. You trusted my word. But I could not trust your word when you denied that you had plotted against my mother. I'm sorry. I know it was a lie. My father admitted it, apparently. Before he died.

'And despite everything, you've done so much for us, and I *am* grateful.' I paused and took a deep breath. This was so very difficult, much harder than I had thought it would be, and Lord Stanton was saying nothing to help me. He walked beside me, eyes downcast. Nonetheless, I forced myself to go on.

'I quite understand that I'm no longer . . . that my reputation is . . . well, that you can have nothing further to do with me,' I tried to explain, feeling the tell-tale heat creeping up my neck and into my face. 'But I did not want you to think that I still think badly of you. Because I do not.'

Such a long speech was exhausting. My breathing was unsteady as though I had been running. Stanton did not reply immediately, and I waited in some trepidation for his response. At last he spoke, his voice quiet.

'I do not need your gratitude, Eleanor. But thank you for your good opinion of me. It is not all deserved. I did not treat you kindly at first either. I am sorry for that too.'

I nodded my acknowledgement of this.

'But, Eleanor,' Stanton continued, and now his voice was stronger, 'what did you mean about your reputation? *That* was not my reason for releasing you from our betrothal. I hope you know that?'

I felt confused for a moment. Was it not? And then I pulled myself together.

'Those slanders must bar me from any marriage for life. I know that. I could not bring such shame on anyone . . . to be associated with such . . . no.' I shook my head firmly.

Stanton stopped abruptly, and I stopped beside him. He cupped his hands around my face and turned it up, looking into my eyes. I was so surprised that I did not resist. His hands were slightly cool against my skin, and I could feel myself trembling at his touch.

'I know the accusations against you were false. I love you, Eleanor, and I care for your happiness,' he said, looking intently at me. I felt my heart miss a beat at his words. 'I released you because I thought you wished for it, not to save myself from scandal,' he said. 'My God, what do I care for that?'

'I . . . I do not . . . anyone would care about *such* a tale,' I murmured, dropping my gaze. Stanton's closeness was affecting me powerfully. I felt I could scarcely breathe.

'Eleanor, look at me,' he ordered. 'Look me in the eyes and tell me you still do not wish to marry me. Tell me you do not love me. If it is still true, say it boldly, like you did at Bath.'

My thoughts were in turmoil. I felt both hope and deep despair. He said he still loved me. Could that be true? But even if it were, I knew I could not bring my own shame upon him. I would have to lie to him. For his own sake, I would have to deny my feelings.

'I do not . . . I could never . . . ' I began. But my voice would not obey me. I could not look into those eyes and utter such falsehoods.

'You do not answer me,' he said softly. Stanton let go of my face at last, his hands sliding down my arms and around my waist, drawing me even closer to him. My heart was fluttering wildly, but I went to him willingly, lifting my face, inviting his kiss. He bent his head until his lips just touched mine.

'Say my name once more,' he whispered, his breath warm and sweet on my face.

'Philip,' I whispered back.

'Kiss me again,' he murmured.

This time, he wrapped his arms about me, holding me close. We kissed gently at first, tenderly, but then his arms tightened around me drawing me closer against him until I felt dizzy with desire. When we finally stopped, we stood holding each other, reading our own happiness in each other's eyes.

'How soon will you marry me?' Stanton asked.

I laughed shakily, leaning against him, resting my head against his shoulder.

'If you are quite sure . . . as soon as you like.'

'I have no doubts at all. And you?' Stanton ran his fingers through my hair, seeking out the nape of my neck and caressing it with gentle fingers. I felt a light shiver of pleasure run through me.

'No doubts,' I promised him.

I remembered my mother's letter.

'My mother marries next month, so perhaps we should wait till after then?'

'Does she indeed? So soon? Well, she deserves happiness. As do we, Eleanor.' Stanton's arms tightened around me once more. 'We can wait those few weeks if you wish it.'

'Philip, I have not yet told you, but I am supposed to leave for Bath tomorrow morning.'

'Then I shall accompany you, and ask your mother's permission to marry you.'

'You already have the king's permission.'

'I shall accompany you anyway.'

He turned. Taking my hand, he began to lead me back to the horses. 'You will be glad to know that you will not need to purchase a wedding gown,' he remarked over his shoulder to me. 'I brought yours from Farleigh. It seemed such a waste to leave it for the king.'

'You did *what*?' I demanded, pulling my hand out of his. 'You brought my gown to London? How dared you do such a thing? I had already told you I would not marry you!'

'I thought you may well change your mind. And you have.'

'You arrogant, conceited . . . ' I began, and then I saw that he was shaking with laughter. 'Oh, I see. You are teasing me.'

He took me in his arms and kissed me once more.

'Yes, Eleanor, I am teasing you. But I really did bring your gown. I am not quite sure why, and I confess I was wondering what to do with it.'

'You may well wonder, for I think you will find I have grown taller this last month,' I told him.

'That will serve me right,' he said with a grin.

'I do not intend to quarrel with you,' I said virtuously. 'So I shall not say another word on the subject.'

'You do not intend to quarrel with me?' Stanton demanded incredulously. He swept me off my feet and threw me up into Arianna's saddle. 'If I were not quite sure I could provoke you any time I choose, I would be seriously alarmed.'

'I am much too happy to be provoked again today,' I told him with a smile.

# HISTORICAL NOTE

✦

*This story is based on real events that took place in the sixteenth century. Many of the characters are also based on real historical figures. I was inspired to write it by the tale of the Lady Tower and the mystery of how Lady Elizabeth escaped from Farleigh Castle. I have been as accurate as possible with names, dates and facts, whilst allowing for the story I wanted to tell. Where research failed to provide information, I improvised freely.*

*Farleigh Hungerford Castle is in Wiltshire and is now a ruin. The property is owned by English Heritage and is open to the public.*

**Marie-Louise Jensen**
**2008**

✦

✦

Marie-Louise Jensen (née Chalcraft) was born in Henley-on-Thames of an English father and Danish mother. Her early years were plagued by teachers telling her to get her head out of a book and learn useless things like maths. Marie-Louise studied Scandinavian and German with literature at the UEA and has lived in both Denmark and Germany. After teaching English at a German university for four years, Marie-Louise returned to England to care for her children full time. She completed an MA in Writing for Young People at the Bath Spa University in 2005. Marie-Louise reads, reviews and writes books for young people. She lives in Bath and home educates her two sons.

✦

# Also by Marie-Louise Jensen

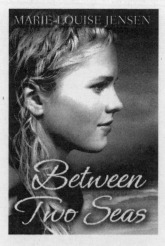

*'Travel to Skagen and find him. Give him my letter. Seek a better life, Marianne! Promise!'*

Bound by a vow made to her dying mother,
Marianne sells her few belongings and
leaves Grimsby. Her destination? Denmark, where she will
search for her father, Lars Christensen—the golden-haired
fisherman her mother fell in love with many years before.

The journey will be long—and dangerous for a young girl
travelling alone. As Marianne boards the fishing boat that will
carry her across the North Sea, she wonders: will Denmark
be the fairy-tale land she has dreamt of?
Will she find happiness there? Will the father she has never
met welcome the arrival of his illegitimate child?

And why didn't he return for her mother,
as he promised he would?

'a riveting read.'
*Guardian*